DO NOT DISTURB

MARY BILLITER

Do Not Disturb © 2016 by Mary Billiter

Do Not Disturb is a work of fiction. All names, characters, events and places found therein are either from the author's imagination or used fictitiously. Any similarity to persons alive or dead, actual events, locations, or organizations is entirely coincidental and not intended by the author.

For information, contact the publisher, Hot Tree Publishing. www.hottreepublishing.com

Editing: Hot Tree Editing
Cover Designer: Claire Smith
Formatting: RMGraphX
ISBN-10: 1-925448-31-2
ISBN-13: 978-1-925448-31-3

10 9 8 7 6 5 4 3 2 1

RESORT
ROMANCES
BY MARY BILLITER

Opening Soon
The Historic Wyoming
Point Resort
Cheyenne WY

"Rule Breakers"

"ESCAPE CLAUSE"
The Point Resort
Newport OR

CANADA

MEXICO

DO NOT DISTURB

"DO NOT DISTURB"
YOUR NEXT BOOK
DESTINATION:
the Waterfront Point
HUNTINGTON BEACH, CA

DEDICATION

When I think back to all that has happened since my breast cancer diagnosis last October 2015, one of the constants has been my little brother, Patrick's, ability to make me laugh. When I started losing my hair, he reminded me that I still had more than him.

During Thanksgiving, when I gifted the men in my life— my husband, brothers-in-law, and brothers—each with a pink tie in honor of breast cancer awareness, Patrick was the only one who tied it around his head and wore it like a headdress during dinner.

The next morning, Patrick woke early to run beside my husband and me in a 5k race because he knew I started training for it before I was diagnosed. He knew how much it meant to me to finish what I had started.

And when I shared my fear of dying and leaving my

husband and children, my baby brother assured me, even promised that I would live to grow old with Ron, see my twins graduate college, my daughter finish high school and my youngest son begin the fourth grade. Patrick was the voice of reason when I had none.

There is no way to ever adequately thank him for being there when I fell apart. So, baby brother, I wrote this book to celebrate what I treasure most about our relationship: the laughter.

And since you were blessed with the best name in the family (Patrick Flanagan Billiter), I borrowed part of it to bring this story to life.

I love you more than you will ever know.

Mary

CHAPTER **ONE**

When did you sneak in line?

Dressed in faded blue jeans and a rust-colored button-down that screamed to be unbuttoned, the anonymous stranger suddenly made the wait for the hotel to open its doors a lot more enticing.

The mystery man stood behind me, and a good foot taller too. *What a package.* Towering over me with dark gelled-back hair and the most amazing hazel eyes, he looked toward me but never really connected. It's hard to explain how one person can look at you and yet not really see you, but that was what he did and I wanted more. I craved eye contact, real eye contact, with this gorgeous guy until it etched up my spine and sat in my throat. *Delicious.*

"Ladies and gentlemen." A booming voice rang overhead. A man with lacquered black hair, a bullhorn, and a really bad tie stood on the edge of the hotel's loading dock.

I straightened my posture and discreetly slid my hands down my gray-and-black-plaid skirt that had a tendency to gravitate up.

"I'm Bill Clark, the director of Hotel Security," the bullhorn-wielding man continued. "Thank you for your patience. We'll be starting the interview process soon."

Thank God. I rubbed my hands together. *It's June. Where's the sun?* I pulled the sides of my black cardigan together. It didn't block the ocean breeze that had a serious bite to it, and worse, it hid my new charcoal-colored tank. *I could accidentally rub up against Mr. Hottie-With-a-Body. That'd keep me warm.* Instead, I slightly turned toward him and discreetly stubbed my boots on the asphalt to waken my numb toes.

I casually glanced past him to the line that had tripled since I'd arrived at seven that morning. I'd been among the first dozen camped outside the hotel's loading dock, waiting for the doors to open. My position, though, gave me easy access to survey the throng of other applicants.

Orange County, the infamous "OC," had rolled out the red carpet for its newest waterfront hotel in Huntington Beach. Attention-grabbing ads ran in California newspapers and radio stations. The mass hiring event wanted what the OC *always* wanted: the best of the best.

I was one of many in the ranks of recent college graduates looking for a paycheck. I had to find a source of income to continue the lifestyle my parents had funded during the six years I was in school. I blame changing my major twice for the delay in my degree. It really didn't matter, though, because since having a gold tassel hanging from the rearview mirror of my new car, supposedly I could function without the safety net of my parents' bimonthly allowance checks. My status of residence independence was yet to be determined.

Though I hadn't recognized anyone in particular, everyone seemed oddly familiar. It was the packaging. *It's always the packaging.* Placing people into imaginary groups—jocks, cheerleaders, freaks, and geeks—was a bad habit I'd picked up in high school and couldn't seem to shake.

Suddenly, I felt the heat of his stare. I glanced over and smiled nervously in his direction. I overdid my fun, flirty smile, and my mouth stretched so wide that I was pretty sure I looked like the Joker, which unfortunately was exactly like my driver's license photo. I don't tend to smile very well under pressure.

Turned toward me, his hazel gaze warmed, I'm sure in sympathy. There were deep shadows beneath his bloodshot eyes.

"Rough night?" The question escaped before I had enough gumption to choke it back.

"You have no idea." He chuckled huskily, beckoning me further into the dark unknown.

I leaned against the brick retaining wall and tried to regain my composure, if not steady my breathing, only my cardigan clung to the gray cinder blocks. *Crappity, crap, crap. I'm stuck.* I tilted my head, hoping he hadn't noticed that I was now a permanent fixture in the loading dock.

"That's rough." *And apparently so is my ability to speak.*

His mouth quirked into another smile, and my knees almost gave out.

"So what are you interviewing for?" I asked.

"Banquets."

"Huh." I racked my brain for what that meant. *A banquet fit for a king. Serve a banquet of food.* Only clichés flooded forward. "So you're a server?"

"No." A slow shake of his head before closing his eyes.

That was fast. I usually don't lose them that quickly.

Then he spoke.

"I'm a banquet captain." He opened his eyes.

"Oh." I nodded as if that clarified things.

"My name's Tim Jansen." He extended his hand, his gaze holding mine.

For a moment I hesitated. *This is trouble.* I carefully stepped away from the brick wall, and thankfully, my cardigan came with me. I placed my hand in his, and his gaze never left mine. *Wowza.* I was dumbstruck, literally, in both senses of the word "dumb." I could neither talk nor think clearly or rationally.

My heart leapt in my chest. My knees felt weak, and I wasn't sure if my legs would hold out.

I broke eye contact and glanced at his hand that held mine— large, tan, warm. He had an instant effect on me. I wasn't sure if I wanted him to continue to touch me or release his grip and its paralyzing effect. I couldn't look away nor could I breathe. My brain and tongue were both rendered useless by the man I'd just met.

Holy hell, he's beautiful. If he asked for anything—the keys to my new car, my place in the interview line, my social security number—I'd have given it to him. *Good thing I can't see how good-looking an Internet scammer is, otherwise my identity would have been stolen weekly.*

"Everyone calls me TJ." He held my hand, his hazel eyes drawn together in thought. "And you are?"

"Um… what?" My brain faded to black.

"Your name?" His smile made it hard to focus.

"Oh yeah. I mean, hi. I'm Katie Flanagan. But everyone calls me… well, Katie." I gave a puzzled shake of my head and felt my face flush.

"You're funny." His eyes twinkled mischievously. "So what are you interviewing for?"

"Um, well, you see." I floundered. "I just quit my job at this radio station, and I've got this car payment, and I recently moved back home with my mom and dad…." His eyes closed again. *I'm putting him to sleep. You twit. You big twit. Shut up and answer the question.*

"I'm interviewing with the Human Resources department."

His eyes popped open in surprise. "Aren't we all interviewing with HR?"

"Yeah. Duh, of course." I shrugged and when I laughed I sounded like a hyena. *Awesome.*

This time, he smiled broadly, and I felt a huge spike in my body temperature. I was either going to faint or spontaneously combust before him. It was hard to know. With each raised eyebrow he shot toward me, my body reacted differently.

"What I meant to say"—trying to regain what little composure I had left—"is that I'm interviewing for a *position* in the Human Resources department."

He nodded.

"Clerk," I blurted. "It's the HR *clerk*. Position."

"Great."

Nope, it wasn't, but I was desperate. I should have lied. Said I was… what? What was cool? I'd never been cool at the same time others were cool. In fact, I wasn't sure cool was the right word. Whether it was my clothes, my hairstyle, or my choice in profession, I'd always felt one step behind and today was no exception. I was on a downhill roll, and TJ had witnessed my bumpy ride into hell.

Hell of another kind erupted when Mr. Clark appeared again with his bullhorn.

"Hello folks. We'll now be accepting applicants in parties of ten. So please count off into groups."

The countdown began. I quickly tallied the heads in front of me and smiled. I was nine and not surprisingly, TJ was a perfect ten. *Suh-weet.*

The countdown continued through the serpentine line that wrapped along the perimeter of the hotel and onto the sidewalk along Pacific Coast Highway. The salty air was palatable. I deeply inhaled and waited for instructions.

"Once you have numbered off, please group together and introduce yourselves to one another. It's important that you know the other members in your group."

Five years of college had trained me to listen to instructors' cues, and Mr. Clark was definitely letting us know a key component to the interviewing process. I just couldn't help being distracted by his hideous tie. It was blaze orange with white dancing skeletons. I mean, who wore their Halloween stuff in June? Not even my mom was that early.

I focused on his face as he spoke into the bullhorn.

"Since you'll be entering in groups," he said, "please get to know one another."

That meant I had very little time to get the 411 on nine other people, including TJ.

I didn't really know anything about TJ other than what my body was responding to, which wasn't something I wanted to share with a potential employer.

Hi, I'm Katie, and this incredible hottie next to me is TJ. He's got a kickin' nickname, a wicked smile, and he wants to be a banquet captain, which could be code for dishwasher for all I know. Hire him, hire me, and make us strip beds together.

I shook my head. *Focus, Katie. There's gotta be someone here you know.*

The interviews were being held in my hometown of Huntington Beach, California. Surf City, USA. Perfect weather, perfect beaches, lined with perfect bodies.

I surveyed the faces in line and realized I was probably the only local amidst the mass of coeds, except maybe for the one I'd dubbed Malibu and her sidekick, Skipper.

Another habit I picked up, only this time from the radio station. I'd been working to be the next Erin Burnett, except I'd always seemed to forget people's names—a *major* drawback in live interviews. My editor had suggested I create word associations or nicknames to remember people. I did and it stuck. Now I mentally baptized everyone with a new name.

"I'd like to see who they're gonna hire to clean the toilets," the blonde, who had the shape, tan, and mane of a Malibu Barbie doll, said while we were walking inside the hotel.

"Oh, I know. I mean really," said her friend, who wasn't as pretty as Malibu. But sadly neither was Skipper, the doll created to be Barbie's younger sister. I understood her pain. In the Mattel world of Barbies, with my short legs, solid gymnast-like build, and brown hair, I was a Skipper.

I was about to mutter something when TJ echoed my thoughts.

"It's too early for this shit," he grumbled.

I smiled, but found my attention returning to Malibu and Skipper's conversation.

"You know I'm going to be seriously pissed if all the hostess jobs are filled," Malibu piped up again.

"Trish, don't even worry. This is the Waterfront Point. They're going to take one look at you and want you," Skipper gushed.

"You think?"

"Please. Are you serious?"

"Oh, you're such a doll." Malibu shook her shoulder-length straight hair. "Do you think they'll recognize me?"

I squinted in her direction.

"Who are you?" I mumbled to myself, but TJ heard me and answered from behind.

"She's one of the Pacific Pro bikini girls."

"Huh." I was really stretching my vocabulary. But what did it matter how I sounded when less than ten yards away was one of Huntington's bikini-clad finest? Sure, the Pacific Pro girls weren't paid, but the national exposure from their bikini calendar was priceless. Something I'd learned at the radio station: It's all about the exposure. In Malibu's case, the Pacific Pro bikinis' exposure gave her more coverage than Sports Illustrated.

"Hmm." I felt myself shrink as I was herded into the hotel. "Funny how that is," I said under my breath. TJ's bionic ears piped up again.

"What's that?" he asked.

"Oh, just that…." I looked up at him and paused before blurting out some random insecurity that surfaced once Barbie garnished a title. *Nope, definitely not first-time conversation material.* "Just wondering if they knew this isn't Hooters."

A broad grin broke across his face. "You're funny."

"Well, hopefully that's what they're looking for in HR, someone funny."

"No, you're smart."

My face must have conveyed my confusion.

"I can tell. It's just something you can tell about someone."

What part of my distorted, rambling repartee gave the impression that I was smart?

"Thanks," I mumbled.

"Don't worry." He gave a pointed glance toward Malibu and Skipper. "They're nothing."

"I'm not worried," I lied, though I wasn't sure why.

TJ yawned and covered his mouth. "Man, I could sleep for two days and still be tired." He rubbed his eyes.

Oh, how I'd love to join you.

Instead, I was crammed into a hallway with nine other twentysomethings. Mr. Clark handed a guy named Chris a sheet of name tags and a black permanent marker. Once the pen was passed around, I read everyone's tag and realized that there were two Chrises in my group of ten.

I don't know what it is about guys named Chris, but I've known more than a dozen in my lifetime and they've all become my best friends. I had two potential BFFs in this group: Chris Colombo and Chris Bogart.

Chris Colombo, the most annoying applicant, oddly reminded me of a Keebler Elf. He was short, frumpy, and for a young man, he had a shock of unruly white hair. The cookie-making man had big aspirations of working his way up to general manager, he informed us, but first he was willing to "settle" for the front desk. I was willing to stick him back into a tree and have him churn out some tasty cookies. I was hungry.

The other Chris or "Bogart," as he preferred to be called, drove a vintage Mustang, and his favorite store was Trader Joes. At thirty-one, Bogart was the self-declared oldest in our group, an engineer by trade, and the nicest Chris in the mix. He had dark hair, like TJ's, only Bogart didn't look like he spent as much time on it. Bogart's hair was cut short on the sides, and the top spiked naturally. No gel, no slick look—just this haphazard bristly mess that looked good. Bogart was an obvious draw for one of the girls in our group, who practically stood on top of him to introduce herself.

"I'm Sandy Schaffer," she said, sidling up beside Bogart. "And this is my very best friend ever, Jackie Portobello. Like the mushroom." Sandy looked at her friend and giggled. "We've been *best* friends since high school."

The guys in the group seemed genuinely interested. So I leaned into the circle to hear the rest of her introduction.

"When we were in high school, we waitressed at Salty's, the seafood restaurant." She nudged Jackie in the side. "Remember this?"

Jackie nodded but wasn't sharing the same smile as her friend.

"One night I waited on this superhot guy, who now plays professional football, I want you to know. Well, he ordered the crabs, but I got so nervous you'll never believe what happened?"

I shook my head along with the circle.

"I spilled the entire plate of crabs in his lap. Of course," she paused and smiled brightly at Bogart, "I helped clean him up, if you know what I mean."

I froze. *Did she just tell us... ew. Please tell me she's not applying to be a waitress.*

"And he tipped me, like, a lot. Can you even believe that?"

Again the circle collectively shook their heads.

Well, there's an image I won't be able to erase. Oversharer. However, I won't forget her name either. What *would* be difficult was not calling her Crabby.

Jackie Portobello or "Mushroom" was up next. But unlike Crabby, Jackie's story was one I wanted to remember. She'd graduated from the University of California at Irvine, where she'd majored in horticulture. She was as organic as her name, refusing to eat meat, poultry, or fish. Mushroom was applying for a job in the Purchasing department to gain insight into the food industry.

Mushroom was tall, blonde, and beautiful. And the only other applicant I noticed TJ talk to. I would too. She seemed nice. Genuinely nice.

To already quote TJ, "it's something you can just tell." There was nothing fake about Mushroom; she was the real deal.

Still, of the nine other members in our motley crew, I had sort of glossed over thinking about his status as a "Chris" in my life, but he ultimately became the one who stood out the most. Maybe it was his cologne, aftershave, or shampoo, but Bogart smelled amazing—clean, crisp, inviting. I checked him out more thoroughly. Broad shoulders, muscular arms, and when the guy smiled, his entire face lit up. I stood beside him, inching a little closer to inhale more of him when Mr. Clark brought us into the conference room.

"Welcome to the Waterfront Point Resort, the most celebrated, internationally recognized, five-diamond hotel brand in the hospitality industry," Mr. Clark said.

"The Waterfront Point," he continued, "is, as I mentioned, internationally recognized. Our guest list is a virtual Who's Who. Accordingly, it is vital to the success of our operation to hire the finest, most qualified applicants to join our winning team. This is your golden opportunity!" He punctuated each word with *serious* conviction.

His enthusiasm was contagious, and I snapped to attention. I was sandwiched between Bogart and TJ, who were also standing tall.

"I know it's been a long morning, so we won't delay the process. Here's how it's going to work. We're going to have one spokesman from each group introduce your team and team name."

"Team name?" Malibu asked in the first frantic tone I'd heard her utter. "You never said anything about a team name." Her blue eyes locked on to Mr. Clark.

"Oh, I'm sure I did," Mr. Clark said.

Yet we all knew he hadn't. He continued to smile while a panel of his colleagues filed in behind him and sat at a conference table.

I quickly counted the suits: five. *I can do this.* I was already recalling the brief introductions we had exchanged in the hallway. There were nine people I had to remember. *I can totally do this.*

Mr. Clark turned and took his seat beside his coworkers.

"In fact…." He pulled his chair forward and poured himself a glass of water. "Why don't we start with you?" Mr. Clark looked up from the table and coldly returned Malibu's icy stare.

Malibu went blank, which is when I stepped forward.

"Hi." My voice trembled. "My name's Katie Flanagan and we—" I extended my hand toward my group, "—are the Huntington Hopefuls."

It was hokey, but alliteration had always worked well on my college English papers, and I was hoping it'd pass here. The hardened stares on the nameless faces sitting at the table in front of me began to soften.

"Whether we've traveled from Culver City," I said and glanced over at Sandy, "or Costa Mesa," I looked at a girl named Carmen. "We're all here with the shared purpose of being employed by the Waterfront Point Resort." I then stole Mr. Clark's opening line. "The most celebrated, internationally recognized, five-diamond hotel brand in the hospitality industry."

I stopped and drew a breath. I had a knack for being able to quote verbatim, which had helped me immensely as a wannabe journalist and was doing wonders for me now.

"So," I resumed, "without further ado, please allow me to introduce the Huntington Hopefuls, or," I added, "your first ten employees of the month." This prompted a good laugh.

Now that the ice was broken, I felt on fire, but I still had to figure out an approach to this assignment. My nickname association would help me remember everyone's names but I had to piece it all together.

I couldn't very well introduce Sandy as "Crabby," though the thought made me smile, which I directed at the panel members before me. Mr. Clark winked in return. His dancing skeleton tie was in full view. Something was written in neon letters beneath the skeleton. I squinted and made out the words "Them Bones." *Perfect*.

Mr. Clark's smile was now growing into a forced grin. "Ms. Flanagan, whenever you'd like to proceed."

I nodded and he winked.

"Ladies and gentlemen, I'd like to introduce our first Huntington Hopeful, Sandy Schaffer. Sandy is extremely gifted at communicating, which will serve her well in her desired field of administration. She has an *ear* for business and people," I said.

"As the *ears* of the Waterfront Point Resort, Sandy will

listen to guest input and be an integral part of the entire *body* of Huntington Hopefuls."

I planted the seed and quickly progressed down the line.

"Chris Colombo," I said, turning in his direction, "is on the fast track to becoming the next general manager. So obviously, he's the *brain* of our operation. He's our thinker and has really thought out his future with the Waterfront Point Resort."

"Tim Jansen, or TJ, and Andy Cates will comprise the *backbone* of our group because of their joint interest in the Food and Beverage department. They would serve as the chief support for the hotel."

Who's next? I pivoted on my heel and spotted Mushroom.

"Jackie Portobello, your future Purchasing Manager, is like the digestive tract because of her eagerness to digest all knowledge related to food products through the division of purchasing."

Okay, normally that'd be a disgusting analogy, but somehow, out of pity, mercy, or plain dumb luck, the hotel gurus smiled back at me.

Five down, too many to go.

"Chris Bogart and Carmen Gonzalez are the *legs* that support the body of the operation. Chris will be the legs of the hotel through the department of engineering," I said, giving a pointed glance at Bogart. "And," I nodded toward Carmen, "Carmen's legs will constantly be moving greeting all our guests at the front drive."

Another moment of laughter allowed me to take a deep breath. *That's right, I'm a clever little minx.* I finished by introducing Malibu and her accessory Skipper.

"And finally the fair *eyes* of the Waterfront Point Resort belong to Trish and Suzi. They are *quite* a pair," I said, punctuating it for effect. "They will serve as the eyes of the Waterfront Point Resort in coveted hostess positions."

I raved about their perception and vision for the hotel. With all the bullshit I was spouting, I was functioning like the bowels of the hotel.

But again, the panel was buying it, so I quickly concluded.

"The structural makeup of an organization is much like the anatomy of the human body. While it's easy to group us as a mass of potential employees, I hope I was able to demonstrate how each of us, individually, adds to the supporting framework that will construct the perfect body of work for the new Waterfront Point Resort."

"The whole is only as good as its individual parts, is that it, Miss Flanagan?" A man in a tweed jacket asked. He was cute, so I smiled in his direction.

"Absolutely." I hoped that my enthusiasm would mask my growing insecurity. I so badly wanted to look back at the other members and ask, "How'd I do?" but I dared not turn around. I kept my attention focused on the panel in front of me.

"Well, Ms. Flanagan," Mr. Clark said, "I like your analogy. We already have a Director of Public Relations and Marketing, but I'm sure if we didn't you could easily, shall we say, fashion the body of work she does." He chuckled and shot me another wink.

What is up with that eye? I nervously laughed at his cheesy compliment.

"So tell us a little bit about yourself," Mr. Clark said and winked again.

Maybe he has some eye condition or a nervous twitch?

"Ms. Flanagan?"

I went blank. Perspiration, which had miraculously stayed at bay all morning, came pouring off my forehead. I tried in vain to discreetly wipe it from my brow. The sweat inched down my neck and began spreading across my body like a rash. *I'm Typhoid Kate.* With my knack for name games, I thought it only appropriate I christen myself.

"Well, I'm Katie," I said and then realized that everyone was staring at me. It was totally different when I was introducing the group because I was removed from the process. I was just "on." Now, I was "on" but not in the way I wanted to be.

"Um…," I stammered. "I'm here for a job." I shook my head and started laughing, that hyena cackle that raises eyebrows and lowers expectations. And I couldn't stop. I had just given nine other hopefuls a chance, and I was completely blowing mine. *Fantabulous.*

Then Bogart stepped up.

"This is Katie Flanagan. She's the only local of the Huntington Hopefuls. Even graduated from Huntington Beach High School, class of…." Bogart paused and cast me a glance with dark bedroom eyes that took the edge right off the morning. "Well, I guess age isn't that important, is it?" His laugher was deep, throaty, and sexy as hell. Nothing like I expected.

I drew in a sharp breath, causing a soft gasp.

Bogart's dark brows rose, a smile curving his lips.

I looked at him with a wide smile brightening my face. "Thank you," I mouthed to the only person in the room who'd stepped up to support me.

He left me dazed. I was spellbound by his presence and the stillness that settled over the room. Bogart also held their interest and mine.

"From my experience," he continued, "the Human Resources department of any organization is the main artery. And Katie, here"—he stepped back in line beside me—"well, she's the heart of the Huntington Hopefuls. Katie wants to be the Human Resources Clerk, but I think she's settling," he boldly claimed. "Because she really should be *running* the Human Resources department."

I can't believe he remembered all my rambling.

"She's a natural with people. That comes from her background in journalism and her love of a good story. But," this time when he looked at me and spoke, he didn't turn again to the panel. He kept his focus on me, and my gaze never left his. "That love is a *hunger* that won't be satisfied by anything less than telling their story right. It's why Katie doesn't just listen to people, she *hears* them. *That's* what gives her heart."

Damn. Did I make him sound that good?

I couldn't respond. I stood speechless as my favorite of the Chrises finished my introduction.

"She's a little shy when it comes to herself, but you've already seen her in action, and if anyone's going to be the first Waterfront Point employee of the month, it should be Katie Flanagan."

My chest was heavy with emotion. I didn't feel deserving of such praise after only having known someone for a matter of minutes.

I reached out and squeezed his hand when he finished. A current of electricity coursed through my body. Bogart's gaze flickered down to me. His brown eyes had a mesmerizing intensity and heat that made me forget where I was. The air between us felt charged. I quickly dropped his hand and turned my attention back to the panel.

"Huntington Hopefuls, you're going to be a tough act to follow," the man seated in the middle of the table said. "Well done." He paused. "Building a strong opening team is vital to the success of our operation." He quickly glanced at his colleagues. They all gave a slight nod.

I held my breath.

"Congratulations. You're through to the next stage!"

I turned and saw that the group was smiling, even Malibu. Then, and I'll never really understand why, I fanned my skirt out and curtsied. I felt my cheeks instantly redden. *Too much?*

"Yes, you did a wonderful job, Miss Flanagan," the man repeated, causing me to quickly straighten my skirt as heat poured to my face. I'm sure it was bright red. *Oh my. Thought I was on a roll. My bad.*

TJ, who seemed to have been staving off chuckles, burst out laughing, as did the rest of the room.

He was still laughing when Mr. Clark gave us an hour to meet individually with our department heads for a one-on-one interview. Whoever made it past that hurdle would proceed to have their photo IDs taken, get to the Huntington Beach clinic for a drug test, oh, and somehow squeeze in lunch. I wanted to skip right to the lunch part, but instead, I met with the director of Human Resources.

My knees were still shaking from the adrenaline rush of the introductions when I accepted her handshake and sat across from her.

"I'm Holly and we all know you're Katie," she said.

I smiled.

"So, before I begin the interview, I wanted to confirm that you know you're applying for a part-time position."

I shook my head. "Part-time? I thought all the positions were full-time."

Her lips pursed together. "No, unfortunately our staffing requirements were determined by the projected volume of business we're expecting for each department, with a little wiggle room in some of our busier areas as we gear up for the grand opening. So, while I agree with Chris's assessment that Human Resources is the main artery of the hotel, our projected volume isn't expected to meet the requirements to allocate three full-time staff members in HR. Not now, at least."

What the hell? Part-time? I couldn't pay for my car loan and hope to get out from living at my parents' house with part-time pay. Unless it was really good part-time pay.

"So what is the rate for the file clerk position?"

"Fifteen dollars an hour." The smile on her face somewhat brightened the delivery. *It's not bad.* Minimum wage was nine. So fifteen bucks an hour to be a clerk wasn't awful. *I mean, how hard could it be?*

"And how many hours a week would that be?" I asked.

"Twenty hours." The chirpy tone in her voice didn't soften the blow.

"Is there ever a chance to work more than twenty hours?"

I asked.

Her hair swayed against her shoulders. "No. Overtime has to be preapproved."

I didn't know what I expected her to say but twenty hours a week, even at fifteen an hour, wasn't going to cut it. I'd clear less than $300 a week after taxes.

"I can't live on that." The statement left my lips without a thought.

Her eyebrows furrowed and her nose crinkled. "I understand." She tapped a purple pen against the conference table between us. "What if I could make the hours just under forty a week?"

I nodded like an eager dog about to get a bone. Hell, I'd bark, roll over, and play fetch if it meant more hours on the time clock.

"The hours wouldn't all be in the Human Resources department, but if you're flexible, I think you'd be perfect for our other part-time position in the Food and Beverage department. It's limited to nineteen hours a week, but that would bring you up to thirty-nine hours every week."

"That'd be great."

"Excellent! I'll coordinate with the Food and Beverage director but I think this will work out well."

"Oh, that would be fantastic. Thank you."

The remainder of the interview dealt with the standard pre-employment questions, which I assumed were developed with the expectation of a certain answer. It was hard to take them seriously, but I tried.

"Katie, can you explain a situation where you were

confronted with a tough personality, and how you handled it?"

"Binge eating works well."

She laughed and fanned away my comment. I provided a more acceptable answer to her question. If I were confronted with a tough personality, I'd take a deep breath and try to figure out ways I could diffuse the situation. In reality, I'd probably first cry in the women's restroom followed by a night of binge eating.

Her next question, though, was my favorite.

"So, Katie, what's your strongest attribute and your greatest weakness?"

"I work too hard, I care too much, and if I could, I'd be at the hotel twenty-four hours a day because I'm just that hard a worker and I care that much." I grinned afterward to really sell it. The sooner I passed, the sooner I could eat.

"Excellent!" Holly waffled on about policies and procedures, had me sign some new employee paperwork to check my references, and then gave me the coveted thumbs-up to proceed in the process. I made a beeline for the security office to get my picture taken. It was right off the loading dock where I'd spent the first half of my morning—hours later, my hunger had elevated to starving.

"Go ahead and sit yourself down there," a man in a security uniform instructed.

I quickly sat in the chair positioned across from the camera. A small mirror hung on the back of the door in the security office. I took a quick glance at my hair. It was growing out, and had actually behaved. I tucked it behind my ears to make it look longer. My highlights were new, adding golden tones to my chestnut-colored bob. Surprisingly, my lipstick was still on and my mascara hadn't smeared. I didn't look half-bad until I smiled. I noticed something black wedged between my front teeth.

"Oh my God!" I leaned forward in my chair. It toppled over and crashed down on me. I didn't care. I scurried out from underneath it, reached up, grabbed the mirror and gasped. A poppy seed from my breakfast bagel that morning had lodged between my front teeth.

"Was this here the whole time?" I pointed to my mouth, looking around for confirmation. But the only other applicant who was through the next phase of the process was the cookie-looking elf. He practically sucked all the air out of the closet-sized space we shared.

"Guess so," he said.

"Really?"

"Uh-huh."

I felt sick. "Why didn't you say anything to me?"

"I thought you had a cap or bad teeth or something," the less-than-magical little man said.

I used my pinkie fingernail to flick it away. "I can't believe it." I was almost in tears. "I've been talking the *entire* time looking like a jack-o'-lantern, and no one said anything to me?" Panic gripped me. *Oh my God, I spoke to TJ looking like this.*

"Okay, Miss Flanagan, if you're ready, the camera is all warmed up and we can begin."

"Sure, now that I have the crater out from between my teeth, I'm all grins and giggles." Humor had found a home, but it wasn't erasing the internal frenzy. *No wonder he kept closing his eyes. I would too.*

"I thought it was a spacer," Crabby Sandy said from the hallway outside the office. She had obviously passed her interview too and poked her head in. "It's not a spacer?"

"Really? You thought it was a spacer?" Elf boy said to Sandy in what I think was his attempt at flirting. It made me pause. *Did he not listen to her introduction?*

"Yeah, either a spacer or really bad teeth," Sandy said.

"You're kidding, right?" Panic and humor were bumped aside for straight-up hysteria. "Does *everyone* think I have bad teeth?"

"It's really no big deal," Elf said. "Your job is in the back of the house. It's not like you need front office appearance."

That's it. How much trouble will I really be in if I throat punch him? I can't believe no one in our group bothered to tell me. *There's loyalty for you.*

"Okay, smile real big for the camera," the man said and snapped my photo as I glared at the elf.

My photo arrived moments later looking more like a mug shot than an ID card. I was staring at it when I felt hot breath on my neck.

"It's not that bad." Bogart stood behind me and glanced over my shoulder.

Heat radiated off his body and against my back. My shoulders dropped and so did my guard. There was this odd familiarity with Bogart, like I had known him my whole life. For a moment, I again forgot where I was.

I turned on the heel of my boot to face him. "Thank you,"

I said. "But it's awful."

His brown eyes smiled along with his mouth. "Hey, those that made it past the final phase are going to raise a pint to employment. Wanna come?"

Over Bogart's shoulder, I saw TJ approach. My stomach did a somersault. *He made it too. He's on the team.*

"Uh… I'm not sure what I'm going to do."

TJ gripped Bogart's shoulder. "Hey bubba, you're going out with us aren't you?"

Bogart nodded. "Wouldn't miss it. I was just trying to get our fearless leader, Katie, to join us."

TJ raised an eyebrow at me. "It won't be a party if you're not there."

I felt my face flush and my heart race. "Well, I can't have that."

TJ patted Bogart on the back. "Let's hit it."

I quickly glanced in the security office mirror and checked my teeth.

"You look great, Katie." Bogart stood beside me.

I grinned and brushed past him to follow TJ.

CHAPTER **TWO**

The beat of the music could be felt outside the building. The faded red bricks of the two-story brownstone in old Huntington vibrated. As part of the revitalization project, the Golden Cub on the corner of Main and Pacific Coast Highway hadn't lost its original façade, but the structural integrity was given a facelift. Or so the banner draped across the entrance announced. The new owners wanted to ensure the Golden Cub would be around for more generations to experience. And an experience it was. Once the double glass doors parted, the polished cement gave way to a brewery, a live band, and a dance floor where a high-energy beat was being played and breathing new life into the decades-old music hall.

I wasn't dressed for a nightclub but that was the beauty about downtown Huntington: jeans and a Hawaiian shirt were enough to get you past the door. Someone could rock a beanie, bikini, and sneakers and get by the doorman. No cover. No dress code. The Golden Cub's lack of velvet ropes and seriously dirty sound system drew crowds that wanted to hear good music and drink IPA with the waves roaring in the background. *Damn, I love Huntington.* I peeled off my cardigan and draped it around my shoulders so that the start of my summer tan showed against my tank top. None of us were dressed to go out, but all of us were ready to celebrate.

TJ hoisted the first pint of frothy caramel-colored goodness in the air. "To the Hopeful Huntingtons or whatever Katie said."

"Huntington Hopefuls," Bogart said as his pint glass clashed against TJ's. The two sat across from each other at the table we had commandeered. Everyone else filed in beside them.

"Ah, whatever. We all got jobs." TJ raised his pint higher.

Bogart raised his pint even higher. "To employment."

My attention volleyed back and forth between TJ's hypnotic good looks and Bogart's brooding bedroom eyes. *My, my, my.* It was like watching a cockfight.

"Here, here!" Jackie said, bumping into TJ's shoulder and pint glass.

Killjoy. I took a sip of my beer.

"Must be nice to have two men's attention," Carmen from Costa Mesa said low in my ear. "I can't usually get one."

"What?" I set my glass down and brushed the side with my thumb. "No, that wasn't about me."

Carmen tilted her head toward the two of them. "I thought we were going to have shattered glass before the toast finished," she said.

"It was pretty intense," I said with a laugh.

"Then the only question you have is, which one do you like better?" Carmen's blue eyes were an exotic contrast against her butterscotch-kissed skin and silky black hair.

"Yeah, that's a question I'll never have to ask or answer." Just as soon as I looked across at TJ, his attention shifted elsewhere. I followed his gaze. Jackie wandered to the pool table. TJ didn't miss ogling her perfect backside sauntering away.

When a group of tanned, blond surfer-looking guys in board shorts, T-shirts, and flip-flops flocked to grab pool cues, TJ pushed away from the table. "I think I'm going to play some pool."

I didn't look away fast enough.

"Don't worry, Katie," TJ said. "My plans still include you."

"Worry?" My entire body flushed and I nervously giggled. TJ walked toward me.

My pint was in my hand and to my mouth within seconds. He stood above me. I set down my empty glass.

"I'm not worried. What would I be worried about?" *Shut up. Just shut up.*

I reached for Carmen's pint, took a hefty swig, and wished I hadn't. A hoppy belch sat at the base of my throat waiting to be released from park to drive.

TJ leaned over, his breath warming my neck. "Good, because there's a special game I want to play with just you."

I swallowed hard and gazed into his hazel eyes. "Really?"

"Uh-huh." His lips were inches from mine.

"And what's that? This game?"

But instead of hearing TJ's honeyed voice echo in my ear, the sound of Jackie's throaty, sexy laugh cut through the clatter of the bar just as the band switched from mash-up hip-hop and dropped to a soft soul and funk. The drum of activity had quieted to a low roar, including the pounding of my heart, which came to a cold stop when I saw the spark in TJ's eyes ignite at her laughter.

"Uh." He stepped away from me and gripped my shoulder like he was palming a volleyball. "Flanagan, catch you later?"

I barely had the chance to acknowledge him before he turned and left. I didn't watch him walk away, but I felt someone watching me. I glanced down the table. Bogart's dark eyes were a beacon. A warning perhaps? I weakly smiled in his direction and raised my empty glass toward him and then turned toward Carmen.

"Yeah, well *that* couldn't have gone any worse." I could barely make eye contact with her. "I can't speak when TJ's around. It's ridiculous. But really, what does it matter? The guy couldn't wait to cue up his pool stick, in more ways than one, and go play with Jackie."

Carmen chuckled and then signaled for the server. "Listen, Katie, the night is still young." She tilted her head toward the bar where Keebler Boy and Crabby Sandy stood side by side. "What about Chris?"

"The Keebler Elf? There's not enough beer or bourbon to ever make that right."

Carmen slapped the table with her hand. The echo caught their attention. Chris and Sandy turned toward us, but so did another Huntington Hopeful, Bogart. I hadn't even noticed he'd left our table.

"Oh, Katie, you're hilarious."

"I'm glad the truth is so amusing because that little man up there…." I shuddered. "No thank you."

"I concur." Carmen's accent was thick with certain words. "But I wasn't talking about that Chris."

"Oh, Bogart?" I shrugged. "He's… I…."

A blonde with razor-cut hair and a tan that she wore as well as her faded 501s, black tank, and Converse set a fresh IPA in front of each of us. "This is from the gentleman at the bar."

She didn't turn, but I knew it had to be Bogart.

Carmen put two fingers in her mouth and gave a sharp whistle. It felt like the entire bar looked over at us. "*Gracias*!" She raised her pint toward Bogart.

"*De nada*!" He raised a pint in return.

I smiled.

The server pulled out her electronic keypad. "So it looks like you ladies are set for drinks. How about some appetizers or dessert?"

"Actually, speaking of dessert," Carmen said. "My friend here is having a difficult time choosing between two guys."

The blonde leaned in. "Which two men are we choosing between?"

"We're not having this discussion," I said.

"The guy playing pool," Carmen said without taking her eyes off the server, who gave a nod in TJ's direction, clearly knowing who we were referring to. "And the guy at the bar. Not the albino. The one with the great ass who just bought us this round."

The server didn't even turn around, but I did look over

her toward Bogart. The heel of his boot was propped on the foot rail that wrapped around the bar, and his hands gripped the edge of the bar's granite countertop. His jeans did cup his ass, but it wasn't just his ass I noticed. The sleeves of his shirt were rolled up and he held on to the bar like he was about to do a push-up. His shirt stretched across his back, revealing muscle tone and definition. He had a perfect V-shaped torso, with a narrow waist that broadened to wide, powerful, ready-to-be-clawed-into shoulders. *Holy. Hell. He'd be fun to climb. I could wrap myself around that and stay a while.* I quickly shook my head. *Gotta be the beer talking.*

"He does have a great ass, and he's a generous tipper," the server said. "The albino's not."

"What about the one playing pool?" I asked.

Carmen and the server looked at me.

I understood the confuzzled stare. But no matter how good Bogart looked, and he did look fine, my attraction to TJ was greater than my common sense and stronger than my will.

"I don't know about him. The girl he's with opened a tab," the server said.

Ouch. I stared into my beer. *Yeah, this isn't going to cut it.* I turned to Carmen. "So your new job is at the front drive. In the valet department, right?"

"Thanks to you, it is."

"So if I need a ride home tonight…?"

"Consider it done."

"I'm betting you have whiskey." I kept the server in my sights while I reached into my purse for my wallet. "But when I say whiskey, what I'm wanting is a good, smooth, we-store-this-in-the-back-for-our-best-customers Irish whiskey. Do you have something like that?"

A slow smile spread across her perfectly tanned face. "Yes, we have a private reserve Irish whiskey."

Now my smile matched hers.

"No more IPA then? Jumping right to the reserve." Her brown eyes were a shade concerned.

"Well, you know those two guys?" I slid my emergency credit card toward her. "I really don't think there's much to decide, but even still, it's a lot to consider sober. And besides, you know what they say."

Both the server and Carmen shook their heads.

"Beer is dear, but liquor is quicker. And the quicker I drink the good stuff, the better I'll feel *regardless* of the outcome."

It's the last vivid memory I had of the night. The rest blurred when I reached the bottom of my first silky-smooth Irish shot.

CHAPTER **THREE**

"Katie, get up, get up, get up. You'll miss mass." I heard my mom in the hallway. Her usual early morning singsong voice had a painful pitch to it. *Shh... quiet.*

My head, buried in a stack of pillows, barely shook in protest because it hurt to shake. Hell, it hurt to talk. "No," I mumbled. "No church."

"My house, my rules," she said from outside my closed bedroom door.

I pulled a pillow around my ears. Coming to after a night of drinking was hard enough. To have my mom chirping happily was torture. My body ached, and I just wanted to go back to sleep.

"Come on, Katie." I heard the rapping of her knuckles against my door, and it might as well have been a log rammed against it for the effect it had on my frayed nerves. "We're leaving in forty-five minutes and you're going with us."

I tried to sit up to explain to my mother that the only way I was going to church was in a casket because I was dying, but I couldn't utter a word. I raised my head, but it bobbed back and forth like one of those drinking birds before it loses its center of gravity. The bird takes a nosedive into a glass of water, and my head did the same thing back onto the pillow. But the pillow had lost its softness. Someone had switched out my feather pillow with a cement slab. Someone was messing with me.

What did I do? Who did I piss off in a past life? Or this life? I pressed my thumb into my temple. *And what did this to my brain?*

Beer or beers? *Oh no.* Whiskey. *Shots. I thought the good stuff wasn't supposed to cause a hangover. What happened?* I rubbed my eyes. Chunks of dried black mascara fell on the pillow. *Lovely.*

I moved my hand off my throbbing temple and tried to massage the constant stabbing in my forehead but it only made it worse. I closed my eyes and hoped death came quickly.

"I don't understand. It all started out so innocently. Really." I didn't know if I was praying or offering penance.

I just needed a job. The radio station hadn't quite lived up to its job fair promise. *Good salary and paid vacation. Ha!* More like indentured servitude. But I'd bought a new, red car based off that false promise. Now I was in car loan hell, which had landed me in an employment line on the first Saturday in June.

So not how I wanted to start my summer. But I had met TJ.

I exhaled and the rank smell of stale whiskey engulfed me. *What was I thinking, ordering whiskey?*

My mom rattled off another warning.

"Katie, get up! You're not missing mass."

She had done the same thing yesterday to ensure I wasn't late for the interview. But if she hadn't been so annoying and woken me up so early, I wouldn't have ended up in TJ's group.

"TJ." It was the first word that didn't make me want to puke. I smiled beneath the bedding. "Banquet captain person." *Whatever that means.*

I slowly lowered the blankets until they were just beneath my chin. I held them tightly, drawing the warmth around me.

I opened my eyes and looked at the white speckled bedroom ceiling. The textured swirls reminded me of popcorn. I stared at the white puffs of plaster until the popcorn blurred, and all I could see were his hazel eyes, feel his breath on my neck, and hear his voice in my ear. *"There's a special game I want to play just with you."*

Does it really matter what he does? Cocooned in warm thoughts of TJ that burned deep inside me, my body stirred for release.

"Katie Maureen, are you out of bed yet?" my mom bellowed from the kitchen.

Any further lurid thoughts of TJ were quickly banished from mind and body.

I lightly kicked back my sheets, looked down at my legs, and squinted. Sand residue was caked on them, and my feet were smudged with tar.

"What the…." I reached down and dusted the debris from my legs.

My mouth was dry and the lingering aftertastes of IPA and whiskey were not mixing well in my stomach.

"Katie Maureen!"

"Relentless." I finally pulled myself into a sitting position and sat on the edge of the bed until I got my center of balance. It got worse when I caught my reflection in the mirror across from my bed. I looked like the bride of Frankenstein. My hair was standing up on both sides and something white was stuck to my head.

"What?" I pulled a strip of Styrofoam off the side of my head. It took a few hairs with it.

"I don't even want to know." I tossed the remnant toward the trash can but missed.

I gingerly leaned forward to pick it up and caught a closer look at myself in the mirror. Black eyeliner was smeared and subtly pronounced the delicate lines that had started to creep onto my face in the last year. *Twenty-four years old and I'm heading downhill.*

I blew out a mouthful of air. "Well, I guess it could be worse…."

And it was. I had almost forgotten about my hideous employee ID, but there it was on the floor beside my trash can. The contents of my purse were strewn across the bedroom. I reached for it with my foot and snagged the laminated photo with my big toe. I inched it toward me.

"Oh, that's pretty." I rubbed my eyes, but it still didn't correct what I saw. "That stupid little elf."

I held the ID beside my cheek and compared it against myself in my bedroom mirror.

"Well, it's a tie. You look like shit today, and you looked like crap yesterday." I flicked the ID card back onto the floor. Maybe I'd lose it and risk a mark on my as yet unblemished employment record to pay for a new one. *Yup, I'm a renegade.*

"Katie Maureen, get up!"

I quickly stood. My body did not agree with the sudden movement. The jolt was too jarring, too unnerving, too quick for my unsettled stomach. "I think I'm gonna be...."

CHAPTER **FOUR**

I barely made it to the bathroom before my stomach convulsed and remnants of Hamburger Hank's, the local drive-through, came rushing out of my mouth like Niagara Falls. Mashed-up french fries and chunks of hamburger and onions were carried to the surface with the help of what appeared to be a chocolate shake. I wasn't sure. It was disgusting and left an indelible splash against the white, glistening porcelain toilet bowl that my mother so painstakingly kept clean.

"Katie, are you making a mess in there?" she hollered in the distance.

I couldn't answer. The bitter, nasty aftertaste of stale beer lingered in my mouth. My pajamas smelled rank and looked worse. But somehow in my drunken state, I had at least managed to change out of my clothes.

I knelt in front of the toilet and put my cheek against

the side of the bowl. *Never again.* The cool exterior was a welcomed relief.

"I'm not going to church." I was trying to convince myself when my mother appeared in the doorway.

"You look awful." She stooped down beside me, and before I could respond, she continued, "And you smell even worse." Her look of concern quickly vanished when she got a closer whiff. "Is that alcohol? Were you drinking?"

I closed my eyes and prayed the ringing would end and the spinning would stop.

"Paddy," she called out to my father. "She's been drinking again."

"Again?" I opened my eyes. "You make it sound like I go out drinking *every* weekend."

"Well there was that time—"

"One time!" *Oh, why did I raise my voice?*

My mom's eyes locked on to mine.

"I was eighteen," I said in a hushed tone. "It was grad night. I had a *little* too much beer."

"A little too much beer? You were sick for three days, almost missed your senior trip to Mazatlán."

"Yeah, good thing that didn't happen. Wasn't like I stayed sober there."

"If that was supposed to be amusing, it wasn't." She looked away and tore off a piece of toilet paper and handed it to me. "Wipe your mouth."

I dabbed my lips as she placed her hand on my back.

"There's nothing comical about getting drunk," she said.

Actually....

My mom's eyes watered.

Crap. "I'm sorry, Mom. I really am."

Her hand gently pressed on my spine. Warmth radiated against my back and felt good, but not good enough to stop the next onset of nausea.

"Oh no." I grabbed the sides of the toilet and once again heaved what resembled the last of the fries. It was hard to know at this point. The acidic beer and bitter bite left behind by the whiskey had stripped my throat, leaving it raw and agitated. It hurt to swallow.

Yet, when my father arrived with a glass of water in his hand, I was willing to give it a try.

"Now, you're not going to like this, Katie Maureen," he said. "But it's the best remedy for what ails you." He handed me the glass. The water fizzed.

"Oh no." I shook my head. "I can't. You know I can't."

My father's cure for anything was Alka-Seltzer. The common cold, sore throat, hell, even a canker sore, he'd pop two tablets into a glass of water and wait for bottoms up. It was vile and he knew it, yet he swore by the "magic fizz-fizz" and damn if it didn't work. Either that or it was my body's way of protecting itself against another shot of seltzer.

I cringed as he held the glass of fizzing water in front of me.

"Now, come on, be a good girl and take your medicine."

"I'm twenty-four," I tried to explain to my two hovering parents who had recently welcomed me back in their home.

"This is cruel and unnecessary." I took the glass, placed it up against my mouth, and closed my eyes. The smell alone made me want to hurl.

"Come on, Katie. You can do it."

My dad could coax a pot of gold from a leprechaun, but no amount of guile would get me to drink that glass.

I shook my head and handed it back to my dad. "I can't."

"I'll leave it here, in case you change your mind."

Not likely. He left the glass on the bathroom counter, right by my head. The relentless fizzing was the only sound in the room, and it exploded in my brain. The sparkling seltzer might look effervescent, but when hungover, it sounded like a nonstop Fourth of July fireworks show.

I was not about to get up off the cold floor and move the glass to another room, so the only way to stop the fireworks in my head and restore the blessed silence was to drink the dreaded drink. *Well played, Father. Well played.*

I opened my eyes and looked up at him. The little patch of brown hair at the top of his round head always reminded me of Charlie Brown. And Chuck was nudging the glass toward me. "It'll make you feel better."

I held my breath and quickly drank the bubbling potion. I shook my head, hoping the taste and the need to vomit would disappear.

"That's a good girl."

My dad smiled and I wanted to cry. Just like Charlie Brown, there he was, stuck in the middle of someone else's mess.

"Now, you know how your mother feels about drinking," he said.

I nodded.

"And I'm not too crazy about it either. But at least you didn't drive home."

Absolute horror must have shown on my face because I clearly felt it in my body. *What?*

"Your car's not in the driveway," he said.

Crappity, crap, crap. Where's my car?

Horror morphed into terror because my father continued, "Perhaps one of your friends from work drove you home. That's the impression your mother got when you called last night."

I called last night? Really? I didn't remember. How drunk was I? *Shit.* That couldn't be good.

"Thank you for calling, by the way," my mother said and brushed tangled hair from my face. "Your friend Chris, I believe?" She looked at me for confirmation. "He sure was a nice young man."

"Bogart?" I asked. "Bogart's not young. Well I mean, he's not old. But he's like thirty-one or something. Maybe thirty."

"Oh well, then he's a real ancient mariner."

"Yah ha ha. Did he give you his *whole* name?" By this time, what my parents thought of me or this situation was a moot point. I had to know whether Chris Bogart or Keebler Chris Colombo had driven me home. The mere thought of being alone with the bad-luck elf caused my head to spin. *And where the hell is my car?*

"No, Katie, he did not give me his whole name," my mother said. "We just assumed you knew the man that was driving you home."

"Oh, I do. I do," I said. "There were two Chrises last

night," I explained. "And I just, well, my memory's a little foggy right now." I gave them my best smile.

It seemed to work on my father, who grinned; my mom wasn't as easy to sway.

"Katie Maureen, this is not the least bit enjoyable for either your father or me. I don't like seeing my only daughter hungover or questioning us about who drove her home," she said.

"I know, I know." I was thankfully interrupted by the sound of the front door closing.

"Anyone home?" my little brother, Patrick, called out.

"We're in here," my mother said. "With your sister, who's hungover from drinking too much last night."

I sank lower onto the bathroom floor and rested my head on my knees as my brother stood beside my father and looked down at me.

"Rough night?" He smiled.

My little brother's thick black lashes made his brown eyes sparkle. A set of similar lashes would easily set me back a hundred bucks. Still, it'd be worth it to have long dark lashes to bat at TJ. *Sexy.*

Patrick stared at me. Sometimes it felt like he could read my mind.

"Hey brat," I said. And he was. My baby brother seemed to have captured the good-looking genes while my older brother, Ian, had inherited the high IQ gene. I was somewhere stuck in the middle. Not too smart and not too good-looking.

"Oh, I'm a brat, huh? Then I guess you won't need a lift to go pick up your car?"

"My car!" Again the pounding in my head, but I had to know. "Where's my car? How do you know where it is?"

"I've got my sources." He winked at me.

I wagged my finger. "Don't do that." I'd never be able to see someone wink and not associate it with Mr. Clark and that tie.

"Someone's testy," Patrick said.

"Listen, the whole point of yesterday's excruciating eight-hour ordeal was to get a job to pay for my new car. Well, I got the job, but joke's on me because I don't know where I left my car."

"Then lucky for you, *baby* sister, that I do."

"Patrick!" I raised my voice and instantly regretted the echo. It ricocheted in my head like I had hollered down an empty hallway, which wasn't too far from the truth. At this point, the space that usually held reason, logic, and rationale was all but vacant.

"All right, settle down," my father said. "Patrick, why don't you take your sister to go pick up her car?"

"I'm not taking her looking like that. Not unless she puts a bag over her head."

"Oh, like your last date?" I started to laugh. Reason and logic may have left the gray matter building, but wit and sarcasm still seemed to be functioning.

I grinned at Patrick and his eyes smiled back. Despite what my mom would say about not having favorites, I did. And Patrick was mine. I grew up feeling protective of him. Now that he had outgrown that need, it seemed to have reversed, with him often coming to my aid, which is why he regularly referred to me as his baby sister. It was sweet in an irritating Patrick kind of way. But at the end of the day, I was still eighteen months older, which gave me big sister rights.

"Your sister will take a shower," my father promised my brother. "But I need you to take her to get her car. Your mother and I have date night this evening."

Seriously? Could my luck get any worse? Date night was something my mom and dad created in their thirty-fifth year of marriage. It was a sweet idea when I was living on campus, but now that I had moved back in, it made me cringe. I never wanted to be home following one of their date nights. It was beyond gross to hear them giggling like schoolkids in their bedroom after one of their infamous date nights. I shuddered at the thought.

"Listen," Patrick said. "Some of the guys and I are heading over to Sullivan's for a couple beers and to watch the game. You're welcome to join us."

It was Sunday and football was as religious to my Catholic family as church, which I would gratefully miss. I smiled at my good fortune.

"That's all fine and well," my mother said. "As long as Katie is home in time to attend the 5:00 p.m. service."

"Five o'clock mass? Oh, shoot, not on Sunday, Mom. That's only offered on Saturday," I said.

"Not anymore," she said. "They just formed a young adult mass every Sunday at five o'clock. Isn't that just lucky for you?"

For the love of all things holy. I groaned. "Okay, everyone out. Show's over. Katie's gotta clean up." When anyone started talking about themselves in the third person, it was never a good sign, but I would talk about myself in the first, second, and third person, singular and plural, and maybe even try speaking in tongues to get some privacy. Bathroom privacy trumped the appearance of self-absorption and insanity. And if it meant clearing out the bathroom, then I'd start talking about myself as if I were the trinity.

"Don't forget the cleanser under the sink for the toilet bowl." My mom pointed to the cabinet.

"Got it." A good sprinkling of the gritty powder into the toilet, followed by a quick flush, and my night of overdoing it would soon circle the drain. *Perfect.*

"Yeah, I'm not sure anything can kill that stench." My brother nudged my father, who tried to conceal his laughter.

Why can't I flush my little brother down the drain? "You're hilarious," I said. "Just be ready to take me to get my car."

"Don't worry. I've got the keys right here." Patrick dangled my key ring like bait. It worked because when I reached to grab them, he reeled them back in to the palm of his hand.

"Later." He shook his index finger at me. "And we're gonna talk later too."

"Great." I shooed everyone out of the bathroom. "Another lecture."

"Be grateful, Katie." My father leaned over and kissed my forehead.

"I am, Dad." I looked into his dark eyes. "I am."

###

After rinsing away the evidence of my drunken debacle, I filled the tub with bath salts. My motivation was twofold: my body ached and my mind was weary. I remembered the first half of the night, but the rest was murky at best.

I dipped my toe into the water. The temperature was perfect. I sank down into the oversized tub and put a warm washcloth over my puffy eyelids.

At some point, there had been a game of darts. I'd lost and had to buy the next round of drinks, but I'd been broke. *Oh no.* I used the emergency credit card my father had given me—not once, but twice. First for the whiskey and then for a round of drinks.

Fan-frickin'-tastic. I raised my hands out of the water like pom-poms and the washcloth fell from my face. *Yeah*! Another lecture on the horizon.

As soon as my mom opened the mail, I'd be toast. She paid the bills the same day they arrived. *Who does that? I mean, what's the point of credit?* Focus, Katie. Focus. *You can always intercept the mail.*

"Darts." I mentally pieced the evening together bit by bit. "Darts, then burgers. What else did we do?"

I gently moved the water around with my hands. Small waves brushed against me.

"Oh, yeah." I snapped my hands and water squirted me in the eyes. I blinked. Burgers. That's when TJ and mushroom girl, Jackie, paired off for a bottle of wine, and I switched from whiskey shots to….

Jager. I slowly rocked my head back and forth against the tub's backsplash. *What was I thinking? Why did I pick up the Jager?*

I sank beneath the water and suddenly the taste of black licorice surfaced in my mouth along with the memory.

But after the *Jägermeister, the rest of the night remained fuzzy.* I did remember a fish bowl and placing my car keys in it. But where was the fish bowl?

CHAPTER **FIVE**

By the time I dried my hair, applied enough concealer to mask the dark circles beneath my eyes, and dressed in my favorite pair of plaid Bermuda shorts and white tank, Patrick was deep into his second stack of pancakes. A plate with the remnants of his first breakfast was pushed off to the side. The aroma of blueberries, butter, and maple syrup turned my stomach.

"Heart attack food," I said as I passed him.

"No, French fries, a double bacon cheeseburger, and chocolate malt will clog an artery," he said.

I whipped around and stared at him.

"That's what I wanted for lunch yesterday, but I ran out of time."

"Well, it's what you had late last night at Hank's."

"I did?" There was no mistaking how little I knew of the previous night. *That would make sense. What I hurled looked like a Hank's combo meal.*

"No," Patrick said. "Actually you had a *double* order of fries."

"No way," I said, now chuckling. "Get out."

Though Patrick smiled he responded, "Katherine, that's nothing to celebrate."

"Katie. My name is Katie." I wasn't keen on any deviation from Katie: Katherine, Kitty, Kay, or Patrick's favorite, dumbass.

"It looked like Hank's coming up, but I wasn't sure we actually went to Hank's."

I stared at him, waiting for a response. I knew when my brother referred to me as Katherine that he was either mad, concerned, or in need of my help. And since I was the one with the missing vehicle, I was thinking it wasn't either of the latter.

"Oh, come on." I elbowed him. "It's a little funny?"

"No, it isn't."

"Well, explain this. How is it that you even *know* what I had for dinner, or lunch, or whatever meal it was for me? And why do you care? It's not like you haven't gotten plowed yourself. I remember your frat parties."

"First, a good friend called to tell me my baby sister was wasted."

"First, what exactly *is* the definition of wasted? I'd wager that everyone's interpretation would be different. Because last night, well, I'd classify it simply as fun… that I can't quite remember." It was the best defense I could muster. Hell, it was all I could muster. "And heads up, I'm *not* your baby sister."

"Secondly," Patrick said. "Whenever I did get plowed, I was at the *fraternity*, not frat house. I wasn't out in public making a complete ass of myself."

"Secondly, I didn't make an ass of myself," I said, though I couldn't really attest to that fact. "And…" I lost track on what number we were on. "Who called you?"

"It doesn't matter."

"Uh, *yeah*, it does. It *totally* matters."

I watched my brother polish off the last mouthful of pancakes and down the remaining orange juice from the carton. He delicately wiped his mouth with a napkin. I laughed.

"Your stall tactics don't work on me," I said.

"You ready?" He eyed my outfit.

"Well, I'm not wearing my prom dress, if that's what you're waiting for." I chuckled.

"Don't get sassy with me, or I won't take you to get your car."

"Lighten up and let's go." I looked around the kitchen for my car keys.

"They're in my car," he said, twirling the keys to his older, secondhand BMW around his finger. "Buckle up."

Patrick drove his car quickly and tightly around the bends and dips that wrapped around Edward's Hill in Huntington. Once rich with oil derricks, Edward's Hill now housed multimillion-dollar estates.

"Did you at least get the job yesterday?" he asked.

"Do you ever listen to me?"

"Huh?"

I exhaled. "Yes. I got the job. Well, two jobs actually, I think." It was another gray area.

I felt his eyes on me.

"I applied for a position in HR but it was part-time, and I think I got another part-time position in the Food and Beverage department. But I'm not really sure where I left my paperwork, so I can't quite confirm what position or positions I have."

I knew my answer would drive Mr. A-type personality crazy.

"But you're going to figure that out, right?"

"Sure. Hopefully when I get my car, I'll find the paperwork. That's the plan."

Patrick nodded but I could tell he wasn't convinced. I rubbed my temples, but it didn't make my brother disappear. He continued to stare at me.

"So who called you?"

Patrick turned into Pacific Crest, an elite private community. The houses all seemed to look alike, but were distinctly different. Or so the real estate agency ads plastered around town announced. Patrick's silver Beemer smoothly pulled into a driveway and parked behind a covered car. The tarp oddly seemed familiar.

Bogart appeared on the front stoop.

Maybe you're not my favorite Chris. I quickly unbuckled my seat belt and jumped out of the car.

"Did you call my brother?"

"Good morning to you, too."

"Where's my car?" I scanned the front drive.

"She's been washed and waxed." He pulled off the tarp. My red car shined brighter than the day I purchased it.

"Wow." I gently slid my hand across the finish. It glided across the polished surface. "That's amazing."

"You're welcome."

That's when the emotional hangover from drinking beyond the point of comprehension settled in, and the pit I felt in my stomach wasn't from throwing up.

"I found your hide-a-key under the wheel well, so I took the liberty of cleaning her up."

"Thank you."

"Yeah, brother, thanks a lot." Patrick and Bogart shook hands with a weird assortment of moves.

When young kids greet each other that way, you know it's usually gang related. But among old farts it's a fraternity greeting.

"How…?"

I was cut off by laughter.

"Pepperdine," my little brother said. "Phi Theta Delta. When I was a pledge, I was hazed mercilessly by Bogart."

"The Malibu campus," Bogart said and raised an eyebrow in my direction.

I stared at Patrick, who may not be as smart as our older brother but who was savvy enough to bank the tuition money he got from our parents to help pay for graduate school. He completed his undergraduate degree in three years and had his Master's by the time I was completing my four-year degree.

So I took my time. Nothing wrong with the six- almost seven-year plan.

"Seriously," I said. "How do you guys know each other?"

"Hey, I may be a grease monkey," Bogart said. "But I is educated."

"Really?"

"Don't look so surprised," Patrick said. "Despite the age difference, Bogart and I were also in the same study group for our Master's program."

"You have your Master's degree?" My tone came out differently than I intended.

"I may be a late bloomer, but the degree is hanging on my wall." Bogart nudged his head toward the house.

"That's *your* home?" Suddenly I felt as shallow as Malibu when she asked about the toilet bowl cleaners. "I'm sorry. That's none of my business."

Bogart and my little brother resumed laughing.

"It's every girl's business," Patrick said.

"I'm not like that," I said, ignoring them both. "But how did you know to call Patrick? How'd you know he was my brother?"

"Aside from the fact that you both have the same last name and you look alike?" Bogart asked.

I held up my hand like a ward against his comparison. "Ew. No."

"Oh, give him a break," Patrick said. "We're cursed with not having a forehead, but a Flanagan fivehead. Hell, your fivehead is big enough to screen a sneak preview."

"Shut the hell up." I turned away from my brother, placed

my hands on my hips, and stared down Bogart. "Seriously, how'd you know to call Patrick?"

Bogart's face softened. "When you were drinking last night, you wanted to text, so Carmen took your phone. She gave it to me when she had to go home and you weren't ready to leave."

I shrugged. "Okay, but that still doesn't explain anything."

"Your phone had a text ready to send to Patrick. So"—his hands splayed open—"I admit I checked your contacts and Patrick's picture surfaced."

"What picture do you have of me? Is it the one on LinkedIn, because that's a keeper?"

I shooed him away like an annoying gnat. "That's right… I was gonna text Patrick that I got a job."

Bogart's laughter surprised me. "Actually, the text wasn't as straightforward as that."

I rolled my eyes, reached into the back pocket of my shorts and withdrew my phone. I slid my thumb across the screen and found the text. "Oh." My voice dropped. "Yeah, okay. So this is your home, huh?"

"What the hell did the text say?" Patrick asked.

"It was mostly emojis." I shrugged. "So it's really not that big a deal."

"Then let me see it."

I knew I'd never get home and back to bed until I handed my moron brother my cell.

He read the text and looked at me. "Thinking about cheese. You remind me of my favorite cheese. I lover you?"

"I was hungry," I said.

"Explains all the food emojis," Patrick said.

"And misspelled words. I was starving."

"Cheese?" An annoyed look crossed my brother's face. He handed me back my phone. "I remind you of cheese."

"Yeah." I smiled. "You're like gouda, short and round." I hip bumped him. "That's for the forehead comment."

Patrick was about to say something when Bogart spoke instead. "Listen brother, at least she didn't say you were something plain like American cheese. Who doesn't like gouda?" He clapped his hands. "Come in and get the nickel tour." Bogart led us along a cobblestone path that actually did seem different from those of the other homes. It led to large, oak double doors that opened widely to reveal a masterpiece in progress.

"I've still got a little work left to finish." Bogart walked beneath a scaffold in the foyer. "Be careful. Watch your step."

"Working on the electrical?" Patrick cocked his head toward the ceiling.

"You got it, brother," Bogart said. "It's a bitch, too." He wiped his forehead with the sleeve of his shirt. My father did the same thing whenever he worked in the yard. I must have been staring because Bogart glanced over at me and smiled. He had a warm, pleasing smile and kind eyes. I quickly glanced down at the Spanish tile that filled his foyer.

"Well, hey, thanks for driving me home," I said to a ruddy-colored square with rounded edges. "Or, driving me to…" I didn't really know what to thank him for. "Thanks." I briefly made eye contact with him. Soft brown eyes locked on to mine. His smile radiated around the room and turned my stomach inside out.

"Well, we should get going." I tilted my head toward my brother. "I've still gotta get to church. Mass." I turned my last comment to Bogart.

"Why the hurry?" Patrick's thick eyebrows furrowed together like one knitted sock that stretched across his wide Neanderthal forehead.

"Mass. I have to go to mass."

"It's not until five o'clock." He stared at me like I'd grown a third eye. Or sprouted a second head.

"I can't go like this." Again I turned to Bogart. "If I could just get that extra set of car keys…." I started to fidget.

"What is your problem?" Patrick shook his head. "Do you need to use the restroom?"

"No. I just have to get to church."

Bogart handed me the spare set. I put them in the pocket of my shorts.

"Uh. Thanks. Thanks again. I mean, for everything. Thank you."

"Not a problem," Bogart said.

I turned toward the door.

"Katie…."

I paused, not wanting to look at him, not wanting to see those brown eyes that seemed to be serious, yet playful, dark, yet soulful, saintly, yet sinful. Eyes that held mysteries that were impossible to solve and irresistible to ignore.

I glanced at him as if he had no effect on me, which I kept trying to convince myself he didn't.

"You may want to stay away from Hank's for a while."

"Oh, you don't have to worry about that. I already paid my price." I patted my stomach. "Learned my lesson."

I was about to beat feet out of his house when his next comment stopped me cold.

"It's not the food I was worried about," he said.

I honed in on those eyes despite my better judgment. "Excuse me?"

"Well, let's just say I worked out a deal with Hank to repair his speaker."

"Speaker?"

"Yeah, apparently you felt like a little karaoke last night," my brother said.

"What?" My fear of the unknown was growing to mass proportions. "What do you mean, karaoke? I can't even sing."

"No argument there," Bogart said.

"Come on." I nervously giggled. "What'd I do?"

"What didn't you do?" Bogart said smiling.

"Oh, God." If dread was an illness, I was beginning to know the symptoms all too well: a drop in the stomach followed by a tightening that pulled deep in the center of the gut to ensure that breathing was difficult… which it now was.

"They have it on videotape actually," Bogart said to my brother.

"You have a video? Do they even make videos anymore?" I said as the pull on my gut turned into a yank that about doubled me over. "This is just a gag, right? You're both putting me on."

But instead of the tension loosening in my stomach and relieving me of my misery, it increased when my brother and

Bogart collectively shook their heads.

"Nope. No such luck," Patrick said. "I had to leave my credit card number with Hank to secure that Bogart finishes the work."

"Work? What did I do? You just said I did a little karaoke. I don't understand. What's going on?" The grip on my stomach magnified, cranking round and round into a twist of bundled nerves until I was one large knot of regret. If I didn't get actual food in my stomach, dry heaving would soon ensue.

"Listen, you leaned a little too much on the drive-through microphone, but it's nothing I can't fix. So come on in, sit down, and have some brunch." Bogart extended his arm toward what looked like a kitchen under construction.

"I broke the mic?"

"Yeah, it was probably your singing," Patrick said.

"Oh, har, har," I said.

"Katie, trust me, the video is harmless and kind of sweet. It's only a few minutes long, and you'll be out of here in time for mass," Bogart promised.

"Awesome." My little brother's face lit up like Christmas morning. He rubbed his hands together. "Goodie, goodie, goodie." He followed Bogart.

Numb. I stood in disbelief that there was a video and I had broken Hank's drive-through mic. *What didn't I do last night?*

An over-the-shoulder glance was cast my way. Bogart's eyes danced. And again that stupid, sweet grin spread across his entire face, the one that made him actually, well, look cute. "Hank's surveillance system is an archaic VHS recorder. It's grainy footage. In fact, if I hadn't been there I wouldn't even have known it was you on the tape," he said. "Come on, have a bagel. You look hungry."

"Oh, all right."

A buffet of bagels and tubs of assorted cream cheese were spread out on top of a clear tarp that covered the tile counter. Rich earth tones popped beneath the plastic. They contrasted nicely against the Spanish-tiled floor. Combined with the pine, hand-finished, custom cabinetry and stainless steel appliances, the kitchen had been upgraded considerably from a standard cookie-cutter model to an intricate modern design.

"I did all the work myself," Bogart said.

"Chris, it's beautiful." His craftsmanship took my mind off my drunken misadventures.

"You like it?" It was the first time I'd heard uncertainty in his voice.

I didn't avoid his eyes, and the words flew out of my mouth as the room overtook my senses. "Your attention to detail is transformative. The color palette and knotty wood design did more than upgrade this space." I paused and took in the beauty around me. "It made it into a work of art."

Bogart stood taller. "Really? You really think so?"

"Absolutely. It's beautiful."

"Oh, for God's sake, Katie. It's a kitchen. I know how much you like food, but it's a kitchen. The Mona Lisa is a work of art. This is simply a place to store vittles." Patrick lightly slapped Bogart on the back. "Listen, we passed the new Taco Bell on Beach Boulevard and Katie almost cried. She thought that was also a work of art. My sister's whack when it comes to shit like this."

"Beauty is lost on you." Though the moment was also lost, I glanced at Bogart. "Your kitchen and the work you've completed are truly inspiring."

"Thank you," he said.

"So where's the video with Twiggy here caught on tape?" Patrick was much too eager to watch my demise.

"Twiggy?" Bogart asked.

I rolled my eyes. "It's my idiot brother's nickname for me. Not because I'm twiggy, but to poke fun at me. And to remind me that I could benefit from losing an extra ten pounds."

"Where?" Bogart quickly scanned my body. His eyes were stuck somewhere between my shorts and my tank top. "You look great." When he looked up, Patrick and I were staring at him.

"I mean relatively speaking." Bogart clapped his hands together. "So let's go watch that video."

We followed him into the adjoining entertainment room that could easily host a movie premiere.

"I forgot something in the kitchen." Bogart disappeared and returned with a glass of orange juice.

"You better drink this first." He handed it to me.

I took a large gulp but instead of the refreshing taste of sweet oranges, my throat tingled from the carbonated effects of seltzer.

"What the hell is this?" I shook the half-empty glass in front of my host.

"Alka-Seltzer and OJ. Nothing beats a hangover like Alka-Seltzer."

"Well, I've already had my shot of seltzer, thank you very much." I stormed to the kitchen counter and slammed the glass down on the ceramic tile. I didn't care if I broke his latest masterpiece. I turned and Bogart was right behind me.

"You should warn someone before you slip them the seltzer."

"Sorry." His eyes were sincere. "I didn't know. I was just trying to help."

"Well, don't." I shook a stern finger. "I'm fine." I picked up a blueberry bagel and ripped a piece off with my mouth, trying in vain to wash away the aftertaste of spiked OJ.

"Enough with the dramatics. Let's watch you caught on tape." My brother lowered his voice to sound like a television announcer.

"Yeah, whatever, little brother. Consider this your Christmas and birthday presents wrapped into one," I said.

Patrick wiggled his unibrow.

"You're really going to like this, aren't you?" I asked, when clearly I didn't need to.

"Damn skippy," he said, using another one of his annoying expressions.

I sat on a barstool and swiveled to face the entertainment that was built out of dark *mahogany wood. It rose to the* ceiling where a red crushed-velvet curtain was tied back.

"As much as I'm enjoying the surroundings," I said and turned to Bogart, "And I really am. Your house *is* one of a kind, but can we just get this over with?"

Bogart nodded and stood in front of the drop-down screen. "Bogart Productions is pleased to introduce Huntington's first contestant for *American Idol*, Ms. Katie Flanagan."

He pointed a remote toward a row of electronics and

pushed a button.

I rolled my eyes, ignoring the hysterics my brother had already lapsed into.

Within moments, my face appeared on the screen. An extreme close-up of my face. I squinted trying to make out what was happening and then in crystal clear black-and-white video, my drunken antics came into full view.

"There's no sound." Patrick looked horror stricken, like he had discovered an empty cookie jar at my parents' house and not simply the absence of audio.

Bogart snapped. "That's right. Hold on." He pressed pause and then cued his iPhone. "Someone recorded her singing on their smartphone and texted me the video. It's too dark to see Katie but you can hear her."

I waved my hands. "That's not necessary. We don't need to hear it."

My pleas fell on deaf ears because Bogart synced the audio to the visual and my drunken antics came into full view, accompanied by enthusiastic singing. The only thing grainy about the video was my inability to dance and sing simultaneously. My voice grew noticeably lower in octaves. I hung on to the drive-through microphone and serenaded the parking lot full of cars. It sounded like an attempt at the Frankie Valli "Can't Take My Eyes Off You" song, but like my cheese text, I really didn't have a clue. I watched in horror as my antics drew comments from the audience.

"Check her out," one onlooker said. "She's trying to be Marilyn Monroe or something."

"Marilyn Monroe?" I asked no one in particular. "How do

you figure that?"

"Well, the tape didn't catch you at first," Bogart said. "When you were kind of breathless and leaning into the speaker like you were…." His voice trailed off.

"Like I was what?"

"Kind of making love to it, I guess," he said without making eye contact with me. I had done the kind of things that made other people cringe. *Awesome. I'm turning into Crabby Sandy.*

"No," another hamburger patron in the audience said. "She's more like Elvis."

I wanted to shut my eyes and erase what I was watching and hearing, but it was like a horrible train wreck. I couldn't look away.

I watched myself twirl while I slaughtered a classic song. My off-key voice sang to the onlookers. I pointed toward someone in the crowd and snapped my fingers as I sang as loud as possible. My head jerked up and down and I moved my hips, like the guy said, in a poor imitation of Elvis.

"That's not even the lyrics," I said, which caused Patrick and Bogart to chuckle.

The more I sang the more obvious my drunkenness was. "TJ, yes, I lover you, TJ."

I jumped off the barstool in Bogart's kitchen and darted to the electronics case. I frantically searched for the Stop button on any of the sleek black boxes while Patrick and Bogart literally held their sides laughing.

"No, no, no," Patrick pleaded. "Don't stop it."

"Katie, it's almost over," Bogart said.

I couldn't look at either of them. I watched the rest of the tape in mortified, abject horror.

I had belted the lyrics loudly and hopelessly off-key. My arms were outstretched and it was clear that I was singing to someone. But who? *Oh, dear God, no. Please tell me no. Please tell me he wasn't there.*

I leaned toward the screen in the direction I sang, and, if it was at all possible, the embarrassment I already felt plunged straight into humiliation.

In the distance, TJ sat on the hood of his truck, watching me.

Now, I know it's a cheesy cliché, but my jaw dropped. For certain my mouth opened and a soft gasp passed my lips. *Oh. My. Hell.* The shocked, almost horrified look on TJ's face made my mouth gape wider, if that were even possible. TJ sat beside Jackie Portobello—with his arm around her no less— and grimaced while I made a complete and utter ass of myself to him and what looked like half of Huntington.

What do I have to do to be permanently relocated by the FBI? A new identity with undisclosed whereabouts was in short order.

"Please turn it off." I was almost in tears. "I can't believe I did that."

My angst fell on deaf ears. I turned around. My brother was rolling around on the floor while Bogart steadied himself against his entertainment console.

They were laughing hysterically. It wasn't helping.

"Stop it," I pleaded. "Come on."

My brother sang the same messed-up lyrics to Bogart as I

had to TJ, and Bogart mirrored his movements.

"I lover you, too," Bogart sang, creating his own lyrics. But why not, I had.

"Okay, enough," I said. "Really. Come on, guys. It's not that great."

"It's classic," Patrick said, coming up for air long enough to ask, "Do you think I could get a copy of this?"

This sent Bogart straight on the floor beside my brother.

"Okay, well, I've gotta go." I looked for the Eject button, pushed it, and grabbed the tape when it popped out.

"No, no, no," Bogart said. "That's mine. Actually… it's property of Hank's."

Patrick held up his finger. "No more. My side hurts. I can't breathe."

"Glad you find this so amusing." I stepped over Bogart and was about to step over my brother when he grabbed my ankle. His sudden movement brought me tumbling toward the floor. I stumbled to regain my footing, but my legs intertwined with Patrick's—or Bogart's. I couldn't be sure. It was like a game of Twister. There were more legs beneath me than a centipede. I held the video tape against my chest and extended my other arm out like I was the Heisman trophy, but it didn't protect the play. I tried to hopscotch my way out of the mush pile, but my fancy footwork failed, and I lost my balance. The video tape flew out of my hand, and I watched in slow motion as it skidded across the tile floor. My body, with my arms outstretched like a diver, came dangerously close to the same fate.

With no way to stop what was inevitable, I did the only

thing I could: I tucked my chin. For some reason, I figured that when I landed face-first on the exposed tile in the kitchen, it wouldn't seem so bad. And at first, it wasn't. *Okay then.* I didn't hear any bones break and I ran my tongue along my teeth and they all seemed to still be intact. *Nice.*

I remained facedown and calm until I felt the warm trickle of blood. I reached up and patted my nose. The pain set in almost immediately. I withdrew my hand, saw that it was covered with blood, and started to cry. I leaned up and blood gushed out of me like water out of a popped fire hydrant.

"Oh my gosh, Katie, I'm so sorry." Patrick scurried toward me. "I was just trying to tackle her," he said to Bogart, who was instantly on my other side.

"I know," he said. "It was an accident."

I dissolved into tears. "Get away from me." My shoulders shook. "Just get away."

"Oh, honey, I'm so sorry." My little brother placed his hand on the back of my head. He stroked my hair, trying to calm me down.

"Kates," Bogart said. It was my mom's nickname for me. No one else had ever called me that but her.

I looked over at him. He was just there: soothing voice, gentle, calm, warm, caring brown eyes. *Those damn eyes.*

"What?" My tone was snappy.

"Let's get you into the bathroom, okay? I have a medical kit in there. Can you get up?"

I wanted to yell at him again but I didn't. Instead I steadied myself against him as he carefully helped me stand.

"Atta girl," he said.

"Katie, honey, I'm so sorry." Patrick's continued apology was annoying until I saw myself in the bathroom mirror. My nose had tripled in size. Blood continued to run and with my hair hanging in my face I was Carrie on prom night. My white tank top was streaked crimson.

"Oh, dear Jesus." I collapsed on the closed toilet.

"You're going to be okay," Bogart said.

I looked up at him, and for a moment I believed him. This guy was seriously beginning to bug me and I wasn't sure why.

Bogart pulled a white box with a red cross out from beneath the sink. He pushed aside bandages, rolls of tape, and ointment, rooting around the contents of the deep storage container until he pulled out a medium-sized ice pack. He squeezed it until it popped and activated the cool ice.

"Do you think you can hold this on your nose?" He knew I could. It was his composure and compassion creating an assurance in the midst of chaos that made me reach for the ice pack and graze his hand in the process.

Bogart reached again beneath the sink and returned with a navy-colored washcloth that he held beneath a stream of water in the sink.

"Okay," he said, "in a few minutes, why don't you take off the ice pack so I can clean you up, and we'll have a look at the damage."

"Damage?" My voice cracked.

"Ah, that's just an expression." Though he didn't sound as convincing as before.

Patrick continued to rub my back. He kissed my forehead. "I'm so sorry."

"I know you didn't do it on purpose," I said.

"I didn't. I swear. I was just trying to tackle you."

"Well, brother, you completed the play."

He nervously laughed.

Bogart withdrew the washcloth from the running water and wrung it out, but before he approached me he stopped. "May I?"

I nodded.

He positioned himself in front of the mirror, I think to block my view. Not that he needed to; my contacts were blurry from crying. He leaned toward me and I removed the ice pack. The washcloth was soft, warm, and welcoming—like his touch against my skin when he gently held the side of my face to clean away the blood.

"There's a little tear." He studied my nose carefully.

"Tear?" My voice rose.

"It's in the cartilage," he said.

"Does she need stitches?" Patrick asked.

"Stitches?" Now I was frantic. I hated needles.

"I don't think they can stitch this. It's right on the nostril," Bogart said to my brother, who stood beside him. They both stared at the center of my face.

I carefully touched my nose. The pain had spread across my face. My head throbbed but I wasn't sure if it was the remnants of the hangover or the tackle.

"Don't touch it," they both said. "Just leave it alone."

"Let me look." I carefully stood.

But they both blocked the mirror.

"Really?" It was all I had to say. Either that or my nose

spoke volumes, because Bogart stepped aside and Patrick followed suit.

"Oh my hell!" It was bad enough when my nose had tripled in size. But the swelling had caused bruising, not only under my eyes, but around my eyes. I looked like an overweight raccoon with a botched nose job.

"No. No. No." I leaned forward to examine the tear of skin in my right nostril. I gently touched the flap and it moved back and forth, causing more bleeding. I lowered my head. "Oh my God." I shook my head, tears streaming down my face along with snot, blood, and who knew what else. "I look awful."

"That's not possible," Bogart said.

I couldn't make eye contact with him. Or anyone. Not like this. Not ever. "I'm a monster."

"Kates," he said and gently cupped my shoulders. His hands were a salve all their own. With his wrists parked on my shoulders, his pulse beat against my bare skin. Despite the tear in my nose and its gigantic supersize, I slowly, carefully inhaled through the one nostril that wasn't clogged or dripping blood. The warm scent of his skin calmed me. Hints of sage, sandalwood and vanilla infused me. Bogart had a clean, subtle scent with an addictive edge that made me want to turn into his neck. With my head bowed down in front of him, I found myself leaning into him until I almost touched his chest. For a moment, I thought he was going to kiss the top of my head. I glanced up and with tears welling at the corners of my eyes, I looked into his, and everything blurred. All I saw was Bogart and all I wanted to see was Bogart. Nothing else mattered.

"Hey," he said.

Every part of me ached, but when Bogart spoke, the pain seemed to subside.

"Why don't you sit back down and let me clean you up a little more?" But his hands still held my shoulders, steadying me. I stayed before him until he let go. Heat radiated off him with an energy that invited me in. It was an energy that drew me to him and made me want to park my ass on the counter, wrap my legs around him, and pull him to me with a force I'd never known. It was an energy that brought healing, happiness, and all sorts of hot sex in one heated moment. And the heat that bounced off Bogart in this little bathroom was crazy. Too crazy. I was lost in what was happening or what should or could happen. All I knew was to look to him for the answer. And since Bogart was much taller than me, that was easy to do.

"Oh, Kates" was all he said. And in that instant, I completely forgot that my brother was in the same room with us.

Bogart's eyes were a lighter shade of brown than mine, but the way he looked at me made me feel something that was foreign, yet familiar. I quickly looked away.

He laughed, reached down, and tipped my chin up, so I had to look him in the eye.

"I won't bite," he said. "I promise."

"Yeah, but she might," my brother said.

I jerked my elbow back and hit Patrick's stomach.

He groaned.

"That," I said, turning toward him, "was for breaking my nose."

"It's not broken, is it?"

"No," Bogart said. "It's just really swollen and the cartilage is torn. It'll take a few days before it returns to its normal size, but it will."

"How can you be so sure?" I asked.

Bogart broke eye contact with me and looked down at his medical box. "I have my EMT license." He fished through the medical supplies.

"Master's degree, EMT, self-proclaimed grease monkey… what don't you do?"

"Well, I'm also an Eagle Scout." He winked.

"Don't do that," I said. Mr. Clark had seriously ruined winking.

Bogart's cheeks turned as red as my stained tank top.

"Eagle Scout, huh? Well, I made it all the way to Cadet in Girl Scouts," I said.

"And that's just because of the cookies," Patrick said. "Except Twiggy here ate all the proceeds."

"Do you want another piece of me?" I cocked my elbow back.

Patrick's chuckle combined with Bogart's made me laugh.

"Okay, now that we've all had fun, can I go home?" I said.

"Let me just put a bandage on you first." Bogart gently applied gauze to my nose. He stood back and studied his work. "Perfect. No one will notice."

"I thought Eagle Scouts weren't allowed to lie."

Bogart smiled.

"Hey, look at it like this," my brother said. "Least you won't have to bother with any pesky autographs."

"Autographs?" I asked.

"Sure," Patrick said, "from your *Solid Gold* dancing last night." He burst out laughing.

"Don't even." It was a losing battle. My *American Idol* moment would go down in the annuals of the Flanagan family.

"Your brother has a point," Bogart said between breaths. "This nose thing is probably the best thing that could happen to you."

"And how do you figure that?"

"Well, anyone who saw you last night probably won't recognize you tomorrow?"

"Tomorrow?" I asked.

"On Monday. We start our new jobs tomorrow."

My face went blank and once again my mouth dropped open.

CHAPTER **SIX**

I delicately dabbed an extra dose of concealer beneath my eyes, which did nothing to mask the purplish bruising. *Concealer? More like revealer!* I could have saved time and just written on my forehead with an indelible marker, "Black Eyes Here! Come take a look!"

I leaned back in my seat and glanced at myself in the rearview mirror, thinking a distant view may make things look better. *Nope.* The only distance that would make that face better was the distant future. A month from now, my face would be back to "normal." *Hell, I'd settle for average today.*

But that wasn't going to happen. I'd have to face the day with a face that would turn heads, but for all the wrong reasons. My nose wasn't broken, but it was in bad shape. It was big, bulbous, and red. *Nothing's going to fix that.* I flipped my rearview back in position and stepped out of my little red sports car I called "Scarlett." It was in homage to Scarlett O'Hara, who was beautiful, smart, and not afraid to make a grand entrance. Just like my car. Unfortunately, it was not the best day to be driving a red car. Most people want to have their cars resemble their personalities, not the center of their face.

The upside to my nose was that my mom showed mercy on me and took me shopping at Nordstrom before mass on Sunday. When her personal shopper, Stella, caught sight of me, she ushered us quickly into a private dressing room, handed us each a bottled water, and brought the clothes to us.

I smoothed the front of my faux-wraparound dress and secured the sash that anchored the jersey together. Another quick glance, though this time in the reflection of the car's side window, and the dark navy polka-dotted dress had a classic, yet subtly playful edge to it that said professional but not stuffy. Or so Stella told me. And since my dress drew enough attention, Stella had paired it with a simple navy pump. I never would have pulled the outfit together. *Damn, that looks good.* I tilted my chin with the confidence someone else's credit card could buy. And perhaps if I cocked my chin like this all day, people would notice my dress and not my nose. *Thanks, Mom.* My first day of work was already looking better.

The hotel's loading dock was a short distance from the employee parking lot. Waves banking against the shore echoed in the distance. The beach was one crosswalk away from the hotel. *So what if my nose is ginormous, my eyelids are bruised, and I look like a demented clown from a Stephen King novel? I have the beach in my backyard. Life is good.*

Mr. Clark, the director of Security, was the first to greet me when I showed up at the door to the Human Resources office. It was directly adjacent to his office.

"So what does the other guy look like?" He nudged me in the side, but gratefully didn't wink while he unlocked the door to Human Resources.

I grinned, preparing for what I could only imagine was the first of many such comments.

"My little brother tripped me," I said. It was the truth but it sounded awful. "He didn't mean to, it just happened."

"Brothers. What are you going to do?"

"Move out," I said.

Mr. Clark chuckled. "You're still living at home?" There was too much emphasis on "still."

I nodded.

"My wife's brother is looking for a roommate. He has this great place in old Huntington. Cute little two-bedroom apartment." He opened the door and moved aside, allowing me to enter the office.

"Thanks, I'll think about that."

"Let me know. He's a good guy. About your age, too. Twenty-five, twenty-six?"

No amount of concealer could erase those damn crow's feet that began at the corner of my eyes and seemed to spread as far as Kansas.

"Twenty-four. I'm twenty-four."

"Like I said, same age as you. Eric's twenty-four, too. What are the odds, huh?"

"Long," I said under my breath, but he didn't hear me, so

I gave him a clueless grin as I scanned the two-room office. The main room had two faux-wood desks butted up against each other. A row of putty-colored filing cabinets occupied the entire back wall. Mr. Clark must have noticed me staring at the cabinets, because again he nudged me. This guy was a winker and a nudger.

"Quite a job, huh?" he said with raised eyebrows.

"Uh-huh."

"I mean, look at it." He pointed and I followed his finger. Vanilla-colored file folders, easily stacked three feet tall, were positioned on the floor beside the desk in the far corner of the room. A lavender sheet of paper was placed on the top of the pile. I glanced and recognized my name.

I picked up the letter. The paper was linen and the name Holly Walker was embossed in black lettering. I fingered the inscription.

Katie,

Good morning! The Executive Operating Board (EOB) stayed out a little late celebrating the completion of our mass hire. So, I won't be in until much later. Perhaps 9:30 or 10 a.m. Janet will be in by 9, so if you have any questions she can assist you. In the meantime, I've left a little filing for you to start.

A little filing? I looked up at Mr. Clark. He was reading the rest of the letter over my shoulder.

I tried to keep the files in alphabetical order. But well, things got crazy. Please start with the A's and work your way through to the Z's. Thanks! See you later!

Holly

P.S. Some of the files aren't hole-punched yet. So if you could hole-punch the papers and place them in order, that would be super! I left Maria Alvarez's file on top as an example.

I placed the stationery on what I assumed was my desk, since it was barren and the other desk was already adorned with knickknacks, and picked up the first file. The label on the tab read: Alvarez, Maria DOH: 06-01-2016.

I wasn't sure what DOH stood for but Mr. Clark, who was now my shadow, piped up.

"Date of hire." He pointed his chubby finger to the acronym.

"Oh, sure. Thanks."

"They should all say June first," he said. "That's when everyone was hired."

"Absolutely." I mimicked the pat responses I had heard during the interviewing process. It was something I'd noticed Holly and the other board members say. They used adjectives like "excellent," "outstanding," and "fabulous" for almost any answer they gave to questions posed to them. "Do you like working in a hotel?" "Absolutely!" "What is it like to deal with guests?" "An outstanding experience."

Mr. Clark turned to leave. "I'll let you get to work. But don't forget about Eric. He's really a great guy and he needs a roommate."

"Eric. Outstanding. Yes, thanks. I'll remember that." I half smiled.

"Until you pass your probationary period, you know, the first ninety days of employment, we won't be issuing you an office key. So I'll be opening your door every morning."

I continued to smile until he left the office.

"Fantastic," I mumbled and placed my backpack on the chair beside the desk.

The top file drawers stood a good foot taller than me. I looked for a stool and came up short. Holly's office was behind the reception area that the recruiter, Janet, and I shared.

"Holly Walker, Director of Human Resources" was stenciled in black on the door.

I peeked inside the room. Her office was considerably larger. A large cherrywood desk, not a pressed particleboard piece of crap held together with glue like ours, was positioned in the center of her office. A lavender bowl on the corner of her desk held a bouquet of heather.

I stepped inside. The air was aromatic with hints of lavender and heather. It reminded me of the bath beads I got every year in my Christmas stocking. Subtle, yet inviting. I inhaled and deeply, slowly exhaled the scent.

Holly's desk blotter was deep burgundy with a matching cup holder that was filled with yellow pencils with plum-colored eraser tops.

"Looks like Barney has a fan."

I jumped and spun around. TJ stood in the doorway to Holly's office in a black tuxedo, which I now knew was one of the uniforms in the banquet department. But damn if he didn't wear a tux well.

"Whoa! What happened to you?"

I reached up and covered my nose. I had almost forgotten about it. The absence of pain was a form of amnesia. Now, I was fully aware of how awful I must have looked as he approached me dressed like James freakin' Bond. And I looked like Dr. Evil.

"Hey, you okay?" He stared at my nose.

I couldn't find the words so I nodded.

"I was worried about you," he said. "You tied on quite a good one."

A video montage of my lounge act at Hank's resurfaced. I felt my face burn with embarrassment.

"Yeah, well, I am *so* sorry about that singing thing." I waved my hands as if that would erase the entire drunken episode.

"Why are you apologizing? I thought it was cute."

Cute? Great. I headed toward the door to pass TJ, but he blocked my exit.

"Seriously, are you okay? What happened?"

"Oh, I'm fine. This…." I pointed to my face. "This was an accident."

"It didn't happen Saturday night? You didn't drive home, did you?"

Does he care? "No, no, no. I got a ride."

"Well, that's good. I would have offered you a ride, but I was already taking someone else home."

Someone that wasn't hammered. Someone like Jackie?

"It's no big deal. I got home safely."

"Chris?" TJ asked.

I shook my head. "Chris?"

"Yeah, did he give you a ride home?"

"Oh, you mean Bogart. Yeah, Bogart gave me a lift."

"That's great. He's a good guy," TJ said.

"I guess."

TJ slowly nodded.

"He knows my brother," I said. "They went to grad school together. He was helping him out by driving me home. I asked Carmen." Bogart had cleared the fuzziness of that night. "I guess she had to leave early, which is why she couldn't be my ride home, so she asked Bogart to give me a lift." I shrugged. "He did and I got home."

"I'm glad to know you got there safely."

"Yup. I sure did. Thank you though for checking." I pursed my lips together. "And again, my apologies. I usually don't drink or act like that—ever."

TJ cocked an eyebrow, which made me lose all composure, and I started nervously giggling before he uttered a single word.

"Somehow, Katie, I find that hard to believe. You were pretty wild."

Wild? You have no idea how wild I can be. Let's kick these folders to the floor, sprinkle heather all over us, and untie my dress. I'll show you wild. But when I looked up at him, he didn't look me in the eyes like Bogart had; he stared at my nose. TJ only seemed to see my imperfection.

"I better get filing." I reattempted to make my exit and pass him.

He put his arm across the doorframe.

"So…," he said, glancing down at me, only this time he

seemed to actually look at me. TJ towered above me, and God help me, he was one tower I'd like to climb. My cheeks flushed and I felt my body temperature spike, stirring the blood in my veins.

"Yes?" I quickly imagined all the many things he might say next. *So... what are you doing after work? So... wanna grab a beer? So... wanna come over to my place? Go for a swim? So....*

"What happened to your face?"

His question lowered my temperature to a chill and brought me crashing back to reality.

"Oh." It felt like someone had drained all the heat from my body. My blood ran cold. "My brother accidentally tripped me."

He nodded, but didn't say anything. That was when I got into trouble. When people were quiet, I somehow felt the need to fill the space. *Beware the jabberwocky.*

"We were picking up my car at Bogart's," I started, "and I had the video and they wanted it back and so he reached out, my brother that is, and grabbed me and I came crashing to the floor. Only Bogart's house isn't finished yet so I landed on exposed tile. Brand-new raw tile that cut my nose, but thankfully," I said, coming up for air, "didn't break my nose."

"Bogart's, huh?"

I shrugged, hoping to downplay any connection between me and Bogart. "Yeah, like I said, he's friends with my brother. In fact, he's like a brother to me. *Completely* platonic."

TJ dropped his arm from the doorway and braced my shoulder. He squeezed it hard like I was his buddy, or worse, sister.

"I'm glad to know you got home all right."

"Thanks, I'm fine." I moved past him and toward the pile of papers and files that waited.

"I'll let you get back to it," he said. "When does Barney arrive?"

"Oh, Holly?" I laughed. "She's not coming in until later."

"So…," he began again in his sultry voice, but this time I didn't allow my mind to run away on some romantic tangent. Instead, I waited for him to continue his sentence while I sat behind my cubed-sized desk sandwiched between stacks of files.

"You've got the place all to yourself, huh, kid?" A flash of his smile and a knowing look; his flirting would be my undoing.

Despite myself, I smiled. "Looks that way."

"I'll come check on you later." He turned toward the door. "You know,"—his hazel eyes twinkled mischievously toward me—"in case you need any…." He purposefully paused and I stupidly gazed.

"Any what?" I took the bait.

"Ice." He grinned like a Cheshire cat. "I'm your man."

"Thanks," I replied flatly and waved him out the door. "Great. Go back to your banquet."

I picked up the first file and looked at the stack in front of me, realizing my chances with TJ were about as likely as me finishing all the filing before the end of my first shift. It just wasn't going to happen. Yet, despite the overwhelming odds of both scenarios, I found myself working in vain for a different outcome when another voice interrupted my momentum.

"So I'm just like a brother to you, huh?"

It felt like my heart plunged to my stomach. I glanced up to find Bogart leaning against the doorframe. He had on a pair of faded blue jeans and a white cotton polo that had the Waterfront Point emblem embroidered in gold. A worn leather tool belt hung below his waist and damn if he didn't look good, which, once again, bothered me.

"Oh, hey, hi," I said, trying to act as if I hadn't heard him. "How's your first day?"

"Not bad, sis." He smiled.

"Come on. How did you even—"

"I may be the *legs* of this place, but I've also got *ears* and you weren't particularly quiet in your rebuttal to TJ of our relationship."

"Relationship?" I attempted to raise one eyebrow but settled for both arching up.

"Correction, friendship," Bogart said.

"Well, we are friends, aren't we?"

"If you say so." Bogart shrugged.

"I do. I do say so. I thought that's what we were. I mean, are. We're friends, right?"

"Sure."

"Hey…."

"Look, it's no big deal. I just came to check on your nose."

"So you make house calls?" I smiled.

"Uh-huh. Let me let take a look." He approached me.

I set down the file I had been working on and stood. Our proximity reacquainted me with his scent.

"What kind of soap do you use? Or is that your cologne?"

I blurted, and then covered my mouth with my hand. *What the hell is my problem?*

His brown eyes drew together as if in thought. "Go ask Mom."

Laughter escaped through my fingers. I dropped my hand. "Funny, that's cute."

Bogart carefully touched my nose like you would if you were checking on a cake while it baked. Though he had workingman's hands, they weren't rough. He patted the sides of my nose and leaned toward me.

A wave of heat flamed in my stomach. I stepped back and instantly lost my balance, slipping on the stack of files behind me. I was midfall when Bogart swooped his arm around my waist and scooped me up.

I gasped. "You're so strong."

"Kates, you don't weigh a thing."

We were closer now than in his bathroom. *Kiss me.* The thought popped into my head and I nervously giggled.

"You know," he said with his mouth inches from mine. "I'm really just concerned with the tear in your nostril."

"Duh. I know that."

Bogart was still holding me when he looked in my eyes. I stared back into his, but neither of us said anything. He let me go.

"Your nose looks fine. It's healing well."

"Oh, okay." I swallowed and quickly regrouped. "My mom said the swelling would go down and the tear would eventually close."

"Well, Mom would know," he said with a wink.

"Don't do that."

Bogart laughed. "Is there anything I *can* do that won't offend you?"

I exhaled. "Uh, yeah, probably not." I playfully grinned. "I'm just not a big fan of winkers."

"Duly noted."

Whatever energy had been there left. I didn't know what else to say. We stared at each other. I liked Bogart. I did, but it was just different with TJ. TJ made my knees weak. TJ made me willing to do things I wouldn't normally do—like serenade him. Bogart was Bogart and my eye contact with him was broken by the annoying voice of another Huntington Hopeful.

"Excuse me."

I smiled softy at Bogart as if to say good-bye before I looked over to find Trish standing in the doorway, only she didn't look quite as Malibu Barbie-ish as normal. She was wearing a black dress with a white bib apron tied around her barely-there waist. A matching white kerchief sat on her head, which caused her fluffy bleached-blonde hair to stick out on the sides. The combination of the uniform and her Dutch-style hat made her look like an overstuffed pastry. When Bogart glanced in her direction, he looked back at me, and we both could not contain our chuckles.

"Excuse me," she said again, her tone growing more irritated.

Bogart stepped aside but not before he reached into the pocket of his tool belt and handed me an ice pack. "Twist it to activate the ice. Then place it on your nose."

I looked at him and again our eyes connected. "Thank you."

He smiled. "You're welcome." Bogart paused, his lips twisting in thought.

"What?"

He leaned toward me. "Just for the record," he said. "I like your dress. I think you look really nice today."

No one else noticed. My chest swelled and emotions caught in my throat. "Thank you."

He grinned and turned to leave.

"So…," I softly called him back. "The polka dots aren't too much?"

"To be honest," he said in a hushed tone. "I like to connect dots."

My stomach did a somersault. I tossed the ice pack on my desk and watched Bogart strut out of my office. As he passed Trish in the doorway, he spoke over his shoulder.

"See you, sis."

"You're just as annoying as a brother," I said but he had disappeared behind the black puff of taffeta that concealed Trish.

"Hello?" Trish stomped one of her black mules on the floor. It was the only fashion-conscious item she wore.

"Yes, Trish. What can I do for you?"

"This is H and R, right?"

I wanted to laugh and remind her that we weren't an accounting firm, but instead I said, "Well, this is the HR office."

"Hello! That's what I said, H and R."

"Yes, how can I help you?"

"Well for starters you can tell me who chose this outfit for me to wear?"

Before I could respond she continued.

"I'm not wearing this. It's ridiculous. Have you seen what they're wearing in the Wave?" She was referencing the hotel's on-site deli.

"Uh, I haven't had a chance to check out their uniforms yet."

"Well, I can tell you it's a helluva lot better than this getup. Who ever thought of this crap anyway?"

"I did," an older male voice answered. I looked past Trish to see Jimmy Johnson, the director of Food and Beverage and my other boss. Jimmy had a shock of thick beautiful hair that had this salt-and-pepper look that really worked, which was great because sadly his face didn't. His cheeks were pitted and badly scarred from what I think was decades-old acne. And when he spoke, his lower lip dragged with the signs of what I could only imagine was a past stroke. Despite a face that looked like it had gone through hell, Jimmy's eyes were a grayish-blue that had the intensity of steel. But something told me underneath all that bravado he was probably malleable. Still, I fought the impulse to stare.

"Oh," Trish said.

"Cielo Grande," Jimmy said, "is our fine-dining restaurant. Our guests come for a formal dining experience, not a T-and-A show."

I held my breath waiting for Trish's reaction.

"Well, I don't know what you mean by T and A but those girls in the Wave have a much better uniform than I do. They get to display their assets."

"As I have already mentioned, your assets are not what I want to showcase in Cielo Grande. Your job is to hostess," Jimmy said out of the side of his fallen face.

Trish let out a mouthful of air and rolled her eyes. She seemed to fear no one.

"In a couple weeks though," he said, "I'll be auditioning dancers for our California Coast nightclub."

"Really?" Trish replaced the surly look on her face with sweetness. "What kind of dancers do you want?"

"I've ordered two large cages to hang from the ceiling," Jimmy said without apology. "I'll be looking for go-go dancers."

"And what's the uniform look like?"

"Oh, I think you'll like it," he said. "White knee-high boots with leather miniskirts and halter tops."

Trish jumped up and down in her black-and-white getup and clapped her hands together. "Yes, yes, yes!"

"Not so fast," Jimmy said. "You don't have the job yet. But if you do well as a hostess at Cielo Grande, and that means presenting a polished Waterfront Point appearance," Jimmy stressed, "maybe, just maybe, I'll consider you for one of the dancer positions."

"Thank you, thank you, thank you." Trish reached out and stroked his arm. "I won't disappoint you."

Unbelievable. Her emotions changed on a dime. Luckily, she left as quickly as she had arrived.

Jimmy watched her leave and shook his head. I had overhead Jimmy on the loading dock the day of the interviews. He'd been smoking a cigarette and talking to Mr. Clark about "all the fake pretense and other bullshit" he disliked about the hotel's management.

He looked at me and tilted his head.

"I thought you didn't like all that Waterfront Point tagline bullshit," I said. I hadn't even started working for him and I was already cursing. Yet somehow it seemed to fit with him.

"You're right, I don't. But I use it when I need to," he said.

I smiled. "Good to know."

A crooked grin crossed his face. "Listen, I just came by to let you know I won't be there at one when you get on your shift. My daughter's graduating this afternoon, and I have to get there early to grab a seat in the shade."

"Where's she graduating?"

"Riverside."

"Oh, I'm sorry," I said.

A graduation in Riverside, California, in June was never a good place to be. The humidity combined with the triple-digit temperatures could turn an afternoon commencement ceremony into a sweat bath. I didn't envy him or his daughter.

"Yeah, me too," he said. "Anyway. I left you a few memos to type and distribute in the mailboxes. Other than that, I thought you could get your desk organized. I left the office supply book and a list of supplies I like to keep in stock. Go ahead and order yourself whatever you need."

He must have seen the only excitement that crossed my face all morning because he quickly added, "Don't go too crazy. We're on a budget."

"Yes, sir."

"I know I'm old, but you're making me feel older. Don't

call me sir. My name's Jimmy. Everyone else around here may give you that Waterfront Point bullshit about Mr. and Mrs. around the guests, but I'm going to tell you now, my clients call me Jimmy, and I expect everyone who works for me to call me Jimmy. Understood?"

"Yes," I said and caught myself from saying sir. "Absolutely, Jimmy."

"And please," he said. "None of that 'absolutely' and 'excellent' bullshit either, got it?"

"Yes… Jimmy."

"I can't stand that crap. It sounds about as phony as it is. Plain English, that's all I want. *Comprende*?"

I wanted to be a smartass and respond with *Si*, but opted for, "Yes sir, I mean, Jimmy."

He smiled and wagged his finger. "No more of that bullshit. Take messages and leave them on my desk. I'll be back tonight to finish up the menus."

"Okie dokie." I glanced at my watch and realized only an hour and a half had passed. "That can't be right," I said to no one in particular and resumed my post behind the stack of files.

CHAPTER **SEVEN**

My week began in a navy jersey dress of classic polka dots and ended in a lemon tweed pencil skirt, a cream-colored matte-silk blouse, and pointy-toe black pumps. Thanks to my mom and her personal Nordstrom shopper, I was on track for getting best-dressed new hire. Add to it, I had also mastered the routine of working in two departments. I was on fire.

I filed from eight to noon in HR, broke for an hour lunch, and then clocked back in and worked from one to five as the Food and Beverage secretary. On Friday, I slid my time card into the punch clock like a pro. *Yeah, I'm badass.*

But that pumped-up, I-can-conquer-anything feeling quickly diminished when I walked into the Human Resources office. No matter how much I filed, there was always a new stack waiting for me. *How many new employees can they hire?*

It probably didn't help that the only work I actually

accomplished happened during the first hour of my day when I wasn't constantly interrupted by Janet, the recruiter. Janet arrived by nine and had somehow gotten the impression that my sole purpose in HR was to serve as her sounding board. Maybe it was the fact that my job as a file clerk was rather mindless. When she discovered I could file and listen at the same time, I suddenly became a captive audience to a play-by-play account of her dating mishaps. I had to admit her escapades often caused me to pause, lose track of my place in the file drawer, look up, and realize her dating exploits were actually true.

"When I decided to get my boob job," she began on Friday morning, causing me to pause, stop, and look up.

"You knew I had a boob job, didn't you?"

It was one of those moments when you know you shouldn't stare but just can't help it. Janet was wearing a tight-fitting designer suit. The jacket wasn't buttoned and now the stretched seam on the jacket and the bulging buttons on her silk blouse made sense. Her long blonde hair couldn't cover the fact that she was, as my brother Patrick would say, stacked.

Janet reminded me of a typical Orange County girl. She drove a white convertible, had an endless tan to match her limitless wardrobe, and was engaged to a guy in Finance but she still played the field. "Just in case," she had once said in a hushed tone. Her boobs blended in well with the rest of her perfect aesthetics.

"I hadn't really noticed," I said. It was truthful. The only mounds I saw were the growing files that had accumulated.

"More applicants," Janet said when she handed me yet

more files to add to my pile, which had tripled by week's end.

"Well, when I got my boob job, Bobby said to me, 'J-J,' that's his nickname for me, isn't that cute?"

"Absolutely." My head was back down in the alphabet.

"'J-J,' he said to me, 'It's like going to the circus and getting two big cones of cotton candy.' That's how he felt about me getting my boobs done," she said. "Cotton candy, can you believe it?"

I gave her a quick glance. "It is original."

I filed what I hoped was the last Gonzalez and moved on to the Hernandez section. I spotted Vasquez at the bottom of the stack. "Shit, I'll never get this done."

"Oh, you can always come in tomorrow," Janet said. "On Saturday."

Pause, stop, and look up. My face held the word I didn't dare speak. *Saturday?*

"You know." Janet leaned over her desk, and the tops of her two large cotton candy cones peeked out of her designer silk blouse. "Holly's allowed to authorize overtime right now." Her voice was barely above a whisper. "I saw the budget. She's slated for like twenty hours of OT."

"Really?"

Janet nodded. "That's why I'm taking my time." She sat back and slowly waved her arm across her desk like one of the prize girls on a game show. "I mean, why should I break a sweat making twenty-two dollars an hour when I could get thirty-three an hour on the weekends? You know?"

I couldn't respond. I was still stuck on the twenty-two dollars an hour part.

"You get time and a half on the weekends," she said.

I quickly did the math in my head. Half of fifteen was seven fifty. Fifteen plus seven-fifty was….

"Twenty-two fifty?" I realized my time and a half rate was fifty cents higher than Janet's starting pay.

"Hey, that's good money for filing."

"Do I need to get it approved? I mean, how do you…?"

Janet shook her head. "When Holly comes in, just go in and tell her that you have a lot of projects and that you don't want to get behind. Then let *her* suggest coming in on Saturday. She likes to think it's her idea. Besides," Janet said as a smug look crossed her face. "If we don't get the work done, someone has to."

"Oh, like she'd have to come in and do it?" I asked. I didn't mind passing up twenty-two fifty an hour if it meant all my filing would be done when I returned on Monday.

"No." She shook her head. "Are you kidding? She'd just hire a temp. She's done it before."

"A temp?"

"Yeah, you know, a temporary assistant from an employment office. But then she's looking at paying that person anywhere between fifteen to twenty dollars an hour and the temp only gets like eight of that."

I couldn't believe what I was hearing.

"So Holly's paid up to twenty dollars an hour for someone to do what I'm doing for fifteen dollars an hour?"

Janet shrugged with a nod.

"Unbelievable."

"Well, you are just part-time, and we try to pay our part-timers well, but sometimes it's not that much."

"You're not kidding."

"It is only filing," Janet said.

"Sure, right. It's only filing." I glanced at the file cabinet that contained a week's worth of my work. Tears pulled at the corners of my eyes. I turned from Janet toward the wall to quiet the hurt that welled inside of me. I didn't know why, but I cared about those stupid files. *It's only filing.* But it didn't lessen the empty, hollow feeling that sat in the pit of my stomach, like nothing I had accomplished that week in HR mattered.

"Hey," Janet said.

I kept my back to her and my head in a file.

"When you hit your ninety days, ask for a raise."

"Really?" I cringed. Asking for money wasn't something I was very good or comfortable with. At the radio station, I watched my friend Chelsea work her way up the ladder while I stayed stationary. It wasn't that I didn't do as good a job, but tooting my horn to seek that promotion or bump in pay just wasn't one of my strengths.

"The rich only get richer," Janet said.

That drew my head out of the file cabinet. I quickly wiped my eyes and looked over my shoulder. "How's that?"

"Look, I've seen your wallet. You have an American Express platinum card, right?"

I glanced at my backpack. My wallet was nowhere visible. "Uh-huh."

"Well, you pay the annual fee, right?"

Well, actually it was my father's card and he paid the fee,

but for the sake of shutting her up, I nodded.

"I don't. I don't ever pay the annual fee."

"Okay...."

"It's why the rich remain rich," she said as if that would clear up any confusion. "I never pay annual fees. I call the credit card company and tell them that I have excellent credit history, which I do, and that if they want to continue to have *my* personal business, which they do, then they will waive their annual fee—which they always do."

"And that works?"

"Absolutely," she said in her best Waterfront Point rhetoric.

"Who knew?" Though I could never imagine my father calling American Express and telling them that he wasn't going to pay their annual fee because they'd be lucky to have Paddy Flanagan as a patron. Nope. Wasn't going to happen. And actually, I was proud of my pop that he paid his annual fees. Someday I'd pay my annual fee too. It just wasn't going to be anytime soon on fifteen an hour.

"It's what makes the world go around." Janet grinned and I wanted to smack that smug look right off her face with a file folder.

Instead, I said, "I'll have to give it a try." I knew I didn't have the balls for such an attempt. Hell, I wasn't even born with any.

"Stick with me and you'll be living large before you know it."

That actually made me laugh. "Sure, will do." I turned my attention back to filing.

"No, come on. Seriously. Start with Holly. Work the

weekend with me. A lot of guys in the Finance department do. It'll be fun. You can even wear shorts."

Working with Janet and wearing shorts were the two least motivating incentives—ever. If Janet had her way, by the time I left that office—if I ever did—my life would consist of working alongside her every weekend. But on the upside, I'd probably be sporting a new set of tits courtesy of some poor schmuck in Finance Janet hooked me up with along the way. Still, while Janet wasn't a draw, twenty-two dollars an hour certainly was.

I returned to my file pile. "Is it just me, or do the majority of new hires have Hispanic or Latino surnames?" It was a comment more to myself, but Janet responded.

"They don't mind making minimum wage."

I whipped my head around to see if she was serious. Her bright blue eyes practically glistened.

"They don't," she said.

"Uh… do you present higher paying positions?" I asked.

Janet's well-tanned face nearly drained of color. "Staff members always have the option to apply for an internal transfer."

She sounded as rote as the employee handbook on fair hiring practices.

"But, Katie, let's be real. For someone without a formal education, they're happy to have a job and be employed," she said.

If I had eaten breakfast, it would have come up. My inclination was to return to filing, but when I looked at the names fanned across my desk, I couldn't stay silent.

"I don't agree. I think Carmen from the front drive has a college degree, but"—I shook my head—"that's not the point. To advance beyond the lower-wage and entry-level positions, staff members have to be educated about advancement opportunities."

Janet's eyebrows rose and she waved her hands frantically like an air traffic controller trying to slow down a runaway plane. "Whoa, whoa, whoa. My position isn't to educate candidates during the recruitment process. Their job is to come prepared to the interview with questions I can answer. Everything they need to know about the position is online, and if it isn't, those are the questions they ask. But to educate each applicant about the hotel.... Do you know how many people we screen a day?"

"I can only imagine," I said, thinking a softer approach might be more effective. "And I know from what you've told me about the recruitment process that hotels have helped establish careers for people in marketing, accounting, and hotel operations. It's really great and provides a foot in the door for a lot of people."

A pleased smile spread across her face.

Yeah, you get more flies with honey, and Janet liked her honey.

"So I get it. I know that to qualify for a managerial or executive position, job candidates need to have certain business and operational skills. And I know that your position as recruiter is to guide applicants through this process, which has been very fruitful in the past." I paused and let her soak in the accolades of my obvious career compliment volleyed her way. "But I was just curious about those other career opportunities, like"—I shrugged—"I don't know, filing. When I signed and accepted the file clerk position, I don't remember anywhere on the job description that stated a college degree was a requirement, yet it pays above minimum wage."

"It does." Janet smiled again.

"So for positions like file clerk or trade positions like landscaping or food prep, is there a way we could post these positions or suggest them to the staff members who are making minimum wage?"

Janet crossed her arms over her chest. "Most of these candidates that you're so concerned about are working part-time."

I shook my head. "Then why am I filing them in the full-time file cabinet?"

"Well," she rolled her eyes, "you shouldn't. They aren't supposed to be filed under full-time because they're like you. They have two part-time jobs, but they're working less than forty hours a week so they don't get benefits. Only the staff members who work a full forty hours should be filed in the full-time cabinet."

My mouth fell open. "So all these candidates"—I picked up the top half of my stack—"are working less than forty hours a week without benefits?"

"Yes, but they get paid decent wages and they're happy. They've got steady hours, and a lot of them get to work in two departments. So they may work in Housekeeping and Laundry and then the other half of the day they rotate to Stewarding."

"Well, that's much better. They make beds for the first half of their day and then they wash dishes for the latter. Awesome." I felt like all the air had left my lungs. *Is this where I'm working? Do they only care about people with college degrees? Or full-timers? What about everyone else?*

"It's really a win-win, Katie. They're getting consistent hours with a top-rated hotel chain."

"Sure. They're almost working full-time hours and stuck at minimum wage. It's a real win-win."

She shrugged. "They could always decline the position."

"Or…" I kept my voice light and cheerful, hoping to make, and not hinder progress, "they could be banquet servers. Heck, they make less than minimum wage, but they get a percentage of the banquet revenue, which puts their hourly rate much higher than minimum at nine bucks an hour. Have any of these employees"—I glanced at the labels—"like Martinez, Nunez or Solis been told they could cross-train and learn a new trade?"

Janet paused and then burst out laughing. "You're adorable. For a minute I thought you were serious."

I was about to say I was serious when Holly walked into the office. Janet shot me a quick glance. I made more money per hour than the people I'd filed away in the wrong cabinet, and I was about to ask for even more. A pang of guilt hit me in the stomach. But then the thought surfaced. What help would I be to any of the people in these files if I had to quit to earn more money somewhere else? I waited until Holly returned with her usual cup of coffee from the employee cafeteria before I brushed myself off and approached her office. I lightly knocked on her door.

"Holly?" I said with uncertainty. I wasn't sure how to approach this weekend overtime thing, but I had twenty-two good reasons to give it a shot.

"Oh, good morning, Katie, come on in." She waved me into her office. "So, how has your first week been?"

"Excellent," I said. "Really good. But I haven't made as much of a dent on my filing as I had hoped." I waited for her reaction. A neutral look on her face prompted me to proceed. "I know how important it is for me to start working on the insurance enrollment forms and the ride sharing program. But I haven't even had the chance to tackle either of those projects. The filing…." The exasperated expression on my face was anything but fake.

"It's a big job," she said and then glanced at her desk blotter. A spreadsheet was tucked beneath the burgundy flap. Her index fingernail, painted in a shade of lilac, skimmed down the column. "Well, you've kept to your twenty hours this week," she said.

I took a sneak peek at the spreadsheet. There was an OT column beside HR. Janet may have had parts of her anatomy inflated, but she was telling the truth.

"This is the time sheet for our department." Holly turned the paper toward me.

Three names, listed in alphabetical order, appeared: Boile, Janet. Flanagan, Katie; and Walker, Holly.

Time clock punches, logged in military time, preceded each name. A running total appeared at the end column. Fifteen was beside my name.

"This doesn't include your punches for today," she said. "Hmm." She drummed her purple fingernails on her desk. "Janet?"

"Yes." Janet appeared in the doorway.

"How are you doing with the recruitment files?"

Janet rolled her eyes, exaggerating her response, "I'm swamped," she said through a smile.

"Were you thinking about coming in this weekend?"

"That's a great idea," Janet said. "Sure, I could do that."

Holly exhaled. "Okay, well, Katie, if you want to work on Saturday, you can."

"Saturday?" I asked, feigning ignorance.

"I normally don't allow overtime hours." Her voice took on an authoritative tone. "But since we just conducted a mass hire, and I have the smallest department with currently the most amount of work to do…."

Janet and I both nodded.

"Jerry, I mean, Mr. Adams," she said, correcting herself. Only the executive board could refer to each other by their first names. "Mr. Adams said he'd approve any extra hours I needed. So if you want to work on Saturday, Katie, you can."

Before I agreed, I wanted to ensure I would be paid the time and a half that Janet had dangled as bait.

"Would that be considered overtime?"

"An excellent question," Holly said. "And I appreciate that you remembered the overtime issue we discussed during your interview. Yes, it would be overtime. So you would make time and a half. Again, I don't normally allow it to happen but we are seriously understaffed, so if you would like to come in on

Saturday you'd be paid time and a half."

"Thank you. That'd be great. I'd love the opportunity to catch up on my work."

"Super!" Holly clasped her hands together. "You can work up to eight hours."

It was more time than I wanted to forfeit of my weekend, but the money was too good to pass up.

When Janet and I returned to our desks, Janet looked over at me and smiled. She leaned forward and whispered, "See, the rich only get richer."

CHAPTER EIGHT

An hour lunch wasn't nearly enough time to decompress from four hours of Janet. I wanted to punch something, and opted to punch out my time card via the time clock. Better to keep my pride, dignity, and most importantly, my job intact. It may only be filing, but right now it was half of what kept me employed.

The best part about the second half of my day, aside from the fact that there was no Janet, was that Jimmy left me alone. Instead of purple notes written in purple ink, like I received every morning from Holly, Jimmy wrote his notes in thick black pen on graph paper. His instructions were clear, the tasks were fun without being overwhelming, and his letters were visual eye candy.

"I was trained to be an architect," he once told me when I commented on his penmanship.

Up to that point, my entire week had been spent writing memos, distributing them in the Food and Beverage department mailboxes, and creating menus on the computer.

"Everything is done in-house." Jimmy stood beside my desk. He placed another box of the thick, high-quality paper used to print menus for Cielo Grande, the fine-dining Italian restaurant, on the corner of my work station.

"The Wave keeps running out of menus. Should I order more paper and run a mass printing?" I asked.

The Wave was the on-site deli that locals often visited because of the teenage girls Jimmy had hired and the uniforms they wore.

"They're using them to write down their e-mail address and phone number." Jimmy shook his head. "But it is free advertising."

The Wave staff wore Hawaiian-print bikini tops with matching sarongs and white tennis shoes. There wasn't any alcohol served in the Wave, but that didn't stop the twenty-one and older crowd from swooping in to look at the locals serving lunch.

Jimmy held up his finger. "Give me a minute." He disappeared in his office, which wasn't more than ten yards away from my desk.

When he returned, he handed me a stack of résumés. "What we need are more servers. High schoolers are perfect for this job, or recently graduated high school girls." He tapped his finger on the stack. "Look for their age. They have to be at least sixteen. The younger, the better, but they have to be able to work."

"Sure, why not. Maybe we can pay them less than minimum wage too," I mumbled.

Jimmy placed his hands on his hips. "Who ate your lunch?"

I glanced up at him. "I'm sorry. I've had four hours too much of Janet. But it does beg the question, isn't she supposed to go through these for you? Isn't that kind of Janet's job as the hotel recruiter?"

Jimmy tilted his head, and his lower lip dragged to the side. "Janet's about as useful as a rash."

I raised my hand and Jimmy high-fived me. "That's what I'm talking about," I said.

"So I gather you're not a fan of Miss Boile?"

"Nope. Not even a little."

Jimmy couldn't hide his smile. "Is she the reason for your foul mood?"

"Let's just say that I don't agree with her hiring practices, or rather her philosophy on the recruitment process. I think her idea of closing the minority hiring gap is to hire as many minorities as she can for the lowest paying positions. It's bullshit." My hand rose to my mouth but the damage was already done. "I'm sorry. That was inappropriate workplace language." Now I sounded like the employee handbook.

Jimmy leaned his tall frame over my desk and gripped the edge with his hands that were tanned and dotted with age spots. "Listen, I like your spunk, but not everyone here would agree with you, especially in regards to the hiring practices. So when you need to vent, come into my office, close the door and vent. But not here. It's too public and you never know who may overhear and misunderstand."

"Thank you. I will."

Jimmy patted me on the back as he stood. "Don't lose that fire. It may come in handy."

I clenched my teeth together but it couldn't hide my smile. "Thanks." I glanced at another pile of files on my desk. "So you want me to weed through these applicants."

"Yes, I'd rather have you sort through the résumés. You know what I'm looking for."

I nodded. "Will do. And how are you going to get these applicants past Janet and Holly? Have you met them?"

A gruff laugh escaped. "Just do your part."

"Got it. So what about the Wave menus?"

Jimmy rubbed his chin while he looked at the Wave's takeaway memo. "Print it on the aqua paper. It costs less to purchase in bulk."

He picked up a piece of the lightweight colored copy paper that was in a black tray on my desk. "I'd bet my next paycheck that there's a lot of these floating around Huntington with phone numbers and e-mail addresses written on them."

I shrugged. "Usually people just program numbers into their cell phones. And no one exchanges e-mail addresses."

Jimmy crossed his arms over his chest. "Then what's happening to all my menus? Why are they all disappearing?"

"Honestly?"

"No, I'd rather you lie."

I felt heat rise to my cheeks. "I think it may have something to do with the pictures of the servers we have printed *on* the menus. There's a server beside each sandwich. So when someone asks for a Sunrise Special, you've got to wonder if they're asking for the sandwich or…."

Jimmy's head leaned back like he was inspecting the ceiling in the administrative offices. "That would make sense, too."

I smiled. "Thanks, Jimmy. So do you want me to remove the pictures of the servers?"

Jimmy vehemently shook his head. "Absolutely not. We've had the strongest sales in the Wave since adding those pictures to the menu. What I want you to do is find more cute young girls in that résumé stack."

"Well, let's hope that's what they wrote down under skill set, cute and young."

Jimmy's sideways smile filled his face. "Okay, okay. Next item."

"What about the Banquet department?" TJ was on my mind.

"Banquets?" Jimmy repeated my question. "We won't start doing any banquet menus until the holidays. Right now, they're getting slammed with weddings. That's the bulk of their business. Weddings. Everyone wants to get married on the beach. And the Waterfront Point is the only beachfront resort in Huntington."

It was the first time Jimmy sounded like a promoter.

"Alrighty then." I swiveled my chair around to face my computer. I moved Jimmy's daily note from beside the new projects he had just assigned to the list.

"Not yet." Jimmy guided me away from my desk. "It's Friday," he announced. "Food and Beverage meetings are every Friday." He pointed his finger toward the back hallway.

"Oh. Okay."

Jimmy and I worked well with one-word responses. He didn't like a lot of chatter. And frankly, after any shift in HR, the quiet was welcome.

He led me to the back hallway and to the service entrance of the California Coast nightclub. The grand opening had kicked off on Monday with a football drink special and continued with promotions all week. I knew this because I had been responsible for typing and printing up the tabletop menus. Each night had a different theme. I was particularly fond of the Wednesday midweek special, "Over the Hump Hamburger Hash."

The chef, who was Danish, took a spin on an American classic and created a Danish burger: a hamburger topped with a fried egg and melted cheese. Instead of a hamburger bun, Chef placed his burger on top of a pile of hash browns. Not surprisingly, the protein-style burger was a huge hit. Jimmy was considering adding it to the menu in the Wave.

Last night was "Thirsty Thursday" and the bitter, strong stench of stale beer greeted me when we entered the dimly lit bar. Jimmy switched on the lights, and the glare bounced off the black lacquered tabletops.

"Belly up to the bar." Jimmy was a chameleon who changed with his environment. There even seemed to be a swagger to his walk when he strode into the nightclub.

He slid a yellow pad of paper and one of his trademark black felt-tip pens toward me at the bar.

"You're here to take the minutes."

I uncapped the pen and watched as the managers and

assistant managers in the Food and Beverage department assembled at the tables surrounding the bar.

TJ was one of the first to arrive. My legs began to sway beneath me on the barstool. TJ put a pad of paper, pen, and folder on a table beside the bar.

"Afternoon, Jimmy." He extended his hand to our boss.

"TJ."

By the time everyone had arrived, they had each shaken hands with Jimmy, including Chef, who tended to be distant and curt. They all paid homage to Jimmy.

Is this how organized crime works? Or is it simply that Jimmy's holding court? Hard to tell. Still, no matter how the men and women felt personally about Jimmy, they showed their respect. Hell, Jimmy demanded it.

One by one, each manager took turns giving a two-minute recap of what was happening in their department. I wrote feverishly to keep up with the quick exchanges. The only time I drew a breath was when TJ spoke.

"We're getting hit hard with weddings," he said of his department. "But we've got our staffing covered."

My pen paused. TJ was focused on Jimmy, who showed no emotion.

"Overtime hasn't been an issue," TJ added.

Jimmy, who wasn't allowed to smoke in the nonsmoking bar, chewed on his pen cap. Occasionally he'd throw out something, but mostly he listened. Finally, in the last ten minutes of the meeting, Jimmy stood and looked at me. He held his capped pen, pointed it toward my notes, and shook his head. I set down my pen and placed my hands in my lap.

"Listen up," he said. "We've had a good week, but this is only the beginning. I've noticed a few things that went wrong."

He paused, turning his body and pen cap toward Bob Stewart, the restaurant manager at Cielo Grande.

"Bob," Jimmy said. "I never want to see guests waiting in the foyer, understood?"

I briefly glanced at Bob, who looked like he was about to respond, but thought otherwise.

"Absolutely," he said.

I cringed. *Jimmy hates the blanket Waterfront Point response.*

"Aisha." Jimmy now directed his pen cap to the bar supervisor. "If I ever come in here again and smell the aftereffects of rank beer and piss, you'll be demoted to a housekeeper, understood?"

Aisha, who was a transferred employee from a Point resort in Egypt, wasn't quite accustomed to Jimmy's style.

"Well, then maybe you should talk to Housekeeping," she said. "I called Cherrie more than a dozen times to have them clean the carpet, but she's 'blown me off,' as you Americans would say."

"I don't want your damn excuses!" Jimmy snapped and I flinched. "I want results. Or is that too American for you?"

"No, not at all," Aisha said, completely unaffected by Jimmy's hollering. "Would you suggest I clean the carpets myself?"

I thought I was going to lose the daily free lunch I had eaten in the employee cafeteria. I sank down on the barstool and lowered my head. I barely raised my eyes to look at Jimmy. His jaw was clenched, his face was the color of a fresh beet, and I could have sworn the dash of salt in his hair had stiffened. I know my entire body did as I anticipated the verbal onslaught that was about to ensue.

Jimmy calmly took a breath and smiled.

"Aisha, if that would ensure that the carpet smelled and looked better, then by all means, roll up your sleeves and have at it."

It couldn't be that easy. I snuck a peak at TJ, who wore a half smile. This didn't seem to bother him, nor did he appear intimidated by Jimmy. Two attributes I wished I possessed, because my stomach was tight with tension. I made a mental note to not eat lunch before the Food and Beverage meeting in the future.

"Chef," Jimmy said.

"Sir?" Chef responded in a thick Danish accent, though his sir didn't annoy Jimmy.

"I'm glad to see you're making use of the meat before it spoils."

"Thank you, sir," Chef said. "Today we served the remnants of Wednesday's Hamburger Hump day in the cafeteria. It seemed to go well."

"Oh gross," I heard myself say out loud and then watched as all eyes found their way to me. I looked over at Jimmy, who had the first smile on his face.

"If you don't like leftovers, you might want to rethink eating in the cafeteria," Jimmy said.

The entire roomful laughed, even Aisha.

"Note taken." My stomach grew queasy thinking of the two-day-old hamburgers the cafeteria cooks had reheated and that I'd eaten as if they were fresh.

"Speaking of leftovers," TJ chimed in. "What's your position on the banquet staff eating the extra plated food?"

Jimmy said nothing.

"I know the Waterfront Point Resort policy on overage," TJ said. "But what's your position?"

It was a bold question. TJ was placing Jimmy in a position to either back the hotel policy or counter it. Jimmy was smart and did neither.

He simply shrugged. "I know how slammed you get, which makes it difficult for your staff to break and go eat." Jimmy looked over at Chef. "How do you feel about this?"

Chef looked at TJ and then back at Jimmy. "I don't mind it so much as long as it's kept in the back of the house."

The back banquet hallway was removed from the guests' view and the kitchen staff.

"I don't want my cooks to see them eating," Chef said. "They're not preparing five-course meals for servers."

"Understood," TJ said, and the entire room got the message. Eat with discretion, but if they were caught they would be on their own. No one, not even Chef, and certainly not Jimmy, were about to lose their jobs over a meal policy infraction.

My work in HR reinforced the necessity of policies and procedures, which prohibited any staff from eating anywhere but the cafeteria. This included the executives, who were continually in violation of this policy, but who had the luxury of an office door they could close whenever they had plates of contraband food.

"Let your staff know," Jimmy said as everyone stood to leave. "Chef will be preparing a menu tasting at the end of July to showcase our fall offerings for all Food and Beverage employees." He turned toward me. "This includes you, Gidget."

I hopped off the barstool and smiled at my sudden nickname.

"Everyone can participate in the menu testing. Gidget, please include that in your minutes."

I wrote down his last directive and followed Jimmy out into the back hallway. No one left the bar until he exited. Jimmy pointed his pen cap toward the loading dock. I walked quickly beside him to keep up with his pace.

Outside on the loading dock, Jimmy pulled a pack of cigarettes out of his white dress shirt pocket. He gently shook it until a cigarette fell forward. He fished it out with his mouth. The afternoon sun bounced off his chrome lighter. He flicked it with his thumb, leaned toward the flame, and took a long drag.

When he exhaled, I found myself inhaling. My mom used to smoke. The first hit off the cigarette always seemed to smell the best. Then it was just gross.

"So what'd you think?"

"I think Aisha has… backbone." I stopped myself from saying girl balls because that was just demeaning.

"The hospitality industry can be brutal. You've got to be tough in Food and Beverage. I don't mind that. It's how she goes about swinging her authority."

Maybe you can speak up to Jimmy as long as he controls how you do it.

"Take that kid, TJ, for example," Jimmy said and I smiled. "He's smart. He knows how to ask a question and get the answer he wants without being difficult. I like that."

Me too.

"But I've got my eye on him."

"Why?"

"He's still young and he's got some proving to do."

"Don't we all?" My thoughts escaped without any filter.

Jimmy's sideways smile surfaced. "I suppose you could be right. But…." Jimmy shook his cigarette at me. I turned from the suffocating smoke. "Proving yourself and playing politics are two different beasts. One will help you grow, and the other will dig you an early grave."

"True that."

"Go ahead and type up the minutes and distribute them."

"Will do."

I headed toward the loading dock double doors.

"Gidget."

I turned on my heel and smiled at Jimmy. A long "Yes" followed.

"You did good in there today."

"Thank you, boss."

"As soon as you get those typed up, get on outta here. It's Friday. Enjoy your weekend."

"I will. Thank you."

###

I returned to my desk to find Barbara Bee, the head secretary in the secretary pool, scrolling through my computer files.

"Whatcha looking for?" *And how did you log on to my computer?*

Barbara held up one finger, topped by a long acrylic nail. It was painted red with gold flourishes on the tip.

Normally someone's brush-off would bother me. But this was Barbara. Barbara had taken me under her wing. In less than a week, I had learned more about the computer's operating system and programs than I had throughout five years of college computer tutorials.

Barbara had the knowledge and the know-how to oversee the administrative area that housed five women, including Crabby Sandy, who was proving her skills may have been better utilized as a server. The girl couldn't type to save her life, and she had claimed to possess top dictation and computer skills. But there hadn't been a typing test, so she was now part of the administrative wing. Sandy, though, was good with handling the multiple personalities she reported to. She never lost her cool and that counted for a lot.

I was the only administrative assistant assigned to one person. The other four women supported the entire catering, sales, and executive staff. There was too much work for too few people, but it was all the hotel had allotted in their opening budget. That meant Barbara often pulled longer hours than the rest of us.

Barbara had thick, black hair that she kept cut short. Her

calico-blue eyes were hidden behind large turquoise-colored glasses. She was extremely skinny and was constantly munching on hard candy. Today she smelled like butterscotch, and the bulge in her cheek revealed the buttery candy tucked inside.

"Hello, Katie." Her focus remained on my keyboard. "How was your first Food and Beverage meeting?"

"Wild."

"They usually are."

Barbara had been the first Waterfront Point employee. She'd worked at the pre-opening office, so she already knew a thing or two about Jimmy and the rest of the executives, though she wasn't someone who would say an ill word about anyone.

"Can I help you?"

Barbara worked the keys on my computer at breakneck speed. "Oh, I'm sorry, Katie. I hope you don't mind?"

"Not at all. What are you looking for?"

"Well, before they got me the blue bomb," she said, referencing her new computer. Barbara named all her computers. "This Halloween machine used to be mine."

My computer defaulted to a black-and-orange screen saver. It wasn't my choice, but I hadn't had time to change it.

"And…." She glanced over her glasses at the computer. "I was hoping I had saved a copy of the critical course."

"Critical course?"

"Every manager and executive is responsible for creating a critical course. It's a blueprint for how they plan to operate their departments and who they anticipate moving forward."

"Hmm." *Interesting. Holly would have one and so would Jimmy. And if it's on my computer....* "Would you have saved it on disk or a thumb drive?"

I glanced at my watch. I didn't have much time left to type the minutes, copy them, and stuff them in the mailboxes. My early Friday was slipping by.

"I already checked my files and I couldn't find it. I've got to find it." She looked at me. "It contains all the budget numbers and the payroll expectations. Jerry will kill me if I didn't keep a copy."

Barbara's desk was outside Jerry Adams's office. The general manager called her to handle the more discreet, confidential memos that were always urgent.

"What about your memo file?" I asked. "I bet it's in there. You have us save everything, remember?"

She smiled. "Everything but the confidential memos. Jerry keeps a copy in his personal file."

"So where's his copy?"

She looked at me from beneath her large-framed glasses. "He 'misplaced' it."

"Oh." I stood quietly behind her and glanced at the clock above the printer. "Do you think I could use your computer?"

"Sure, darling. Go ahead. Do you know how to log on?"

"Not a clue."

"Just hit Control-F and that'll get my computer back up."

"Thanks."

The administrative area was a narrow workplace with a strip of desks that ran the length of the room. My desk was the first in the row of desks. So whenever anyone walked into the administrative area, I was their first point of contact. *So much for Keebler Boy Chris's back of the house philosophy and where I fit. He's so full of fudge.*

The administrative area also served as the hotel's business center. The business center hadn't been built but that hadn't prevented it from being advertised as an on-site service amenity for the hotel guests. Barbara had decided we would pool together to meet guest requests. Luckily, we hadn't been interrupted today by a guest needing to fax, copy, or overnight a document. Because once a guest arrived, all other work ceased.

The Waterfront Point Resort policy stated very clearly that "a guest always comes first." It was a fine policy, but try explaining that to Jimmy or the other executives who always wanted to come first, guest or not. Balancing the scales between the executives and the guests had already proven to be a challenge some of the administrators, like Sandy, wanted no part of.

"Hi Katie," Sandy said when I sat down at Barbara's desk, which was directly in front of her.

"Hey Crab— Sandy." I was still breaking myself of the nickname associations I had created during last weekend's mass hire. It was hard to believe only a week had gone by and not a month.

Though gum was not allowed to be chewed by any staff member, I could always hear the cracking of Sandy's gum. It was a sharp, constant snapping that drove me crazy.

Smack. Crack. Pop. "So you going to the club tonight?"

"What club?"

"The Coast."

I turned around. "You mean California Coast?" *The stanky smelling bar I just left?*

"Hello! That's what I said, the Coast."

I was always behind on the hip new names the other admins were creating for the hotel outlets.

"I didn't think we could go to the bar? We aren't allowed to be on the property outside of work." Damn if I didn't sound like a carbon copy of the policies and procedures handbook Holly constantly quoted.

"We can if we have an executive sign a pass."

"A pass? Who would sign that?" My boss and executive, Jimmy, appeared beside the new desk I occupied.

"You got the minutes typed?" He didn't have a cigarette dangling from his fallen lip but smoke clung to him nonetheless.

"Well, uh, Barbara needed my computer...," I began and then settled for a simple answer. "No, not yet."

"Okay, well get moving. It's Friday. I've still got to line up the entertainment for tonight."

"Jimmy?" Sandy cut in.

He nodded in her direction.

"Me and Jackie wanted...."

This should be good. Incorrect grammar and a special request all rolled into one.

"Jackie and you wanted to inquire about what?" Jimmy asked with his hands on his hips. His body language should have told Sandy that this was not the time to ask for anything, but Sandy wasn't the deepest thinker and she resided in the shallow end of the admin pool.

"We were wanting to go to the Coast tonight. But we need a pass to be able to go. And Jackie and me," she said, again incorrectly, "wondered if you'd sign one for us?"

I watched frustration inch across Jimmy's face like it had in the Food and Beverage meeting. Only this time, before he blasted off he paused.

"I'll sign it once. But…" He tapped his finger on the edge of her desk hard. "If you misbehave or carry on like you own the place, it'll be the last time you ever go to the Coast again."

"Super!" Sandy's high school cheerleading days were in full glory.

"What about you?" Jimmy directed his question toward me. "Aren't you going?"

I shrugged. "Oh, I don't know."

"TJ's going," Sandy said.

I shot a glare in her direction.

"Oh. So it's TJ you're interested in?" Jimmy said with a crooked smile.

"No!" I said much too loudly and defensively. "I'm not interested in anyone."

"You're a horrible liar, Flanagan," Jimmy said.

"It's one of my better qualities," I quickly snapped back and then bit the inside of my cheek. *What am I doing?*

Jimmy grinned. "There's that fire of yours. Listen." He leaned toward me. "I'm going to leave a pass for you, too. Just like I did for TJ." He winked toward Sandy, but Jimmy's wink didn't annoy me. Jimmy's wasn't anything like Mr. Clark's. "So just in case you decide you want to go, you've got a pass."

"I'm not interested in TJ."

Jimmy waved away my rebuttal. "No funny business for you either."

I nodded as he walked toward his office and closed the door.

"So what are you going to wear?" Sandy resumed smacking her gum.

"Nothing, if I don't get this work done."

"Geez, I was just asking."

"Well, I don't know what I'd wear." I hit Control-F and waited for the blue bomb to boot up. Within seconds a memo appeared before me on the computer screen. It was from Jerry, the general manager, to my morning boss, Holly, the director of Human Resources.

"In response to your memo dated June 3," it read. *"I do not see the necessity for an additional full-time person in Human Resources. The staffing of a full-time recruiter and part-time file clerk is sufficient to meet your needs. Additionally, I'd like you to distribute the following memo to all executives.*

I scrolled down to the memo that appeared beneath the e-mail memo to Holly.

As part of our annual budget, one of our "controllable costs" for the next year is overtime. Additionally, we want to make sure we keep our part-time employees in part-time status so keep their hours under forty each week.

To meet our projected budget requires we hit these controllable costs. Beginning in the fourth quarter, overtime will no longer be authorized.

No more overtime? I read the confidential memo and my

heart raced. *When does the fourth quarter begin?* I mentally blocked the year into quarters. *October.* I had from now until October to bank as much overtime as possible?

Jerry's memo continued. *To improve our bottom line and hit our estimates, we want to have a solid fourth quarter. Our fourth quarter numbers will be reflected in our year-end report that will be publicly released in February. Our goal is to provide strong year-end numbers. As a reminder, we only pay bonuses if we meet or exceed our year-end target.*

Bonuses? What the hell? So by cutting the line staff's extra earning potential, they get a bonus? Bastards. I continued reading.

Folks, we've been doing okay, but in order to hit our year-end target, this is what we have to do. Our forecasting and bookings are strong with a higher volume of business expected in the fourth quarter. Our expected occupancy rate is high during the holidays and through the first part of January. But in order to meet our budget and for people to get their bonuses, no matter how busy it gets, you have to keep part-time staff under forty hours without, of course, sacrificing customer service.

So get creative. And remember no overtime. Let's work together to hit our numbers and make it a December to remember!

There was a postscript following the three-paragraph blocked memo that Holly was in charge of distributing.

P.S. Where are we at with the Christmas party planning? This is a good project for your part-timer.

"Oh, sure," I said under my breath. "Just have your

overworked part-timer plan the Christmas party. When will I have time to do that? I won't be able to work the weekends when the fourth quarter starts. So I have to cram more into my four-hour shift? Nice."

"What was that?" Barbara said as she approached her desk.

I quickly hit the Print key and saw a printing icon pop up, indicating that the memo I had just read had been sent to the printer we all shared. I don't know why I did it but I had, and now Barbara was closing in on me and her memo. I simultaneously hit the Control and S keys, which switched the screens on her computer. A blank screen appeared. It was a trick Barbara had taught me if I was ever working on something personal. I could switch screens and no one would be the wiser.

"You okay?"

"Just rambling to myself." My adrenaline surged and it felt like heat radiated off my body, announcing to the world what I had just done. "You finished with my computer?" I tried to sound normal, but it was difficult with my heart beating so loudly I could hear it in my ears.

"All finished," Barbara said.

"Did you find it? The critical course?"

"No, I don't think it's there."

"I'm sorry." I pushed back her chair and stood up.

Barbara moved toward me. My stomach tightened. "I think I'm going to go grab a soda." She reached past me under her desk for her purse. "Can you catch the phones?"

"No problem." I smiled tensely. I waited for Barbara to pass before I grabbed my notepad of minutes and walked briskly toward the printer. Sandy stood beside it.

"Barbara," Sandy started to call out her name when the memo popped up with Barbara's initials on the bottom of the page. The initials identified each secretary.

"I've got it." I snatched the memo out of Sandy's hands and placed it on top of my notepad.

Sandy let out a puff of air. "Sheesh. You don't have to be so pushy."

"Sorry. Printed by accident. Minutes to do and it's Friday."

This caused her to smile. "I make mistakes on Friday too."

Sweat was inching down my neck by the time I reached my desk. I still didn't know why I'd printed the memo. My reaction was instinctual.

"Katie?" It was Sandy again.

"Yes?" I asked without turning around.

"Do you have that memo?"

Memo? My breathing intensified to a rapid pace that almost aligned with my heartbeat, which spiked so suddenly it felt like I was about to have a heart attack. My scalp instantly felt like it was on fire, and I wasn't entirely sure it wasn't. And if I'd stood, I was sure I would have passed out because without warning I felt light-headed. *Memo?* I couldn't respond.

"Here." Sandy appeared at my desk. "You forgot the rest of it." She handed me a set of papers.

"Thanks," I managed with a brief glance up to grab the documents.

Sandy cracked a bubble before she walked away.

Critical Course appeared in bold type on the top on the first page.

"Oh my God." My voice was just above a whisper. I flipped through the small stack. "It must have been attached to the memo." It was either good fortune or dumb luck, I wasn't sure which. I just knew I was acting in a manner unfamiliar to me. I stashed the copies along with the GM's memo in the back of my legal pad. I ripped off the top pages of minutes, placed them on the top of my desk to deal with, and wedged the bulky legal pad into my backpack.

Security. Mr. Clark always checked bags before anyone departed the property.

"Katie," Jimmy called from behind his closed door. "How you doing with those minutes?"

"Just about finished." I grabbed the mouse beside my computer and clicked open a new document. I began typing with the same light speed that Barbara employed. I may not have mastered many computer skills, but the keyboard I had. Journalism had honed my ability to type raw notes while my mind could be engaged elsewhere.

You're going to lose your job.

My fingernails were not acrylic, but they hit the keys and tapped out the minutes like an old telegraph machine. Rat. Tat. Tat.

I could *lose my job. But I'm going to lose overtime hours in four months anyway. What's the difference?*

"The difference?" My voice startled me. "You took something that wasn't yours." I took a deep breath. *Keep it together, Katie.* The staccato nature of my keystrokes began to sound like Morse code. Dit. Dah. Dit. Dit. Dah. *Go home, read the critical course and the memo again, and then decide what to do.*

I finished typing the minutes, grabbed them off the printer, and was photocopying them when I noticed Mushroom Girl, Jackie Portobello, standing by the water fountain. She was tucking her blouse into her skirt. Suddenly it was that simple. She glanced in my direction and smiled.

"Hey, Katie, you going tonight?" She walked toward me.

"Tonight?"

"The Coast. A bunch of us are going after work. Well, actually we're thinking of grabbing some dinner at Hank's...." Her voice trailed off.

"Uh, I don't think I'm allowed back at Hank's for a while." I shook my head. "Hey, I'm really sorry about that. I had a bit too much to drink, and I wasn't acting like myself."

And I'm still not acting like myself, but this time I'm 100 percent sober.

"I never thought anything about it." Jackie's eyes could not lie.

I stepped away from the copy machine. "Thank you."

She simply smiled. She reminded me of Bogart with her easygoing nature.

"Most people don't get banned from a fast food joint." I laughed but my chuckle fell flat. "Or serenade half of Huntington."

This time she laughed and it made me smile.

"We could always go somewhere else for dinner," she said.

"Who's all going?"

"Sandy will be there. And I know she invited Chris from the front desk. So I think he may be going, but I'm not sure."

"Oh." I was not too enthusiastic about the prospect of hanging out with Sandy and/or Chris.

"Come on," Jackie said, "it'll be fun. TJ and I are going." And there it was. *TJ and I.* My stomach dropped. It was bad enough to see them on the video together, but it was a whole other matter to hear their relationship confirmed.

"Fantastic. Sounds like a lot of fun," I lied through my forced smile.

"Maybe we could get Bogart to go?"

"If you want to." My tone turned defensive.

"Didn't he drive you home last weekend?"

"I guess. I don't really remember."

"Oh."

"Yeah, he's like a brother." *There it was again. The sibling alibi.*

"Really? I thought you two—"

I shook my finger before she could finish her sentence. "No, no, no. We're just friends."

"Katie, where are those minutes?" Jimmy called down the hall.

"Right here." I popped my head out from the copy room. "I'm just putting them in the mailboxes."

"I better get back to work, too," Jackie said. "We had a ton of deliveries in Purchasing today."

I grabbed the pile of photocopies off the tray in the printer. They were warm. I held them against my chest.

"Think about coming tonight, okay? It'll be a blast."

"Thanks. I might."

I held on to the minutes and stared at the wall of mailboxes.

White labels with names typed in bold black lettering appeared under each mailbox. *How many of these people will lose their overtime? And what's the deal with keeping hours under forty a week? What am I missing?* The executive board mailboxes were on the top and the managers and assistant managers trickled down from there. I looked at the last row of mailboxes. The assistant managers. *They're salaried. I bet they'll be the ones stuck working longer hours.*

The boxes began to blur. I started stuffing memos in everyone's box. I didn't look anymore at who was who or what belonged where.

I grabbed Jimmy's mail and walked it to his office. His door was open. I placed the mail on his desk.

"I've got to use the ladies' room," I uncharacteristically informed him.

"Have a great time," he said without looking up.

I grabbed my backpack and headed for the women's locker room. No one was there. A shift change would soon be happening and then it would be standing room only. I locked myself in one of the bathroom stalls before opening my backpack and retrieving the documents. Folding them in half, I sandwiched the thick, leafy pamphlet of papers in between my blouse and skirt in the small of my back. It wasn't a perfect fit but it concealed the notes. I bloused my shirt and exited the stall before evaluating my appearance in the mirror.

You'd think in the twenty-first century it'd be easier to smuggle out confidential papers. Load them on a thumb drive, disk, anything other than a wad of papers. Even leaking it out on a computer would be easier. *Pull an Edward Snowden.*

But there wasn't time. There just wasn't time. *Plus, Barbara would notice something saved to an outside drive.*

I turned in the mirror. The papers were secure and couldn't be seen.

Hell, stashing papers in my back is the best I've got.

I walked back to my desk and with each step I felt the papers begin to shift. *Shit.* I threw my bag into my shoulder and held it and the papers with one hand, and then crossed all the fingers on my other hand.

"Okay, I'm off." I shut down my computer and put my pen back in the top drawer beside the new stapler and box of colored paper clips I had ordered from the office supply catalog. *Why not make it a real heist and grab the stapler.* I giggled.

Jimmy looked up from his desk.

"Sorry. Just thought of something funny."

Sweat began to form on my upper lip. I grabbed a tissue off my desk and pretended like I was blotting my lipstick. "See you Monday, Jimmy."

My legs were stiff as I walked down the row of administrative desks and said the rest of my good-byes.

"See you tonight," Sandy squealed. "It'll be a blast!"

I grinned wide-eyed.

"Thanks for your help today, Katie," Barbara said. I nodded. The guilt stabbed at me. It didn't help that so did the packet of papers tucked into my back.

I swiped my ID card through the time clock, punching out exactly at five. My backpack and I made it through the security checkpoint. I was walking down the loading dock, having completed my first full week of work and my first theft, when I felt a hand on shoulder.

"Stop, you," the voice said.

I froze. *Oh my God. I've been caught. Who do I call? Patrick? No, maybe Ian? Mom?* I contemplated which brother would be the kindest.

The hand was still on my shoulder. I turned to find Derek, the security officer, who had just flagged me through to leave.

"Yes?" My voice cracked.

"You're needed in the office." He guided me back up the loading dock. My pulse pounded with each step.

Cameras. They must have cameras in the locker room. Is that even legal? Does it matter? Crap. Crap. Crap.

My throat tightened, and I felt sweat trickling down my back. *Great. Not only am I caught, but the documents are going to bleed onto my blouse. They'll probably confiscate my wardrobe for evidence, like they did with Monica Lewinsky. What have I done?*

I walked into the Security Office and saw Mr. Clark. He wasn't smiling.

"You wanted to see me?"

"Not me." His voice was flat. "The big kahuna wants you."

My body was paralyzed with fear. *The big kahuna?* Did he mean Mr. Adams, the general manager? Or the local police chief?

Mr. Clark picked up his phone and dialed an extension. "Yeah, I've got her," he said. "Okay, see you in a minute."

"Go ahead and take a seat."

I sat down. The packet of papers pinched my skin. The

discomfort was a welcomed distraction. *You deserve it. You stole something that's not yours. No matter how justified you feel. Where's your trust that things will work out? Are you trying to ruin this? Oh, dear God, please help me.*

The minute or two I waited passed painfully slowly. I imagined the payroll office was cutting my first and final check. Human Resources was pulling the file I had put together of my limited work history. And Janet was probably already placing an ad for a new file clerk, though that was probably the only upside of this situation. No more filing.

"Here he is," Mr. Clark announced. I turned and looked out in the hallway outside the security office. Jimmy stood with his hands on his hips.

Shit.

"Thought you could get away, did you?" His crippled face looked more disfigured, yet somehow sad, too. I had let down the one person in this entire stupid hotel I actually liked.

"You can't leave that easily, Flanagan."

"I'm sorry." I could hear the tears in my voice. I lowered my head.

"You're going to need this."

I looked up. A white card with an aqua-colored wave printed in the center was in the palm of Jimmy's hand. My name was written beneath the emblem in his perfect penmanship. "It'll get you into the club tonight."

"Oh my gosh."

"No need to get all emotional on me."

I wiped my eyes. "Thank you." I exhaled. "Thank you so much." I looked at the card and then back up at Jimmy. "Can

I go home now?"

Jimmy laughed. "Yeah, go on home. If you go tonight, I want you to have fun, but remember." He wagged his forefinger. "No funny business or the privilege is revoked. *Comprende*?"

"Yes."

"You're a good girl, Katie. I trust you or you wouldn't have this pass."

The sharp corners of the paper dug into my skin.

"Hell, you wouldn't even be working for me if I didn't trust you," he said.

I stood up and gently smoothed the back of my skirt. The papers miraculously hadn't slid down my back or fallen out of my skirt. "Thanks again, Jimmy."

He nodded. "Get going and have a good weekend."

I smiled, turned, left the hotel, and walked to my car. I remembered hearing Bogart and Mr. Clark discussing a work order to install security cameras in the employee parking lot. I knew there were eyes everywhere. I waited until I was a few blocks away from the hotel before I pulled my car over to the side of the road and collapsed against the steering wheel. *What the hell have I done?*

CHAPTER NINE

My head rested on my steering wheel and my breathing had somewhat returned to normal when a rap on my car window shattered the silence and my steady intake of oxygen. Startled, I jumped. My nerves were shot, and the sound ricocheted through my body like a ping-pong ball. On the verge of crying, I looked out the driver-side window. Bogart stood with his hand on his tool belt and a wide grin on his face.

"What? What… what do you want?" I snapped.

He cupped his hand around his ear, and I was actually grateful he hadn't heard me. *I'm a mess.* I turned the key in the ignition and hit the automatic window button but nothing happened. My hand clenched into a fist and before I knew it I was hitting the steering wheel. "Are you freaking kidding me? What the hell!"

Bogart reached for the car handle and opened the door.

"Hey" was all he said.

I stopped attacking my steering wheel and dropped my hands, but remained silent. A packet of papers remained wedged between my skin and skirt and the pressure in the small of my back from this self-imposed stress was making me lose my shit.

Bogart knelt in the doorframe of my car. "You okay?"

My hair moved back and forth across my face. Then paranoia seized me. I glanced over his head and scanned the street for cameras or cops.

"What's up? Are you waiting for someone?"

"What are you doing here? Are you following me?" I asked.

Bogart laughed. "No, I was taking a walk of the hotel's perimeter and got off course when I saw your car."

"You could see my car from the hotel? Can the hotel see me from here?"

"Katie, what's going on? I just got sidetracked. I was lost in my thoughts, and before I knew it I was a few blocks from the hotel. I saw your car on the side of the road, and I thought maybe you had broken down or something."

"Are you off work?"

"No, I'm working nights. My shift starts in a half hour."

"Oh." I exhaled and my last bit of energy seemed to leave with my breath.

"But I've got thirty minutes."

"Can we go somewhere?"

"As long as you have me back in a half hour." He raised an eyebrow. "Think that'll be enough time for you?"

"Oh brother." I laughed aloud. "Getting you back for your shift won't be a problem."

"Well, just for the record," he said, "a half hour would have been fast for me, too."

My belly shook with laughter and released the pressure that bore down on me like extra weight.

He patted my knee before standing. "That's better." With his arm draped against my car door, his soft brown eyes shone against the purplish early evening sky. "Where we headed?"

"Buckle up and find out."

As I pulled away from the curb, Bogart pushed a button on the console of my dashboard. "Try your window now."

My side window slid down. "What did you do?"

"You must have hit the Lock key."

"Thanks." I looked over at him. "You always seem to come to my rescue."

"It's my job."

"Hmm."

"So what's the emergency?" Bogart's eyes studied me.

"Yeah, well, I did something really stupid."

"What did you do?"

"I kind of borrowed some confidential papers that may belong to Mr. Adams."

"The general manager? You stole from the general manager?"

"I didn't steal." I held up my hand. "I'm *borrowing* them."

"Well then, borrowing, my mistake. Does Mr. Adams know you borrowed these papers?"

"Not exactly. Listen, if you don't want to hear this I'll find someone else."

"Like who? Patrick? How do you think your brother would react?"

"I have other people I could talk to."

Bogart rubbed the stubble on his chin.

"I do. You're not the only friend I have at the hotel," I said.

"But remember,"—he leaned in close—"I'm like a brother to you."

"For crying out loud, I don't even know why I picked you up."

"If this is what you consider a pickup, you've got to work on your game."

"Oh! Would you get serious! You make me so mad."

"All right, all right." He pointed to a strip of beach along Pacific Coast Highway. "Pull over there."

I turned into the Bolsa Chica Wetlands conservatory parking lot and cut the engine. The wetlands were bordered on one side of Pacific Coast Highway and oil fields and houses were on the other. It was an ecological reserve coastal sanctuary for wildlife and migratory birds. A wooden bridge crossing and a mile trail loop provided a walking tour of the Southern California acres-long wetlands. Despite the Pacific roaring in the distance, oil derricks churning for profits, and the rush of Highway 101, it was serene. And leave it to Bogart to direct me there when I had no idea where else to go.

I reached into the back of my skirt, pulled out the folded papers, and wiped them on the hem of my skirt before handing them to him.

"I'm impressed. Very covert."

"I know." I lightly whacked him on the leg with my hand. "That's what I thought."

He unfolded the papers and began reading. I leaned toward him, and his scent was better than any air freshener I could hang in my car. *What the hell does this man wear? And what does the rest of him smell like?* My eyes roamed his body. *His chest... hairy or not?* The row of buttons on his shirt didn't give anything away. *But I bet it smells amazing.* Again I followed the buttons that stopped at his tool belt. *One simple release of the buckle and....*

Bogart snapped the papers and broke the trance his aftershave, cologne, or whatever the hell it was had me in. I curtly shook my head. *Focus, Katie, focus.*

He quickly shuffled his way through the stack. "They're planning on limiting how many hours they eat versus paying overtime," he said.

"I don't understand. What does that mean?"

"Okay, let's say for example that Google was going to book the hotel for a corporate retreat."

"As long as interns Vince Vaughn and Owen Wilson show up with Team Google, I'm down with that."

Bogart shook his head. "Great movie, but not the point."

I smiled.

"It could be any company that is hosting its function at the hotel. Regardless of who it is, when the sales team lands a client function, they forecast billable hours expected for the event. From catering to rooms division, they project how many billable hours they will require for the event, and that's factored into the cost. But until Google," he looked at me and grinned, "or whoever shows up on property, all it is is a forecasted prediction of labor hours. Sometimes it's less and the hotel comes out ahead, but since this is our first year in operation, it's not likely."

"That MBA of yours is really helping me understand this."

"Thanks but your economics lesson is far from finished."

There was a cadence to Bogart's voice that made listening to him effortless. He held my attention with rapt interest.

"The key here is that when Google signs their contract, they've worked with the sales team on an agreed price. Other than incidentals, like extra plated food, that price can't change once Google is in house. If the hotel runs over the projected labor forecast, the hotel eats the hours."

"Oh, that's what you meant by eating time."

"Yes, because the hotel can't bill in areas unless Google, or whatever company, asks for something not originally specified in their contract. But that's not likely, which is why upper management is taking the overtime issue out of the equation. If the hotel eats hours from poor projecting, it won't be incurred in overtime costs. And that will make their year-end, bottom line look better and their bonuses bigger."

"Can they do that? I mean, is that legal?"

"Basically a company can't deny overtime if it's incurred. But I've worked at places where a manager presents the option of comp time, meaning the employee can have the hours off with pay later in the pay period. That's happened."

"So the hotel really isn't eating time because the employees who could be making time and a half, instead are given time off."

"Exactly. But"—Bogart raised his finger—"an employer should not pay comp time in lieu of overtime pay even if the employee requests it. And in California, overtime is required when employees work more than eight hours in a day. It's not based solely on more than forty hours in a week."

"But it happens." My voice sounded as empty as I felt.

"Not yet I don't think, but when Mr. Adams wrote 'get creative' and dangled the executives' bonuses as bait, I'm sure some executives will direct their managers to work employees off the books."

"Either way, the employee loses," I said.

Bogart held the leaflet of papers and shook them with conviction. *Sexy.*

"All employees lose," he said. "Because what's likely to happen, is that certain salaried managerial employees, who are exempt from the overtime provision under the Fair Labor Standards Act, will work the overtime."

"I knew it!" I elbowed him. "When I was filing the Food and Beverage minutes, I thought midmanagers, like Aisha or TJ, would be hung with the overtime."

"It's the more likely course so that the Pointe doesn't have to forfeit time because that would reflect badly when the year-end report is issued. And again be reflected in their bonus because it's tied to the year-end report."

I leaned back in my seat. "Unreal."

"Well, the only people who benefit from this are the executives. No one under a manager contract is included in the bonus pay."

"Contract? You mean the job description and policies and

procedures paperwork everyone signed at orientation?"

Bogart shook his head. "No, this is a contract."

"I've never even seen a contract in anyone's files. And trust me," I said. "I've seen *everyone's* file."

"Not the managers' or the assistant managers' files."

Again, I swatted his leg. "You're right. How'd you know that?"

"Because I'm under contract."

"You are?"

He pressed his lips together tightly, like he was embarrassed. "I have a two-year contract with the hotel."

"You do?"

"Yup, it was part of my negotiations with the hotel."

"Do other people have this kind of contract?"

"I don't know if they negotiated as well as I did, but yeah, other managers are under contract."

"Assistant managers too?" I thought about TJ, whose file I realized I had never seen.

"Assistant managers, managers, department heads, all salaried employees are under contract."

"So it's just the lowlife hourly wage slaves like me that are getting the overtime shaft come October?"

"Let's not forget benefits. That's the bigger issue here. The real reason they want to drive home that part-time employees work less than forty hours a week is the benefit issue. Once an employee works forty hours in a week, they are considered full-time and are benefited employees."

"I wondered why that was such a big deal. So by limiting the overtime, they're ensuring we're never eligible for health benefits."

Bogart thumbed the pages. "Based on this report, the hotel isn't providing health insurance to half of its employees."

"Yeah, but they could argue that we're part-time."

"And the counter to that is that all the"—Bogart air-quoted with his fingers—"'part-timers' are working one hour shy of full-time."

I shrugged. "Hey, it was either that or twenty hours a week. And granted math is not my friend, but thirty-nine hours are way better than twenty."

Bogart gently touched my arm. "I'm not blaming you. You made a good decision in a tense-filled situation. There were hundreds of applicants lined up. I would have done the same thing."

"I doubt that, but thanks." I softly smiled at him.

"Katie, don't be hard on yourself. The hotel knew what they were doing."

"I understand healthcare benefits are important but with Obama-care, I'm able to be insured under my dad's plan until I'm twenty-six. So, while I'd like to have healthcare benefits, it's not a huge hardship if I don't. Not yet at least. I know that sounds awful, but it's the truth."

"It's not awful and I think it's great you have coverage with your dad. But there are a lot of working parents who don't qualify for that option."

"Oh, geez, I feel like a jerk. What do these employees do?"

"You're not a jerk. You didn't know. But when the hotel fails to provide affordable healthcare to all its employees, when an employee gets sick, their only recourse is to turn to our public healthcare system," he said. "And we *all* end up footing the bill through our taxes."

"I had no idea." It was mind-boggling. I massaged the tension in my forehead, but no amount of ibuprofen was going to knock away this ache.

"The hotel was kind of banking that you and 150 other new hires wouldn't be the wiser."

"I'm kind of embarrassed. I've been concerned with overtime, which is ridiculous because I haven't even logged any yet, but there're twenty hours slated that I'm eligible to grab at time and a half and I know it sounds greedy, but I really don't want to lose them—especially when I just found out about them. And it seems to be the only benefit we have."

"It's understandable. I wouldn't want to forfeit them either," he said.

"So what do we do?"

Bogart smiled. "*We* can't do anything until I go back to my business law books and research this in greater detail."

"But you'd do that? This doesn't even effect you. I mean not really. I know you're salaried so you may have to work longer hours, but you could walk away from this and from…" My voice trailed off before I said, "Me."

Bogart leaned toward me. "Listen, I'm honored that you would trust me with what you found. And you're right, the hotel is dividing its employees with salaried managers, who will be hit hard in the fourth quarter. So this impacts all of us. The only people who gain in this situation are the executives who want to meet their bonus cap. So yeah, I'll do whatever it takes. I'm in it to win it."

"Well, count me in. I'll do whatever to right this wrong.

Maybe I'll get health benefits out of it."

"Health insurance, retirement plans, special benefits, like tuition reimbursement, these are just some of the benefits you're being denied by working one-hour shy of full-time."

"Damn. Tuition reimbursement? I could get my master's degree? All I get is the free meal in the cafeteria and even that's leftovers."

Bogart chuckled. "If it makes you feel any better, there are 150 people on payroll that share part-time status with you."

"I can't believe it," I said.

"But—" Bogart sat back in his seat and flipped through the critical course. "—you actually might be saved."

"How?"

"The part-time Food and Beverage administrative assistant is slated for additional hours. It may become full-time in the New Year."

"Really? Where do you see that?" I inched closer to him in the car and inhaled. *I think I'm becoming addicted to his scent.* He moved closer to me and pointed to the section in the paperwork under the heading Food and Beverage. The only jobs slated for full-time status were in the Stewarding department and the Food and Beverage administrative office.

"Well, if I can't get full-time as an admin, I could always go wash dishes," I said.

"Nah, they'll probably rotate a housekeeper up to the kitchen," Bogart said and I laughed.

"You have *no idea* how right you are," I said. "So this isn't a minority hiring issue. It's a 'let's look good on paper' issue and get a bigger bonus at year-end."

Bogart nodded.

"I guess the upside is that no one is losing their job. They just won't be able to bank overtime. Or be eligible for benefits."

"Looks that way."

"Is HR slated for any additional time in the New Year?"

"Kates,"—his voice dropped with concern—"you read Mr. Adams's response to Holly's memo. She was already trying to get full-time status for the position, and it was shot down."

Awareness sank in. *Holly's trying to save the position, not me. It's "only filing" as Janet would say.* Still, in a week's time I felt invested in my work in HR. I felt like I knew the employees because I knew their files. The Pacific Ocean was across the street. The white tips of the waves were all that could be seen through my car's windshield. The magnitude of the waves wasn't visible, but the wrath of their destruction when they broke against the shore could be heard for miles. *You don't have to see the crash to know it's going to happen.*

"How'd you come across this?"

I stared out the windshield, wondering how long I could stay adrift before the tide brought me back into shore.

"Kates?"

I slowly exhaled and looked at Bogart, taking in every detail of his face. The shadow of his beard that always seemed to be there regardless of the time of day. His brown eyes that told his mood simply by their color. And his dark eyebrows that drew together often in thought, but now confusion.

"Purely by accident. I was working on Barbara's computer, and the memo popped up on her screen. I panicked, printed it, and then panicked again when Sandy handed me this stack of papers. The critical course must have been attached behind the memo because it printed out, too."

"So you decided to become Erin Brockovich and take off with it?" His voice was light, but the shade of brown in his eyes was serious.

"I don't know what I was thinking. I wasn't actually. Something inside me told me that I had to have it."

"I'll have to remember that." The heat in his voice reflected what I saw in his eyes and shifted the conversation.

I glanced at his lips. They looked soft, especially his lower lip, which had a luscious fullness, like an invitation to nibble. His eyes penetrated me with their intensity. Neither of us spoke, and in that silence, I moved closer to him. *Do you taste as good as you smell?* But I waited, held by his gaze.

He reached across and brushed hair away from my cheek.

"Those eyes." He framed my face with his hands, and I felt protected, even isolated, from the storm I knew was heading my way. I wasn't someone who would sit idly by while 150 people and I had even more earning potential cut. It was bad enough that we didn't have benefits, but to take away our overtime? Hell, I hadn't even logged any, and I was already banking on that income. But with Bogart beside me, my shoulders relaxed, my stomach softened, and I leaned into his touch.

"I've got to get to work," he said softly, without moving his hands.

I nodded.

"Hey." He leaned closer. "Don't worry about your overtime

or benefits. We'll work something out."

Again my head brushed against his hands.

He moved toward me and our lips were about to touch. I stared into his warm brown eyes when our bodies suddenly jerked forward. Instead of our lips connecting, our foreheads nearly collided.

I braced my arm against the steering wheel and stopped myself from hitting Bogart or the dashboard. I turned around. A surfboard was sandwiched against the hatch of my car.

"What the…?"

"We've been hit." Bogart unbuckled his seat belt and jumped out of the car.

I fumbled with mine and joined him at the rear of my car. The bumper was caved in, there was a dent in the back hatch, and when Bogart removed the surfboard the fin had cracked the window, leaving behind a web of fractured glass.

"No." I shook my head. "Are you kidding me?"

"It's okay," Bogart said. "At least we weren't injured."

"Dude." A young guy got out of his car. "Man, I didn't see you."

"I guess not. How can you not see me? My car's red and I'm parked big as life," I said.

"I was checking out the sets and I didn't see you. Man, I am so sorry," he said.

"Sorry? You're sorry? Well that's just great! He's sorry." I turned toward Bogart, who was holding up his hands.

"It's okay," he said to me calmly. "Hey, buddy," he addressed the blond surfer, who was wearing his wetsuit. "Do you have insurance?"

"Totally." The surfer returned to his car. The back zipper to his wetsuit was down and exposed his tanned backside—all of it.

"Well, at least he's got a nice ass," Bogart said.

I swatted him on the arm as I laughed aloud. "He does kind of have a Coppertone tan thing going on there doesn't he?" I glanced past Bogart for a better look.

"Hey, hey, hey." Bogart tried to block my view.

I giggled. "Doesn't matter. This is karma. You know that, right?"

"It isn't karma. It's just bad luck. The guy was pumped to go surfing. He wasn't looking."

I rolled my eyes. "I stole something, so now karma is repaying me."

Bogart shook his head. "It doesn't work that way. You haven't hurt anyone intentionally. Karma is usually cause and effect. And this isn't the same thing. This was just bad luck."

"Here it is." The surfer returned and handed Bogart his insurance card.

"Wellington?" Bogart looked at the plastic. "Like the tools?"

"Yup, that's my dad. Hey, I'm sorry, my name's Wes." He extended his hand to Bogart. The two men shook hands.

"I'm Katie." I reached out my hand. "It's *my* car you hit."

"Katie, I am so sorry," Wes said, shaking my hand. "I really am. But I'll make it right, okay?"

"We know that." Bogart turned to me. "Katie, do you want to go get your insurance card?"

I turned toward my car.

"And if you have a pen and paper," Bogart added.

I grabbed my insurance papers and a notepad from my glove box.

Bogart and Wes exchanged information and phone numbers.

"I'll probably do the work myself." Bogart surveyed the damage. "It's mostly cosmetic," he said to me. "Still, it'll cost a little for paint, a new bumper, and back windshield. The windshield is probably the only thing I can't do by myself, but it's still easy to outsource. Would you want to settle this outside of our insurance companies?"

"Oh, dude, that would be excellent. My Dad would really dig that. I've already had two fender benders this month."

I stared at this Wes guy.

"I'm not a flake." He looked at me. "And I'm not stoned," he said, answering my second thought. "I just get hyped about the waves. It's my addiction."

"Understandable," Bogart said. "The sets are coming in good. Look, we'll let you get to them. I'll call you with the estimate, fair enough?" he asked both me and Wes.

"It's good with me," Wes said.

"As long as you get my car back to normal. It's brand-new."

"I know and I will," Bogart said. "You trust me, don't you?"

I nodded with a smile.

Bogart helped Wes put his surfboard back on the hood of his car, and we watched him slowly pull out and park his car down the strip from where we were.

"So." Bogart placed his hands in the back pockets of his jeans. "I get off work at midnight." He moved closer to me, backing me up against the side of my car.

"Really?"

"Really." He leaned toward me but didn't crowd me. That was the thing about Bogart; he kept giving me this space to decide. *But why? What is there to decide?*

I looked up at him. His dark hair had collected moisture from the fog that was beginning to roll in and it accentuated his spiky hair. I reached up and touched it.

He met my hand with his and intertwined our fingers. Bound to him, I waited—for him to kiss me, to press into me. Hell, at this point he could lick me. *Do something. Anything.* My body hungered for his lips. For his hands to canvas my body and own it. To make it his.

But instead he softly spoke. "I've got to get to work."

"Oh. Shit." I fumbled to free my hand from his. When I did I glanced at my watch. "Crap. It's after five."

"Don't worry. I'm salaried, remember?"

"Right." The confidential memo. The elimination of overtime. Everything resurfaced. *Wonderful.*

"Listen." Bogart reached down and held my hand. I drew closer to him, wanting more. Wanting him.

Instead he fished in his front jeans pocket, withdrew a set of keys, and placed them in my palm.

"Drop your car off at my house and have Patrick drive you home. Or," he said without making eye contact, "you could always stay at my house until I get off work, and I could drive you home later."

"But what would I do?" I pressed into him. He pressed back. Our bodies touched and he didn't pull away. It felt welcoming. *Now we're getting somewhere.*

"Here's your chance to riffle through my drawers." He nervously laughed.

"But wouldn't that happen later?"

His cheeks tinged red.

"Kates," was all he said, and he stepped back.

What?

He removed the garage door opener from his key ring. "This'll get you into the house." He handed me the device. "If, you know, you're interested."

Oh, I'm interested. I playfully raised my eyebrows and tucked the remote in the back of my skirt.

"Oh, hey, look at you."

"Yeah, I'm a regular Jane Bond," I said, laughing at myself.

"So…." There was a subtle change in his voice. "If you want to come by at midnight, that's great. If not, no big deal."

No big deal? "Okay." I slowly exhaled, when what I wanted to do was lean up and kiss him. Or have him lean down and kiss me. But nothing in his body language gave me the impression that he was going to kiss me or that he would kiss me back. And it wasn't a risk I was willing to take. Our moment had passed. I think our attraction was mutual. *But maybe not? No big deal? Maybe there's nothing there for him. Maybe we are just friends? I have played the friend card—a lot.*

"So… work?" he said with a smile.

Oh. My body felt deflated, like air leaving a balloon. *Yeah. Friends. He sees us as friends.*

I nodded. "Sure, yeah, work, absolutely. Let's go."

CHAPTER **TEN**

When I pulled into the loading dock of the Waterfront Point Resort, I looked over at Bogart.

"Thanks for being there today. I mean, with the papers and then the accident." I rolled my eyes.

"Hey, don't worry. I'll get your car looking great again. And we'll figure something out about this job thing. Let me think about it for a while, okay?"

"Of course. Yes." Off to the side of Bogart, the loading dock was in full view. The door into the hotel opened and TJ emerged. My heart rate suddenly spiked. *What the hell?*

It surprised me, but there was something about the guy that caused a physical reaction. Bogart turned me on, but in a sane, normal, keep-your-clothes-on-in-public kind of way. But TJ? My history with TJ had already shown what I was willing to do for that man. He seemed to stir the blood in my veins into a mad, sing-to-half-of-Huntington frenzy. It made absolutely no sense.

"So you've got the clicker and if you want to drop by later…," Bogart said.

"Yeah," I said, and found my tone subtly shifting. "I was actually thinking about going to the Coast tonight."

"Great, then I could see you there. We get calls all the time to fix the air conditioning."

I nodded, barely listening, as I watched TJ palm a volleyball in his hand.

Bogart glanced in the direction of my attention. "Oh. Well, yeah, that makes sense."

"What?"

"Nothing. I've got to get to work." He reached for the door handle.

"I don't understand."

"Katie, don't insult what we could have together."

What we could have together? "What? What do you mean?" I reached for his arm, but he pulled away.

"I can work on your car tomorrow. It's my day off, so if you drop it off, just leave the garage door opener on the kitchen counter."

"Bogart. Wait."

"I gotta go." He opened the door and left without another word.

Even though I knew it was wrong, I still looked in my rearview for TJ. I spotted him leaning against his truck in the parking lot. And though instinct told me otherwise, I backed up my car and drove in his direction. I rolled to a slow stop before him.

"Hey, what happened to you?" he asked when I pressed the passenger-side window button.

"I got rear-ended." I casually glanced over my shoulder to the loading dock to see if Bogart was still there. Thankfully he wasn't.

"Accidents seem to follow you," TJ said.

I reached up and touched my nose. The swelling had all but gone, but it was still tender.

"Seems that way."

"I was heading to the beach to play a few sets of V-ball, wanna join me?"

I looked down at my skirt. "I'm not quite dressed for volleyball."

"I've got an extra pair of shorts and a T-shirt in the truck." TJ tilted his head toward the cab. "They'll probably swim on you but you're welcome to them."

"What about Jackie?"

"What about Jackie? She's my friend."

"Huh."

"I don't know what the big deal is. We had a good time last weekend. That's it."

I didn't say anything.

"I don't have a girlfriend. And," he clarified, "I don't want a girlfriend."

I said nothing and in my silence, TJ filled in the gaps that I usually cluttered with idle chatter.

"I just broke off an engagement." His voice was tender. "I just wanna have fun. I don't want to hurt anyone. Jackie's a sweetheart, but we're just friends."

Friends. The ol' friend card. I knew it well. But really, could men and women truly be friends, especially when one of them was attracted to the other? This wasn't a Nora Ephron *When Harry Met Sally* thing where the sex part got in the way; it was about the entire dynamic. I was attracted to TJ the way a diabetic was to sugar. We both knew it was bad for us, but it didn't stop the craving. TJ wasn't offering anything more than fun and friendship. The fact that I found him attractive was my problem. *Isn't that all I had thought Bogart and I had, anyway?* Friendship.

A burning sun bled above the tide, and the beach was all but empty. The choice before me was mine. *Why not?* I wasn't hurting anyone. It was just a harmless game of volleyball.

TJ politely turned around while I shimmied out of my pencil-straight skirt. Bogart's remote fell, landing in the dirt. I reached over and picked it up. Holding it, I rubbed off the dust. I looked up at TJ, whose back was to me, and tossed the remote in my car, not wanting to think about it. I then pulled up the shorts that did swim on me but found comfort in the space. It was when I unbuttoned my ivory-colored silk blouse that I caught TJ's reflection in the side mirror of his car.

"Hey!" I squealed. "No peeking. This is purely a friendly game of volleyball."

He chuckled. "Come on, I'm not dead."

"You will be if you don't keep your eyes on the beach."

"Jimmy was right about that fire," TJ said.

"Jimmy." I drew the cord to the shorts and secured their hold around my waist.

I threw my clothes into my car, covering Bogart's garage

door opener, hit Lock on my remote, and walked barefoot beside TJ. We crossed Pacific Coast Highway and found the only volleyball net still standing past five on a Friday evening. The weather was perfect. We rallied the ball back and forth over the net.

"You're not bad."

"Don't sound so surprised."

We played for an hour before the fog hindered visibility.

"You've got a powerful serve," he said as we sat on the beach. The waves crashed up against the shore, inching closer to our feet each time.

"I've got two brothers who are extremely athletic."

"Must be nice."

"Sometimes. I'm probably the only girl who actually understands the rules of football, rugby, soccer...." I noticed TJ staring at me.

"I'm rambling."

"Not at all. I like hearing you. You're smart."

It was what he had said to me on the morning of our interviews. Smart.

"That's a good thing," he said.

I shrugged. "Thanks."

"So are you going tonight?" he asked.

"To the Coast?"

"Yup."

"I thought you guys were going to grab a bite to eat beforehand." I glanced at my watch. It was already 6:30.

"Yeah, Jackie coordinated something like that. I'm meeting her at seven. I was going to go grab a shower at home first.

Wanna join me?" A devilish grin danced across his face and flashed in his hazel eyes.

"Uh, yea, no." Friends didn't shower together. *Or do they?* I stood up and brushed off my shorts. "Think I'll pass."

"I meant what I said." TJ stood beside me. "Jackie and I are just friends."

I didn't know how to respond so I didn't.

"We'll be at Hank's if you want to join us."

I was grateful for the limited lighting that hid my embarrassment. "That's what I heard. I don't think I'll be going back to Hank's anytime soon."

TJ chuckled. "I thought your singing was cute."

"I was super drunk."

"The Coast has a great drink special going on tonight."

"I know. I type the menus."

"That's right." He lightly punched my forearm. "You're just a regular Girl Friday, aren't you?"

"Something like that. Hey, walk me back to my car. I hate the dark."

Again he laughed. "It's not dark and I'd never make any girl walk to their car alone."

We raced across the stream of headlights on Pacific Coast Highway and back to the employee parking lot.

"I hope I see you tonight," TJ said.

Even though I knew better, I believed him.

CHAPTER **ELEVEN**

A riptide was a strong undercurrent in the ocean that could pull even the strongest of swimmers down. It was also the name of a new drink the Coast bartender, Max, had created for the grand opening of the Waterfront Point Resort nightclub. A mixture of vodka, lemonade, and some blue liqueur blended together for a deliciously sweet and wickedly powerful beverage.

I was working on my second oceanic concoction when TJ, Jackie, Sandy, and Chris Colombo walked into the bar. Trailing behind them was Carmen from the front drive.

"Carmen from Costa Mesa!" I called out, smiling. She returned the smile.

"Where you been?" I asked when she grabbed the stool beside me.

"I'm a working dog," she said. She was wearing a baseball

cap, only this one was embroidered with the hotel's emblem in gold.

"Nice hat," I said, tipping a nod toward her.

"It's part of the uniform," she said. "I'm on in an hour."

"Nun-uh. Really?"

"Yup. That's okay. Friday is the best night for tips. Look around you," she said, and I did. The bar was packed with twenty-, thirty-, and forty-year-olds who were getting progressively louder, looser, and more liberal with their wallets.

"I caught a fleet of Beemers," I said of the lined valet lot that occupied the main drive leading to the hotel.

"That's nothing," Carmen said. "You should see the Hummers I get to drive."

I laughed. "Only you would be turned on by a Hummer."

"Hummer?" TJ chimed in, joining our conversation.

"Relax, Romeo," Carmen said. "We're talking cars, not your favorite pastime."

"Oh, you're just so funny," TJ said, wrapping his arms around Carmen and squeezing her. She tried to resist him but he was twice her size. He kept hugging her until she started to giggle.

"Mercy, mercy," she wailed, and he relented.

"Whatcha drinking there, Flanagan?" he asked, pointing in my direction.

"Riptide," I said above the roar of music.

"A fruity, girly drink."

"It's not so girly." I offered him a taste.

He took a sip, and his lips puckered afterward. "That's got

quite a kick. I'll stick to tequila," he said, ordering a shot of Patrón. "Max, gimme the gold. None of that other crap."

"Coming up," his Food and Beverage colleague said, returning with a shot for TJ and a fresh riptide for me.

I slid a twenty toward him on the bar.

"It's not good here," Max said. He hadn't charged me for any of my drinks. "You're on the team," he said of my alliance with Jimmy, who held a position in the back of the room, surveying the crowd.

"Thank you, but this is it," I said, holding up my third blue-tinted cocktail. I wasn't sure how many shots were in each drink, but I was one shot away from forgetting the drink's name and two away from forgetting my own name.

"She's good for one more," TJ said, elbowing me. He slid his hand across my bare back and a chill ran down my spine. "Nice."

I had opted for a black spaghetti-strap curve-hugging dress that dipped low in the back and hit all my high points without revealing any of my flaws. It was my favorite go-to piece in my closet. My toes had a pedicure shine and were painted a shade of tangerine that popped in my slim, silver-toned ankle-strap sandals.

Baby oil added shine and moisture to my tanned skin. I was having an unusually great hair day, having blown my wavy locks straight and then tucked them behind my ears. Large silver hoop earrings dangled and glistened. But no little black dress was complete without the smoky eye, and my dark eyes smoldered. A light gloss covered my lips, and when I caught my reflection in the mirror behind the bar, I knew I had it going on. Nothing looked better in a bar than a simple black dress and a summer tan. Or so the handful of riptides had convinced me.

TJ leaned toward me, placed his hand on the small of my back, and whispered in my ear, "You really look hot tonight. Save me a dance."

My knees felt weak as I nodded before he slipped away and joined Jackie at the table they had secured in the corner of the room.

"Wanna join them?" I asked Carmen.

"Sure."

We fought our way through the crowd to their table.

Surprisingly, Chris was the first to stand up when we approached.

"Ladies," he said, extending chairs for both of us. Normally I would have been impressed, but he bothered me. Maybe it was my experience with him and the whole poppy-seed-stuck-in-my-teeth thing that he hadn't told me about, but he was annoying. Still I acknowledged his gesture. "Thanks, Chris."

"Can I get you another drink?" he asked me.

"No, I'm good. But maybe Carmen," I suggested.

He looked right past her.

"What about you, Sandy?" he asked, bypassing Jackie, who was deep in conversation with TJ. It looked heated, but not in the fire-things-up-let's-get-out-of-here kind of way.

The volume in the bar suddenly dropped by octaves. I turned toward the center of the stage to find Jimmy with Bogart beside him, adjusting a microphone. Bogart was bent down and his jeans hugged his ass.

"Nice," Carmen commented.

"Bogart?" I asked, looking at her.

"You see anyone else with an ass that nice in here?" she said.

I glanced over at TJ. The backside of the barstool and TJ's ass were front and center. And sadly, TJ's was rather flat in comparison.

"He's the whole package," Carmen said.

Again I asked, "Bogart?"

"Yeah, Bogart," she said.

"Huh." I knew how I felt when I was around Bogart, which was welcomed, safe, even turned on, but I hadn't taken it past that because Bogart hadn't either. *Aren't we just friends?* I was so confuzzled.

Carmen slowly shook her head. "Hey, if you don't see it, I'm not going to point it out."

"No, really. Come on. I think he's cute," *and I had wanted to kiss him today.* "But what makes him the 'whole package'?"

Carmen stopped staring at Bogart's ass long enough to look at me.

"TJ's a nice guy," she said, to my surprise. "He's extremely good-looking, even hot, and he's probably a good guy. But he's young. He's still playing the field. He doesn't even know what *he* wants yet."

"*Young*? He's our age. I mean, he's close to our age. He's only a few years older. But Bogart? He's like thirty or thirty-one," I said, and figured the age difference between us. "Well, he's at least six years older than me, I mean, us. Six. That's kind of a lot, don't you think?" *When did his age ever matter?*

"I'd rather be with someone who knows what he wants now than with someone who thinks he knows what he wants only to find it passes with the next wave of perfume."

"Wow, that's harsh," I said.

"Reality usually is," Carmen said, returning her gaze to Bogart.

Well, Bogart may not be mine, but he's not yours either.

"He's fixing my car," I blurted out.

"That's great," she said, not breaking eye contact with Bogart's ass. "Is he dating anyone?"

"Who?" Sandy chimed in.

"Bogart," Carmen said.

"The old guy up on stage?" Sandy asked, placing her hand up to her ear. The music had restarted on the loud speakers, making it hard to hear, but it was also Sandy. And Sandy had double-downed on her drinking.

"No, not Jimmy. She's asking about Bogart." I looked beside her at Chris, who hung on her every word. I waved my glass toward him and smiled. His shock of white hair seemed to move along with his eyebrows.

"Want another?" he asked.

"Uh, well." I hesitated. Now that I called him over, I felt foolish. "Okay, maybe just one more. Thank you."

"You like Bogart?" Sandy asked Carmen.

"Sure, what's not to like?" she said.

"I think he's seeing someone," I lied.

"Bogart?" Sandy said. "No, he's single."

"How would you know?" I snapped as Chris walked past us.

"Because I asked him."

"When?" I said.

"Tonight," Sandy said, bouncing in her chair to the beat of the music. But like everything else, Sandy was one chord behind.

"When did you see him?" I asked.

"He walked up the drive with Chris and me," she said. "Said he was coming to check on his sister."

"He said that? He doesn't have a sister," I said, though I wasn't certain. "What else did he say? I mean, how did you find out he wasn't dating anyone?"

"I asked him. I asked if he was here with someone and he said, 'No,' that he was here checking on his sister."

"Really?" I said.

"Yeah, really. I thought it was sweet, actually," Sandy said.

"Yeah, real sweet." I looked back toward the stage.

"Who cares," Carmen said with a lilt to her voice. "He's single and that's all that matters."

I eyed Bogart. He did have a nice ass. But it could have been the jeans.

When Bogart got the microphone working, Carmen put her fingers in her mouth and whistled. "Way to go, Bogie!" she shouted.

He glanced in our direction and gave a thumbs-up with a smile. He had a pleasing face because he had a modest quality about him that showed in his expressions.

"All right, settle down," Jimmy announced on stage. "The Waterfront Point Resort is proud to present a local band, making their debut at the California Coast. Please join me in welcoming Surfside," Jimmy said loudly and clearly into the microphone. He stepped aside as a group of five long-haired, flannel-wearing, ripped jeans, Doc-Marten-stomping grunge types took the stage behind their instruments and began the first in a set of mainstream guitar rock. The music was heavy, the lyrics were raw, and the energy was electric.

Chris returned with my fourth riptide and a glass of wine for Sandy.

"Thank you," I said and slid money toward him. He waved it away.

"I never thanked you for last weekend during the interview process," he said. "You killed it and we all got hired. Some groups didn't have that same luck."

Didn't see that coming. Maybe he is uncommonly good.

He raised his glass toward mine, and we met in the middle. "To the first week of employment," he said.

"Cheers!" Carmen, Sandy, Chris, and I toasted, and my heart sank to the bottom of my empty stomach.

Carmen was part-time and so was Sandy. They didn't know that by Halloween their extra earning potential would be cut. I had slowly nursed three riptides, but I took the fourth one and threw it back.

"Damn, girl!" Carmen said.

I wagged my finger. "Don't 'girl' me. You were supposed to drive me home last weekend and you didn't. And if there was *ever* a time I needed a ride home, last weekend was it. So if tonight I need a ride home, I don't care what's going on— *you will* be my ride home. *Comprende*?"

"*Si*. When my shift ends, I'm your ride home."

"*Gracias.*"

"*De nada.*"

I knew I was no longer sober, but I wasn't fully drunk—yet. I was also still seated. And my glass was empty.

"Wanna dance?" The request came from behind me. I turned to find TJ. He didn't look like himself. His hazel eyes were glassy and sad.

"You okay?" I asked.

"Let's dance," he said, holding out his hand.

I looked around but didn't see Jackie.

"Where's Jackie?" I asked before accepting his hand.

"She left," he said.

"Why?"

"Listen, I don't really want to talk about it right now."

I hesitated and then took his hand, leaving Sandy, Carmen, and Chris behind.

TJ led me through the crowd and to the dance floor.

I was not a very good dancer so asking me to dance was the equivalent of asking me to streak naked across the room. In both situations, I felt hugely awkward, insecure, and downright lame. But it was TJ. *TJ asked me to dance.* Suddenly I found my feet barely touched the ground as I moved easily and effortlessly next to him. Sure, the four riptides didn't hurt as I lost all inhibition and boogied. *Do people still boogie?*

"You've got the most amazing eyes," TJ said above the roar of the room. "Why do you hide them behind all this hair?" he asked.

Because I like hair? I shrugged.

"Cut this shit off," he said, and I mentally made a note

to call my hairdresser in the morning and whack it off. *Who cares that I've been trying to grow the shit out?* I'd probably look better without hair. Don't most girls? TJ had that kind of effect on me. I was powerless. Lost in the haze of his eyes and suddenly wrapped up in his arms, I leaned over and kissed him.

He responded by lightly biting my lip and laughing. "Not here," he said into my hair. He grabbed my hand, leading me away from the dance floor and toward the back entrance. I wasn't thinking clearly. Hell, I wasn't thinking at all. An entirely different part of my body was dictating my every action.

Alone in the back hallway of the hotel, TJ pushed me against the wall and kissed me. It was sloppy and not what I had imagined. He wasn't passionate and romantic. His lips didn't linger on mine. Hell they didn't linger at all. How could they? His lips were paper thin, paltry, and barely left an impression. *Did he always have thin lips?* But what his lips lacked his tongue made up for in size. It was gargantuan. His tongue darted in and out of my mouth like a hummingbird on speed. But I pushed this all out of my mind. It didn't matter. It was TJ. *TJ was kissing me.*

I tilted my head back against the wall, exposing my neck, giving him a new area to kiss. His cheek grazed against me roughly. I winced, my shoulder instinctively rising, blocking his prickly chin from rubbing against me. I turned to him, hoping our lips could softly connect and slowly discover each other. But his mammoth-sized tongue continued to roam free, wreaking havoc wherever it went.

So instead, I deeply drew a breath, wanting to know TJ's scent, and what I inhaled almost made my eyes water. Maybe it was because he was around food all day, but the closer I got to him, the more I smelled raw onions, garlic, and rotten cheese that seemed to waft together in an aroma of bad feet. I tucked my chin and turned my head, hoping to catch a breath of fresh air, but his damn tongue found me again. And I was drawn back into a battle with his mouth.

His hands swam along my body, inching up my dress and beneath the thin layer of cotton that stood between him and my strapless bra. He reached around and in one snap unhooked the clasp. Though I wasn't very busty, his swift move released the pressure holding the underwire bra that pulled me into a fuller cup size. I felt myself come tumbling out. His hand was there to catch my right breast and squeeze it.

"Gentle," I whispered in his ear as his other hand wrapped around my back and down to my G-string as he grabbed my exposed ass and began groping it. All I could surmise between his tongue darting in and out of my mouth and his hands across my body was that things were moving fast. Too fast.

"Slow down," I said as I tried to savor the moment. Hell, as I tried to catch up to him and allow my body to respond to what was happening.

"Shh," he said in a rare instant when his mouth wasn't slobbering all over me. He unsnapped the row of buttons on the front of his jeans. The button fly parted and he was full-on commando. His cock rose between us. I stared at it in shocked disbelief, not because it was anything extraordinary, since sadly there wasn't anything grand about it, but simply because he had whipped his dick out in the back hallway of the hotel. *Oh my God!*

He pulled me toward him and lifted my leg around his waist.

"We can't," I said, very conscious of our surroundings and what he thought what was about to happen. I didn't have a condom, I wasn't on any birth control, and I'm pretty sure they had cameras mounted everywhere in this place.

"I've had an AIDS test," he whispered in my ear.

My body shut down and froze instantly. It reminded me of when my brother Patrick had dumped a bucket of ice water on top of my head when we raised funds for the ALS ice bucket challenge. For a minute I was paralyzed, unable to reconnect with my muscles, my speech, and my brain. *AIDS test?*

It was just the reality check I needed to pull myself away from TJ and out from beneath the riptide effects of his charm.

"Well I haven't," I confessed. "I mean, I've only been…. It doesn't matter," I said. "I can't do this. Not like this."

TJ ran his hands through his hair, parting the thick black layers.

"What's wrong?" he asked. "I thought this is what you wanted."

Oh God. The alcohol helped make it sting a little less, but not much. "Not like this. Not *ever* like this," I said.

He moved away from me and buttoned his jeans. I was adjusting my dress and looking for my bra when the back door to the bar opened.

"TJ," Jimmy said. "I think Max could use some help in there."

"Not a problem." TJ headed toward the bar without ever looking back.

I stood against the wall somehow hoping Jimmy wouldn't notice me. Hoping I was as invisible as TJ had made me feel. Instead Jimmy walked toward me, bent down, and picked up my black strapless bra off the floor. When he reached me, he handed it to me.

"This isn't like you, Flanagan."

Tears replaced words as I accepted it and lowered my head. I couldn't face him.

"Go use my office and clean yourself up," he said.

I nodded, crossed my arms over my chest, and buried my bra before I walked away.

Jimmy's office provided the respite needed to gather my thoughts. *What just happened?*

I put on my bra and brushed my hair with my fingers in the glass reflection of his framed artwork. I turned off the lights in his office and went to the side of his desk that faced the wall. I sank down the back of the desk onto the carpet beside an open case of Merlot. Three spaces were missing in the cardboard box. They were sample splits—or half bottles of wine, I had learned in my first week of work—sent to Jimmy for Cielo Grande.

The four riptides were wearing off fast, and I wasn't sure I was ready to face the rest of the night sober. I reached into the box and grabbed a small bottle. I leaned over and slid open

Jimmy's top drawer for the wine opener that I knew he kept beside his black felt-tip pens.

Before working for Jimmy, opening a bottle of wine was tantamount to shooting off a rocket indoors. I had no clue what I was doing, and the results were usually disastrous. But now, after a week of watching him during wine tastings, I peeled back the silver foil and flipped down the small wire "key"—as Jimmy called it—that was pressed up against the neck of the bottle. But that was as far as I got.

What am I doing? I held the bottle and brought it to my nose. The faint aroma of dark cherry and vanilla rose to my senses, washing away the smell of TJ. But another drink, from a stolen bottle no less, wouldn't erase what just happened. I placed the unopened bottle back in the box.

I glanced at Jimmy's bookshelves. A coffee maker and mug with some distinguished honor etched on it propped up a stack of books on food pairing. Jimmy always had a fresh pot, of some new flavor a vendor sent, brewing. I stood up and poured a strong cup of black coffee. I closed my eyes, and drank, imagining this hellish night, wishing it was nothing more than a bad dream.

The first sip went down smoothly. It was a dark chicory roast with a hint of vanilla that allowed me to escape into a world where I hadn't just had my boss hand me my bra. Or have TJ walk away without even looking at me. Or think that all I wanted was some back hallway hookup. It was a world where I never looked at him on that loading dock or ever looked away from Bogart. *Bogart.*

My chest shook and I bit my lip to stop it from trembling.

What have I done? What the hell was I thinking?

I kept the cup to my mouth, hoping the caffeine would sober me and make sense of my last two drunken weekends and the choices I had made. Maybe the coffee could calm me and assure me that all wasn't lost, but it didn't provide any answers. It only sank me further into darkness.

"Katie?"

I opened my eyes.

"It's Carmen." The door to Jimmy's office opened and lights flickered on.

I squinted.

"You in here?"

I nodded with my head against the back of Jimmy's desk. She couldn't see me. I was hidden where no one could see. I set down my coffee cup and raised my hand. "Over here."

She peered around the desk and her shiny luxurious black hair swung from behind her baseball cap. Her blue eyes softened. "You okay?"

I pinched the snot from my nose, wiped it on the carpet, and shook my head. "I totally blew it tonight."

Carmen knelt down beside me with my black purse in her hand and hugged me. "Katie, we've all been there. Right guy, but not the right time. TJ's a good guy, but he's *just* not right for you. Not now."

"Not ever." I covered my face with my hands.

"Oh, Katie, I'm so sorry." Her arm braced me, and I leaned in to her for strength.

"Me too."

"Do you want to hear something funny?"

I lowered my hands and looked at her. "Jimmy found someone else in the back hallway almost having sex?"

Her honey-colored skin looked like it drained of color. "*Ay, dios mio.*"

Granted my Spanish was rusty, but I knew Carmen wasn't thanking God for my good fortune.

"Are you in trouble?"

I raised my shoulders to my ears. "Not sure yet." I waved the empty coffee cup. "Thought coffee could cure it. Ha."

"*Qué está pasando?*"

"English, please."

"What is going on?"

I shrugged. "I don't know."

"I saw you leave with TJ and then you didn't return so I got worried."

"Do you think anyone else saw us leave?"

"Anyone else like Bogart?" she asked.

Even though my belly was full of riptides and coffee, it felt hollow. There was a gulf between the moment Bogart and I had shared in my car at the wetlands and what had happened with TJ in the hallway that was so wide it physically hurt. Maybe Bogart and I were just meant to be friends. But he never made me feel cheap. Or secondary. Or disposable. Yet, wasn't that what I had made Bogart feel when I dismissed him for TJ? I stared into Carmen's almond-shaped eyes. "Do you think Bogart saw me leave with TJ?"

"I don't know."

I nodded and the gulf widened.

"I don't think so. Maybe Sandy did, but that's doubtful

too," she said, laughing.

"What? Why?"

"Her and Chris *Colombo* took off for a walk on the beach," she said and we laughed aloud.

"They are such an odd pair," I said.

"It is ironic isn't it? Mr. Future General Manager is out on the beach with someone who's nothing more than a secretary," Carmen said.

I tilted my head. "I'm nothing more than a secretary. And file clerk."

"Yes, and I park cars. But neither of us introduced ourselves to a group as 'settling in jobs' that we thought were beneath us, did we?"

"Point well taken." I exhaled. "Still, they seem happy. Sandy and Chris."

She raised an eyebrow. "What did you call him? The Keebler man?"

"I did," I said, smiling. Despite all that had gone wrong with the night—and there was plenty—I looked at Carmen with a full grin. "And if Sandy likes him, then I guess a little elfin magic goes a long way."

Carmen's laughter was rich, welcome, and lifted my spirits. She patted my knee. "Okay, I'm your ride home."

"Is your shift over?"

"No, but Jimmy suggested I drive you home."

I nodded. "Thank you."

She helped me to my feet where I checked myself again in Jimmy's framed art. I wiped his coffee mug with the hem of my dress and placed it beside his stack of books. We left his office and the hotel through the front entrance, which employees were never allowed to do. But I figured come October, it wouldn't matter how I entered or exited the hotel; as long as I didn't incur overtime or benefits, I'd still be welcome.

CHAPTER **TWELVE**

Fog. If it stayed on top of the ocean, that would be fine. But fog wasn't stationary. It moved from the ocean to the shore to the beach. Even that would be okay. But when fog found its way onto Pacific Coast Highway, it didn't gradually weave onto the two-lane road like an oncoming car intersecting into traffic. *Hell no.* Fog banked itself onto the highway with the insistence of an annoying trucker that thought it owned the road simply because it drove the biggest vehicle on it. *I hate fog.* It surrounded Scarlett on all four sides, taunting me like a trucker. The only way to get away from it was to push past it. Add to it the ocean breeze from PCH carried salt in the moist air that clung to my windshields, it made visibility even more of a nightmare.

"Carmen, I can't thank you enough for driving, and I am so sorry its freakin' freezing in here." I rubbed my arms. "I got rear-ended today, which is why I'm having you drive me to Bogart's house. He wanted me to drop off my car."

The defroster was flipped to the highest setting, and hot air blasted against the front windshield, but it did nothing for my shattered back windshield. Cold air sneaked through the cracks, biting me on the back of my neck.

"It's not a problem." Carmen drove in the direction of Bogart's subdivision. Another valet driver followed us in a hotel car.

"I don't know if this is a good decision or not, but…." It neared the midnight hour, and Bogart would be getting home from work. At some point, I had to phone my parents and tell them the rest of my plans for the evening, which I didn't even know. It was the only request they'd made when I moved back home.

"I don't necessarily need to know what you're doing," my mother had said. "But if you're not going to make it home, I do need a phone call so I won't worry."

I must have remembered her appeal last weekend when I phoned home. I couldn't recall.

When Carmen turned in to the Pacific Crest subdivision, I couldn't quite remember which house was his.

I palmed the passenger side floorboard and located Bogart's garage door opener. I held it in my hand while Carmen slowly drove down the first street.

"Okay, it's a two-story," I said and hit the automatic window button. I leaned my head out of the side window as I canvassed the neighborhood.

Where the hell is it? For the life of me, I couldn't remember which house was Bogart's.

I squeezed the garage door opener in frustration.

"I think that's it?"

Carmen whipped my car around and pulled up the emergency brake.

I pressed the garage door opener but the garage door didn't open. I looked at Carmen. "I can't remember his house."

"I radioed Bogart before we left the property. He should be off his shift soon. Can I leave you here until he comes and gets you?"

I nodded. "I won't drive. I'll just wait for him. Thank you so much for driving me."

Carmen leaned over and hugged me. "Tomorrow's another day."

I tried to smile.

She cut the engine to my car and handed me the keys. "Wait for Bogart."

I nodded.

She stepped out of the car and disappeared in the fog.

I slid into the driver seat and started pressing the garage remote to see if any garage door would open. I rolled down the driver-side window and reached toward the opposite side of the street, clicking the remote. I got out and walked up and down the first street in Bogart's neighborhood, and not one garage door opened.

"Maybe it's broken. Or cold?" I got back in my car and rubbed the remote against the palm of my hand. The glare of oncoming headlights blinded me.

"Cut your lights," I said, but not loud enough for the driver to hear me.

"Lost?"

"Bogart? Bogart, is that you?" I squinted, but all I saw were white spots from the headlights.

"Kates? What are you doing?"

"I was looking for your home."

"It might help if you were on the right street. Follow me."

"Will do."

I glanced at my dashboard. 12:45 a.m. *Crap.* I carefully followed Bogart's Mustang to his house. It was on the other side of the track. I'd had Carmen make a left when I should have had her make a right.

Bogart pulled his car to the side of his driveway, making room for me to enter the garage. I cut the engine and quickly tilted the rearview mirror. My makeup was smeared, my hair was damp and curly from the fog that had seeped into my car, and the smell of alcohol couldn't be masked. *This is a disaster.*

I sat for a moment to collect my thoughts. The last time I was there I'd tried to leave as soon as I arrived. I pressed my hands against my face, trying to think of the right thing to do, but the answers wouldn't come. I stepped out of my car and followed him inside.

"I'm hungry." The words popped out of my mouth.

"How much have you had to drink?" He turned, looking at me.

I shrugged. "Not much."

"Katie."

"Really. I only had like three, maybe four drinks. And my last drink was coffee, which Carmen could verify."

"Hmm."

"May I use your phone to call my parents?" I asked. "My cell died, and I didn't bring my charger with me."

"It's on the counter. Code is 1234." He cocked his head toward the iPhone. Bogart wasn't his usual playful self.

"Are you mad at me?" I tapped in my parents' phone number.

He crossed his arms over his chest and said nothing.

"Hello?"

Her voice was groggy. "Mom?"

"Katie?"

"I woke you up. I'm sorry, Mom."

"It's fine. What's wrong?"

"I'm okay." I swallowed, but the knot in my throat remained.

"Let me go to the kitchen."

I heard the rustle of blankets followed by my mom's bare feet on the hardwood floor.

"Sweetheart, where are you? Whose phone is this? I didn't recognize the number."

"I'm at Bogart's house. It's his cell phone. Mine died. Bogart drove me home last weekend. Patrick knows him. They went to grad school together."

"Honey, you don't sound like yourself. Are you all right?"

I lowered my head and felt the sting of tears. *Oh, Mom.*

"Do you need me to come get you?"

I nodded, but the words were stuck. *Oh, Mom, I'm a mess.*

"Kates, let me come get you."

A hot tear rolled down my cheek. I knew my mom would

come for me, but I didn't want her to see me like this. Not again. *I've got to get my shit together.* She doesn't deserve this. *Hell, no one deserves this.*

"Katie?"

I sniffled and found my voice. "I'm here. My car was hit this afternoon but I'm okay. It was only cosmetic damage. Bogart was with me when it happened and he's going to fix my car. But I have to leave it here." My parents hadn't been home when I returned from playing volleyball with TJ, so they didn't know about my car.

"Oh, I'm so sorry."

"Yeah, me too. I think I'm going to stay at Bogart's."

No sooner had the words been spoken when I felt his tap on my shoulder.

"Hold on, Mom." I turned around.

A cold stare met me. "I'll drive you home or you can borrow a car."

"The fog's really bad so you could drive me home in the—"

"Tonight," Bogart said.

Suddenly it felt like an ice-cold bucket of water had been poured over me—again. My heart jumped to my throat. His comment startled and shut me down simultaneously.

"Um, okay."

"Katie?"

"Yeah, Mom. I'm back." I turned from Bogart's unforgiving eyes. My chest began to shake, but I quieted the inferno that threatened to erupt. "Mom, don't bolt the door. I'll be home tonight."

"Are you sure? Have you been drinking?"

I nodded.

"Katie, if you've been drinking, I'll come get you."

The kindness in her voice was a salve. *She wants me. She loves me. So why do I keep doing this?*

"Thanks, Mom but I've been drinking coffee and it's been a few hours since my last drink. I'll get a ride home if I'm not okay."

"Kates, please be safe."

It hurt to breathe. Tears streamed down my face faster than I could wipe them away. "I will."

"Okay, sweetie. I love you."

"I love you too, Mom. I'll see you soon."

I slid my thumb across the screen, disconnecting the call, and wiped my eyes before I faced Bogart. When I did, he crossed his arms over his chest and stared at me. *Okay, it's my move.* I handed him his phone. "Thank you." I paused, considering how my next question would land and decided to go for broke. "I thought you wanted me to stay?"

"Katie, I saw you and TJ tonight."

Though my Catholic upbringing lent toward confession, I decided to wait and determine what required an explanation. Or apology.

"He asked me to dance," I said.

"Katie."

He could have been bluffing. Carmen had said she didn't think anyone else had seen us leave.

"What? He asked a lot of girls to dance."

"Funny how you were the only one he screwed in the back hallway!"

I hadn't known Bogart for very long, but I knew he didn't raise his voice. His tone again frightened me and my fear turned to anger.

"He didn't *screw* me."

"Really? What would you call it?" He took a posturing step toward me and placed his hands on his hips.

I couldn't breathe, feeling my fight-or-flight response kick in. I came out fists raised.

"What I call it is none of your *damn* business. You had your chance with me in the car at the wetlands. But what did you do?" I took a step toward him and felt our bodies nearly touch. The heat bounced off us like a nuclear reaction. He didn't move and neither did I.

"You. Did. Nothing. You didn't kiss me. You didn't tell me you were interested in me. You didn't tell me you wanted more from me. From us. No, you waited, didn't you? You waited until *after* TJ walked onto the loading dock so that you could play your little head game and walk away and tell me we could have had something together. What the hell is that?" I opened my hands in front of him like I was releasing a time bomb.

"*That's* the biggest screw of the night. So go ahead." I fanned my hands out and nearly swiped him with them. "Judge me. See one glimpse," I held up a finger, "of what you *think* you saw between me and TJ and cast judgment. But don't for a second think you're innocent in any of this, *Mr.* Bogart."

Bogart opened his mouth, but paused. "You're right," he said, stepping away from me. "It's none of my business." He took another step back, distancing himself from me even further.

I gasped. "I'm sorry," I said through tears, but it was too late.

"There's nothing to apologize for," he said calmly. His anger had held the possibility for passion, but the stillness in his voice now had the certainty of indifference.

He doesn't care.

"Bogart," I said gently and approached him. But he backed away from me as though I had slapped him.

I've lost him.

"I have an extra car you can drive home, unless you don't feel up to driving," he said.

I barely shook my head. His reaction to me was sobering. "No, I'm okay. I'll just drive my car home. If I could get that insurance information…."

"Katie, I'm going to fix your car. I'm just not going to fix you." His comment blindsided me.

The air was knocked from my lungs. *Oh my God.* Tears pulled at the corners of my eyes and fell down my face. I quickly wiped them away. I had no one to blame but myself. I had made such a mess of my life in such a short time. I didn't know how it had gotten so unmanageable so fast, but it had.

Bogart stared at me.

"If I can just get the keys, I'll leave," I said, trying to maintain my balance when I had just turned my world on its axis. I no longer knew which way was up. And the one person that I had unknowingly come to rely on as my compass, my North Star, looked at me with such hatred and contempt that I had to leave before I fell apart. *What have I done?*

Bogart disappeared into his kitchen and returned with

a key ring. I took the keys, grabbed my clothes and other belonging out of my car, and pulled myself into the cab of his green 4x4 truck. As I drove away, my only thought was what could have been.

CHAPTER **THIRTEEN**

"I've got ninety-nine problems and he ain't one," I said in response to my little brother's question.

He kept staring at me.

"Patrick, I know you like Bogart, but he doesn't want anything to do with me. Trust me. If he sees me in the hallway, he turns and walks the opposite way. And even then, we barely make eye contact. I can't blame him. I was a train wreck," I said.

"Bogart's a good guy."

"I agree. I like him." I paused. "But I blew it and I'm finally making some peace with that. I can't go down that rabbit hole again wondering what could have been, or I'll never find my way out." I wiped crumbs off the kitchen counter and avoided my brother's inquisitive eye contact. I hung my mom's dish towel back on the hook. "Besides, I've got bigger issues. How can we save 150 people from the overtime ax?"

For the last three months, it had been my constant thought. I'd buried my head and my life in work. My endless summer was filled with stacking files, sorting every Saturday, and spitballing ideas with my brother on ways to save the part-timers.

"Tell them they are getting cooked like this bird," my brother said, waving the large chicken leg at me.

I giggled. No matter how badly I felt or how dim things seemed, Patrick always found a way to make me feel better.

"So these are people who don't even know they need saving, right?" Patrick said with his head in the refrigerator.

I wagged my finger at his backside. "No, because I made the employee bulletin board like you suggested." I pulled out a chair from the kitchen table and sat down. "It's hung right outside HR, and I post all the open positions on it. So now everyone knows what full-time jobs are available."

"That's a start." Patrick held a chicken leg in one hand and a diet soda in the other. "But I suppose your job postings are in English." He bumped the refrigerator door shut with his hip.

"Yes, but," I pointed my index and thumb at him like I was firing a shot, "I sat next to a housekeeper at lunch and asked if she'd help me translate the postings. So now they're in Spanish too. Every week we eat together, and she helps me with the new list." I lowered my hand and drummed my fingers on the table. "So whatcha think about that?"

With a mouthful of drumstick, he raised his eyebrows in approval.

"And I started that Facebook page under an alias like you suggested and invited all the employees I could find online to be my friend. But not everyone has accepted my friend request. I mean a lot have, but not 100 percent. It's kind of a bummer because I've posted a lot of pictures and comments promoting all the hard work of the part-time employees. You know, to rally the troops."

"Social media is big now. But I agree, it's not advisable to use your real name and have the hotel let you go because of some clause you didn't know existed when you signed your new hire paperwork that says you can't post hotel stuff online. It's better to be safe than sorry. But getting everyone in an uproar on Twitter or Facebook would be key to your cause," Patrick said.

"I'm working on it. I did a lot of research online to see how other companies market their benefits, and I realized what doesn't work."

"Like what?"

"Well, for starters, a lot of companies provided a bulleted list of all of the benefits they offer, but it almost made my eyes glaze over. And if I'm trying to capture the part-timers' attention, I want every perk to stand out. So on my page, the banner reads, 'Benefits of your dream job.' If nothing else, it should get their interest."

"That was smart."

I was almost speechless—almost. "Thanks. Each week, I highlight a new benefit and create a catchy phrase to go with my post like, 'Go Ahead, Be a Know-It-All.' And then I discuss the tuition reimbursement benefits."

"What name did you use for your profile page?"

I cringed.

"Katie, what did you do?"

Both my hands raised like stop signs. "Okay, before I tell you, I have to explain this to you." I clasped my hands together and held them tightly because I wasn't sure how well this next part would go over. "I don't know if you realized it, but there're *a lot* of rules to follow if you want to set up a fake name on social media. You have to have a first *and* a last name. I read all the life hacks about how to do this without getting flagged by Facebook as a spammer. But since I wanted to conceal my real identity, this was the only way to do it."

The loud pop of his soda caught me off guard. The can was to Patrick's mouth in seconds. He nodded as if following my every word, when I knew he was just waiting for me to cut to the chase. I exhaled.

"As I was saying," I dropped my hands to my lap and smiled in his direction, "there's a lot to do to create a fake name and set up a page. I entered a bunch of names like Mary Dawn, but they were already taken."

"Mary Dawn? What are you, a porn star?"

I waved him away, but he didn't disappear.

"No, I was trying to be cheerful, like, a merry dawn. A new day."

He shook his head. "I don't know why you make everything so difficult. Why didn't you just go with Sister McFattybutt?"

"You're an idiot." Though my laughter wasn't very convincing.

Patrick grinned. "So, Mary Dawn, what'd you end up with?"

"Well, after I had used up all the fake identities I could

think of, I went to get a coffee."

"And?" Patrick tore off another chunk of chicken with his teeth.

"I saw the featured beverage of the month and I thought what the hell. So I came home and Facebook accepted the name!" I clapped my hands. "It was awesome."

"You still haven't told me the name you used." Both his hands were full. When he wasn't ripping chicken off the bone, his other hand brought soda to his mouth. His hands worked in perfect synchronicity. It was like watching a juggler, only my little brother's deftness was keeping several food and beverage objects in motion at the same time by alternately tossing one into his mouth. He was midsip when I blurted out my identity.

"Pumpkin Spice."

Dark cola spat across the kitchen. I held up my hands but I was hit by his cola spray.

"Ew, gross." I wiped my forehead on my shoulder.

"Pumpkin Spice?" He actually set his soda can down. "I think I like Mary Dawn better."

"It could have been worse."

Patrick's brown eyes widened.

"I could have been Maple Delight and that would have sounded like some Canadian dessert. Or Michigan Cherry. That was also in the pastry cabinet."

"So instead you went with Pumpkin Spice? You couldn't have been Mocha Latte, or actually, with your pasty white skin, Vanilla Frappé?"

I glanced at my arms. My summer tan had all but faded

with all the hours I was logging at work.

"No, I'm Pumpkin Spice."

"It's a wonder anyone friended you."

I raised my eyebrows. "Brother, you'd be surprised. Granted not everyone accepted my friend request, but I did pull in some new friends and followers. A little spice goes a long way, if you know what I mean?" I giggled.

The horrified expression on my brother's face made me chuckle.

"Oh, relax. It's just a faceless name, and the Facebook page hasn't sparked the interaction I was hoping for. I feel like I'm back at square one. I don't know what to do to connect the part-timers and explain what's going on. You know, to unify them."

Patrick wiped his mouth on the kitchen towel.

"That's not a napkin," I said.

"And you're not Pumpkin Spice, but as you said, sometimes we work with what's in front of us."

I rolled my eyes. "You're absolutely no help."

He pulled up the chair beside mine. "Listen, since social media is flopping right now, the old-school way is the employee break room. That's where shit happens."

"I agree and for us it's the cafeteria, but they have cameras in there and even if they aren't recording sound, I literally feel watched."

Patrick nodded. "Well, then have a party and invite 150 of your closest friends."

"A party?"

"Yeah, you've been talking about finding an apartment

forever. So start looking and then have a housewarming party." Patrick pushed out his chair and headed in the direction of the cookie jar.

"It's empty," I said.

His eyes got as large as quarters. "What?"

I shrugged. "You know I eat through my stress." I pointed toward the cupboard. "There're crackers."

"No, thanks." He sat back down. "If you're not up for putting on a party, have a few people host a happy hour and shit will fly."

"No, I like your idea of a party. I just don't know if it's the best time for me to move out. I have free room and board. And my overtime is going to come to a crashing halt in three weeks."

"What's the harm in looking?"

I tilted my head at him. "Oh, I don't know, that I'll see something I like that I can't afford."

"Katie, you're not losing your job, and you've already passed your ninety-day probationary period. You get paid semi-monthly, right?"

I raised my shoulders to my ears. "We get paid on the first and the fifteenth. I don't know what you call it, but I call it payday." I slapped my leg when I laughed.

Patrick rolled his eyes. "That's semi-monthly. So with your regular earnings, you're netting about a thousand each paycheck."

"That's right! It's just over a thousand after taxes."

"All right, so that's two grand a month and your car loan is four hundred a month, right?"

I nodded.

Patrick titled his chair back and reached behind him to the glass table in the adjoining family room where Mom kept the house phone. A pad of paper and a jar of pens were beside the cordless phone. He grabbed a pen and the notepad Mom used for her grocery list. He wrote fast and furiously on the pad and then slid it toward me.

His chicken scratch was hard to read but the bottom line wasn't. After deducting my car payment, insurance, food, gas, even a little fun money, I was left with a balance of twelve hundred a month for rent.

"You've got to find an apartment where utilities are included. It'll be tight, but it's not impossible," he said.

"Wow. Do you really think I can find something for twelve hundred in Orange County?"

"It won't be the heart of the OC, and it'll probably be a studio apartment in an older section of Huntington or Fountain Valley, but yeah, I think it's possible."

I pushed away from the table and ran to my bedroom. I returned with my laptop. After it fired up, I did a quick search of available apartments in Huntington.

Page after page scrolled by and there wasn't one apartment for under fifteen hundred. I shook my head.

"It's a nice thought, brother, but until I'm full-time and eligible for a raise, I can't swing it."

"Keep an eye on the newspaper because, believe it or not, there're still a lot of private owners who advertise in the paper and not online. They're older and just do it the old-fashioned way."

"Dad would be so proud," I said of our father, the sports writing newspaperman.

Patrick stood. "I've got to go. I'm heading to Sullivan's for dinner."

"Dinner? You just polished off a King Henry-sized chicken leg."

He snapped his fingers. "That, little sister, was my appetizer. Steak is the *entrée*."

"Enjoy." I leaned back as he walked by and he kissed my fivehead.

"Don't give up," he said in my ear. "On the apartment or Bogart."

"Love you, too."

He threw the paper toward me as he left. "That's not love, little sister. I'm tired of you mooching off Mom. There're never enough cookies left when you're around."

I laughed, opened the paper to the classifieds, and began circling anything that looked promising. *Maybe Patrick is right.* I'd find an apartment, host a party, and unify the troops. And while I was at it, I'd cure cancer, end poverty, and shave my legs.

CHAPTER **FOURTEEN**

Finding an affordable apartment in Orange County, especially in Huntington Beach, was like trying to catch the perfect wave in Surf City, the town's official nickname. Everyone would be after it, so I would have to be in the perfect position, the right place at the right time, to catch it, because only one surfer would be able to ride that perfect wave to shore. So when an affordable apartment came on the market, I likewise had to be in the right place at the right time to get that perfect wave of an apartment before anyone else had a chance to see it.

Usually, surf side apartments cost an arm and a leg, and an affordable one usually meant there was a corresponding crime scene photo where someone literally lost an arm and/or a leg. I'd have to have the luck of the Irish, a four leaf clover, and a unicorn's horseshoe to find an ocean view apartment that didn't require a leprechaun's pot of gold to rent it. Or gallons of bleach to rid the place of chalk outlines and other remnants from the former tenant.

Still I was stupidly optimistic. After all, the one advantage to all work and no play was that it allowed me to earn a good chunk of money to put down for first, last, and a security deposit. Better yet, focusing on an apartment allowed me to stop focusing on Bogart. It compartmentalized my thinking, which left me little time to remember our last night together. A painful pang resurfaced anytime I did. Working overtime shut out those thoughts and let in new possibilities, like apartment surfing. Independence was possibly mine if I could just catch the perfect wave.

During my lunch hour, I drove past the places I'd circled in Sunday's classified section. Nothing promising resulted. I headed back toward the hotel and the last posting on my list. Leaves blew onto Main Street and crunched beneath the tires on Bogart's green truck. I dubbed the loaner the Green Machine because it wasn't big enough to be a Hulk and it wasn't cute enough to be a Kermit. And until Bogart returned Scarlett, I was stuck with good, 'ol reliable Green Machine.

It had neared the end of my lunch break when I drove past a two-story blue cottage on my way to find a duplex off B Street. A group of workmen ate lunch beneath a maple tree.

"It can't be...."

I glanced in my rearview and caught sight of a For Rent sign staked beside the tree. I quickly flipped a U and backtracked to them. I hopped out of the Green Machine that I had oddly grown fond of in the three months it was taking Bogart to fix my car. Apparently, Scarlett's red licorice paint color had been out of stock for months. She was one of a kind. So, while Bogart waited for it to arrive from the manufacturer, he had taken to doing other things to Scarlett. What, I'm not sure. This had all been conveyed to me by Patrick, who seemed to always bump into Bogart at Sullivan's. I still barely said "Hello," to Bogart, and he barely acknowledged me. I told myself we were mutually respecting each other's space and needed to civilly communicate and work in the same hotel. But I knew I was full of crap. I missed talking to him. I missed looking into his eyes and knowing what kind of day he was having. Or the way he could make me laugh. I shook my head, erasing that pang that surfaced again, and approached one of the paint-speckled workmen.

"Hi. I'm sorry to interrupt your lunch, but I was wondering if those are apartments." I pointed to the upper balcony.

"They sure are," an older man said. He stood up, brushed off his hands on his pants, and introduced himself. "My name's Ed Rowain."

"I'm Katie. Katie Flanagan." I firmly shook his hand. "Are you the owner?"

"How'd you know?"

"Lucky guess." I smiled and then paused before I asked the dreaded question. "Is it already rented?"

"Nope, just had someone move out. Care to take a look?"

"Oh my gosh. That'd be great." I quickly glanced at my watch. My lunch hour was almost up, but I was less than five minutes away from the hotel.

"We'll make it quick," he said.

"No, don't. I'm just on my lunch break."

"You can always come back."

"No." I might have found the perfect swell, and I wasn't about to drive away. As we ascended the stairs, I asked the next dreaded question. "What's the rent?"

"Eleven fifty a month, includes utilities and water," Ed said.

"Really? Eleven fifty. Like eleven hundred fifty dollars." I sounded like an idiot. But I wanted to make sure I hadn't imagined what I wanted to hear.

"That's correct, eleven fifty."

My heart skipped a beat, and I almost missed a step on the staircase.

"Careful," he said.

I nodded and smiled so wide it hurt.

"What about the deposit?" I asked.

"I usually get first and last month's rent," Ed said. "And a twenty-five-dollar credit check."

I quickly figured the total to move in. I had saved three grand. It was the most I had ever squirreled away. Something to be said about free rent, groceries, and not going out.

Ed opened the white front door. "It's only a studio."

"That's okay. It's just me."

I walked behind him for the tour of the apartment. The walls were in the process of being painted a soft cream that offset the rich, two-tone, caramel-colored Berber carpet. The kitchen and main studio were trimmed in pine. It reminded me of Bogart's house and the care he had taken to customize his first home.

The bathroom was laid in a reddish-brown tile that led to

a built-in, oak armoire. The aroma of stain filled the small space.

"Just put a fresh coat of sealer on it." Ed carefully slid his hand across the smooth finish. "It's for your hand towels and such."

"It's beautiful." I stopped in front of the older tub that had a rod for a shower curtain. It wasn't much, but it was clean and would do the job. "It's perfect."

We returned to the main room. The kitchen was off to the side. It didn't have a dishwasher, and there was a large empty space beside the dated cupboards that had a charming appeal to them.

"Now you've gotta furnish your own refrigerator," he said.

"Oh, sure." I couldn't even begin to imagine how much a refrigerator cost. *Eating's overrated.*

"The *Nickel and Dime* is always advertising used ones," Ed said.

"That's a great idea." I'd totally forgotten about the free weekly paper that was 90 percent classified ads. *Bonus.*

A small, narrow strip off the kitchen served as the only balcony. *It's big enough for me.* The studio was framed by large picture windows that rose above the tree line and provided a straight view to the ocean. From my bedroom, I could see Catalina Island. I almost cried.

"I'll take it!" I paused. "I mean, if it's still available." I held my breath. "It is still available, right?"

Ed laughed. "It's all yours."

I reached over and hugged him. "Thank you so much. You won't be sorry. I'll be the best tenant you've ever had."

"I hope so, because the gal that left was just wonderful. She's getting married," he said, eyeing me.

"You don't have to worry about that. I'm not dating anyone," I said, my voice trailing off.

"Not yet," Ed said optimistically. "This apartment is a magnet for men. Every tenant I get moves out in six months because they're getting married."

"Not going to happen. I'll sign a year's lease if you want me to."

"No, I think we better keep it to six months," he said.

"As long as I can renew when six months are up."

"The place is yours as long as you want it."

"Thank you, thank you, thank you!" I checked my watch. "I'm late. Can I come back after work and leave a deposit?"

"Leave me a deposit tonight, fill out the credit application, and unless you've committed some horrible crime, the apartment's yours. We're aiming for October fifteenth. We're working on a few units."

"Oh." My voice dropped. *It's only the beginning of September.*

"Everything okay?"

"Yes." I shook my head. "I'm sorry. I was hoping to be in by the first of October so I could have some friends from work over."

"And these friends won't be friends after the first of the month?"

I laughed. "No, they will be. We just have some changes coming up at work, and I wanted to have one last hurrah before it happens."

"Summer's last blast, huh?" Ed said.

"Something like that, yeah. But it's okay. I'll figure something out."

"Well, you're welcome to start hauling your things here. You can use the garage where I store my stuff. I'll be the only other person besides yourself who would have a key. But you won't be able to move in until the fifteenth. I can't push my guys any harder than what we're doing."

"The fifteenth's great. I'll swing by after work with a check."

"See you later. We'll be hammering away on it."

"Is anything wrong?" I asked, realizing maybe there was some gross handicap I hadn't noticed. *Where's Bogart? Bogart would know what to ask.*

"Nah, just regular wear and tear. It was time for new paint and carpet in the hallway."

I raised my shoulders to my ears and smiled. "Thank you so much." I shook his hand. "So it's mine, right?"

"It's all yours."

"See you after work," I reconfirmed before I flew down the staircase and toward Bogart's truck.

I hauled to work and clocked back in from lunch twenty minutes late.

"I was afraid you got lost," Jimmy said when I appeared at my desk. We had been working in a state of minimal conversation since he caught me in the back hallway. So much had changed. I'd lost my confidence that day and hadn't been able to get back on track. Today felt like a turning point.

"I found an apartment." I heard the energy return to my voice. It had been dead for so long.

"That's wonderful." Jimmy patted me on the back. I looked up at him and smiled.

"Thank you."

"You've really been working hard and it's paying off," he added.

"I hope so."

"When do you move in?" Jimmy asked.

"Not until the fifteenth."

"Why the long face?"

"I was just hoping to have a party before then."

He questioned me with his eyes.

"I was aiming for October first to get some friends I've met at work, other part-timers to come over to the house and hash some things out." I glanced up at him and his gray-blue eyes studied me. *Crap. Me and my big mouth.*

"Hash things out?"

I exaggerated an eye roll. "I meant party things out. Any who, what's on the agenda today?" I said in a singsong voice, hoping to redirect his attention off my stupidity.

"I'm glad you asked." He clapped his hands together. "We have to get going."

I looked at him.

"The Food and Beverage meeting? It's not Friday."

"Remember, I changed it because I'll be out of town. It's my birthday."

"I completely forgot." My face flushed. I spaced on both his birthday *and* the F&B meeting? *Great Flanagan. I don't need to lose the only job that may become full-time in the New Year. Shit.*

"It's okay, you're just on time."

I grabbed my pen and notepad and followed Jimmy to the Coast nightclub.

I had grown accustomed to the smell of stale beer and cigarettes. Even though there was a no-smoking policy in the club, nicotine found its way into the bar, polluting the upholstery and carpet and staining the walls. A yellow tinge had begun to build on the wall covering. It was one of the items Jimmy had down to discuss: renovation work.

The Coast was the most attended food and beverage outlet in the hotel, and as such, it was already showing the most wear.

As usual, TJ was one of the first to arrive. The awkward stage between Jimmy, TJ, and me had thankfully passed. Now he greeted me with a handshake as he did Jimmy.

"Flanagan," he addressed me.

"Johnson," I said in return, which always made him smile.

My attraction to him had left that night in the back hallway. Besides, it was rumored by Sandy that he was steadily seeing her best friend, Jackie. They made a good pair. Sandy and Chris, who had escaped to the beach together that night, remained an item three months later.

It was a case of opposites attracting. Sandy, who easily stood over five feet eight inches and wore bright fuchsia-colored suits, towered over conservative Chris, who barely cleared five feet and was always dressed in Armani. Sandy's hair color that switched as often as her wardrobe and salon-baked skin clashed with Chris's fair face and shock of white hair. But they were supposedly "in love," and Sandy hinted that plans for a New Year's Eve wedding were in the works.

At times, I envied what Sandy and Chris had. During those times, I threw myself into filing or some mindless activity to preoccupy my thoughts so that my envy wouldn't turn to self-pity. When that didn't work, I bent Carmen's ear about the lack of luster in my life.

"It'll happen," she always said, and I banked on her assurance.

I glanced at TJ and was quickly reminded of the need for patience. My impulsiveness had created a train wreck out of my life, and I liked that it had been a while since it had last derailed.

"Okay, well, my watch says two," Jimmy said as he opened the midweek meeting. There was a skeleton crew assembled.

"The menu tasting for the winter soups and entrees will be held on Friday," Chef announced.

I smiled. It was the only time I ate well at the hotel. I had long ago forfeited day-old cafeteria food in lieu of bagging my own. I brought my sack lunch into the employee cafeteria and tried to meet someone new every day, but mystery meat wasn't going to get the best of me ever again.

"Tomorrow, we're hosting the breakfast buffet for the overnight crew," TJ said of the monthly event that my other department, HR, coordinated. It had been my idea, which Holly credited herself with creating, something I learned she did quite frequently. My proposal was to recognize the overnight staff, who weren't able to enjoy many of the employee amenities offered to the daytime staff, by providing a catered breakfast once a month.

Jimmy hated the idea because it pulled employees away from his designated breakfast functions, but Mr. Adams, the general manager, strongly supported the concept and so it continued.

I came in early during the monthly functions and helped decorate the allocated ballroom or meeting room where the overnight crew were sequestered with continental breakfast. I set my cell phone alarm to remind myself of tomorrow's early call. The meeting, thankfully, ended as uneventfully as it began. Short meeting equaled shorter minutes and getting out of work early. *Score.*

###

Despite the early wake-up call, I couldn't sleep. After filling out the credit application and leaving a deposit, I returned to my parents' house and immediately fired up my laptop. I parked myself at their kitchen table browsing the Internet for prices on refrigerators.

"Whatcha doing, Twiggy?" My brother Patrick snuck up on me.

I shrieked. "Don't do that!"

He laughed as he held my mom's cookie jar. A snickerdoodle hung from his mouth, and another one was less than a bite away.

"It's customary to sit down and eat," I said. "And close your mouth when you chew."

Patrick ignored both of my suggestions and instead opened his mouth, revealing a back row of silver fillings. As a teenager, he'd had a thing for jawbreakers, and he'd often allowed the hard candy to sit, slowly dissolving in his mouth. By the end of his freshman year in high school, he had rotted two of his back teeth. It was the only time I had ever seen him uncontrollably cry. The pain from the dentist was enough to ensure he never ate hard candy again.

"You're disgusting," I said, though I smiled in his direction. Our mom was a lousy cook, but she was a great baker, and our house always smelled of fresh-baked cookies, cakes, and pastries. My crafty little brother had beaten me to the new batch. It was the Flanagan curse. We all had a sweet tooth, and my mom knew how to satisfy the craving. She never seemed to tire of making an assortment of wonderful offerings.

Patrick and my dad could eat to their hearts' content and never gain an ounce. For that matter, so could my older brother, Ian, but I wasn't as lucky. I just looked at sweets and the digital scale started to scroll higher and higher, like a gas pump filling up an SUV.

"I got an apartment!"

His head remained buried in the cookie jar.

"Patrick, stop shanghaiing the cookies and listen to me. I got an apartment!"

"I heard you," he mumbled, his hand digging through the assortment. "Ah-ha!" He fished out a leftover chocolate chip cookie. "I knew you were in there."

"Hey, what about my apartment? Isn't that great? I took your advice and found one."

"Where's it at and how much is it going to cost me?"

"It's in old Huntington and it's not going to cost you anything." I elbowed him in the side.

"Where in HB?"

"Down on Main by Tenth Street," I said proudly. "Patrick, it's so cute."

"That's always important."

"Stop. Be happy for me."

"I am, I am. Now how much is it going to cost *you*? Did you stay within the budget I factored?"

Patrick's work in the finance field kept him checking the balance sheet of everything. Over the weekend, it was how many cookies I had eaten compared to him. He was clearly making up for that deficit. Now it was whether I had adhered to the financial plan he drafted on Mom's grocery list.

"Eleven fifty. Utilities and water included. Isn't that amazing?"

"You're not in the redevelopment section," he stated rather than asked.

"No, but it's still a good section. It has brand-new paint and carpet and this quaint bathroom."

"Huh. That's really good. You'll be able to afford rent, your car payment, and living expenses."

"Yeah, it'll be nice when I actually drive the car I've been paying for. Hey, when *is* Bogart going to be finished with my car anyway? It's been three months. I'd really like it back."

"I talked to him tonight, actually."

"Really? Where? Did you guys go out? Did he call you?" I found myself a little too curious about Bogart's whereabouts.

"Well, Detective," Patrick deadpanned. "I met the suspect at nineteen hundred hours after work for some drinks."

"Very funny." I ignored his lame humor. "Where did you meet him?"

Patrick arched one dark brow.

"Sullivan's."

"Only decent pub in town."

"Only *Irish* pub in town," I said.

His mouth twisted into a smile.

"So what'd he say about my car?"

"You're going to love it. He tricked out the engine and gave it more horsepower. It's going to hum."

"But my car was fine. Why'd he do that?"

"Trust me," my little brother said. "You're going to thank him."

"What about the paint?"

"Yup," Patrick said with a mouthful of cookies. "It finally came in, and he just finished spraying a second coat. He had to repaint the entire car."

"What?"

"Relax, he did you a favor. The morons couldn't match their own color so they sent him something close and Bogart stripped and sanded your car so it'd be an even coat."

"Wow" was all I could say.

"Yeah, you'd better thank him."

"I would if he ever spoke to me," I said, but my remark sailed over Patrick, who had disappeared into the refrigerator.

"Are we outta milk?" he asked frantically.

"Mom and Dad are out of milk. I don't know what's in *your* refrigerator."

"Come on." He grabbed his coat and keys.

"Where we going?"

"I need some milk."

"So?"

"So you're going to run in for me."

"No way. Look at me. I'm in sweats and a T-shirt. I look awful."

"You won't see anyone. I'm just going up to the corner." Patrick lived to support the twenty-four-hour convenience shop a block away from our parents' house.

"Well… I haven't had dinner."

"And…?"

"If you buy Hank's, I'll go in and get your milk."

"Hank's? That's clear across town."

"Yup."

"Katie, Katie, Katie, do you really feel like you need Hank's?" He gazed at my thighs.

I gazed at the balding spot on his head. "Listen, Charlie Brown, I haven't had Hank's since—" I stopped midsentence. I wasn't about to reminiscence about my singing debut, which would only backfire on me.

"All right, all right. But only because I feel sorry for you."

As we headed toward his car, he began singing. "I lover you, my beautiful baby."

"Break any noses lately?" Catholic guilt was a charm that worked well on Patrick.

"So, dinner," he said. "It's on me."

"Yeah, it's on you."

I grabbed a half gallon of whole milk and practically gagged watching Patrick guzzle the thick white liquid.

"Ew. How can you drink that?" The only milk I drank was in milkshakes, and I was less than a mile away from ordering an extra-large triple-chocolate shake. My mouth watered just thinking of the sweet, yummy chocolate concoction. I didn't care if I had to eat celery sticks for the next two weeks; tonight I was going to really splurge.

Patrick pulled into the drive-through, which was surprisingly empty. Hank's was always busy.

"They're still open, right?" Panic seized my voice and appetite.

"They're open twenty-four hours. Yes, they're open." Patrick tossed the empty milk container into the trash can beside the drive-in marquee. The carton disappeared inside the metal tin.

Lucky shot. "Okay, I'd like—"

"I know," Patrick cut me off. "Double bacon hamburger with grilled onions, large fries, and a triple-chocolate shake."

"Oh, if only you weren't my brother…."

"Disgusting. Don't make me hurl."

"I was joking. And I will *not* let you spoil my mood." I danced in my seat. A new apartment *and* Hank's all in the same day. Life was good.

"All I need now is a new refrigerator. Any suggestions?"

"Go to the store and buy one?"

"You think?"

Patrick ordered my food and added a burger and fries for himself. "A refrigerator…. Let me think." He pulled forward to the window to pay. He grabbed a twenty from his ashtray. A thick stack of bills was wedged in the silver compartment. "I do have a few contacts at Guy's Appliance Shop."

My little brother had contacts all over Orange County; it

was just a matter of whether he wanted to pull in one of the many favors everyone seemed to owe him.

"Guy's, huh? That's high-end, isn't it? I just need a basic refrigerator. White… no, tan… no, white," I said, trying to remember the color of the linoleum kitchen floor. "White, definitely white," I said, and noticed Patrick had become unusually quiet.

I followed his line of vision and saw Bogart. Only he wasn't alone. He was sitting beneath an umbrella table with Carmen. The same Carmen who had driven me to Bogart's that fateful night three months ago. The same Carmen I called and complained to. The same Carmen who told me "It'll happen," when I bellyached about my love life. The same Carmen I trusted… was now with Bogart.

My stomach fell and my appetite went with it. Nausea crept to the back of my throat.

"Katie," my brother said. "I didn't know they'd be here."

I looked at him. "What do you mean *they*?"

"They were together tonight at Sullivan's. I didn't want to tell you because I knew it'd hurt you."

"Why would it hurt me?" My tone was clipped, defensive, and my body felt hot. But it wasn't from anger. It was feeling like I was going to break out in a rash at any moment.

"Kates," Patrick said, using Mom's nickname for me. "I'm sorry, sweetheart."

That hollow emptiness that I had worked three months to avoid returned in one swift moment. "It's okay. I'm okay. I'll be fine." I wasn't and it got worse when Bogart glanced over his shoulder and spotted us.

How could you be with her? I hoped my eyes could convey what I held in my heart. *Why her? Why not me?* Sadness pooled in my stomach. *Oh. This is how he felt when he saw me with TJ.*

Carmen glanced our way. She wasn't wearing a baseball cap and her glossy black hair was down, framing her petite face and accentuating her almond-shaped blue eyes. A soft, inviting smile played on her lips. I'd never underestimated her beauty, but her attraction to Bogart I had. The ache in my chest deepened.

I'd been able to let go of Bogart and what we may have had because he wasn't with anyone. The possibility of what still could be had always lingered in my mind. Now that he was with Carmen, my emotions returned to that night in June when I left his house and his heart. *I've been replaced.*

The car inched forward and Patrick grabbed our food. As we drove past their table I looked away.

"I'm sorry," my brother said, rubbing my knee.

"It's okay."

"Hey, why don't you show me that new apartment of yours?" His sounded desperate to change the mood and topic.

"Not tonight. Maybe later. Thanks, though," I said.

My brother's heart was always in the right place. I knew he wanted to make this better for me, but all I wanted to do was go home, fall asleep, and hopefully forget about the whole night. I had to do what Bogart had done and finally move on.

CHAPTER **FIFTEEN**

"So what's on the menu?"

I turned to find Bogart in line with the other overnight crew.

"When did *you* return to working nights?" I asked. He'd either answer or grunt and turn away. We'd been civil to each other, but this was the first real conversation I'd initiated in months.

"We rotate every quarter. It's my turn to pull graveyard."

"Huh." My stomach stirred. There were two more breakfasts left in the quarter that guaranteed I'd come face-to-face with him again.

Bogart picked up a plate off the buffet station. "What looks good?"

"Everything, actually," I said. "Chef does an amazing eggs Benedict, if you like that. Or there's traditional oatmeal."

Bogart gave a slow, weary shake of his head.

"Okay, how about an omelet? You tell the cook how you like it prepared, and they make it from scratch."

"Nope."

"Pancakes? Waffles? Danish?" I rattled off a list of our offerings.

But Bogart rejected each one.

"What do you want, then?"

His eyes honed in on me before he set down his plate and pulled me toward him.

I gasped.

"You," he said. "I want you. I've always wanted you."

My stomach fluttered like a thousand butterflies had taken flight. "Really?"

"Really."

"But what about Carmen?"

"We're just friends."

"So there's nothing…."

"Nothing. How could there be?"

I smiled as he leaned toward me. Our lips were about to touch when his mouth opened wide and blared like a broken car alarm. Frightened, I jumped and popped open my eyes. The cell phone had pulled me from my dream. My bedroom ceiling was above me and not Bogart. *It was a dream.*

I wanted to shut my eyes and drift back into Bogart's arms, but the second wave of alarms sounded, reminding me that I still had to coordinate the breakfast with TJ. *Fan-freakin'-tastic. The guy I used to pine for, I see all the time, but the one I really want to see, I never do.*

###

Autumn continued to show itself in Huntington. A crimson tide of leaves littered my parents' driveway. I kicked my square-toed black boots through the foliage and smiled.

"It'll be a good day," I tried convincing myself. "I can shop for a refrigerator and new bedding. Bedding that no one will see, but hey, by mid-October I'll be in a new apartment!" I had to redirect my thoughts to something other than Bogart or Carmen. *Please let me get through the day without seeing either of them.*

Carmen began her workday when mine ended, so it shouldn't be a problem bypassing her, but Bogart…. I drew a deep breath, and crisp fall air awakened my lungs with purpose. Bogart was another story. His shift schedule changed frequently. There was no telling when or if I'd bump into him.

###

I pressed into the top rung of the ladder and stood on the tips of my boots. The small hook in the ballroom ceiling was just out of reach. *Crap.* I braced myself against the metal ladder and stretched until I was able to loop the tip of the tissue-paper autumn wreath into the hook. *Yes! Gotcha!*

I released the festive swag, and colorful fall leaves hung high in the air. The overhead decorations popped in color with vibrant orange, burnt sienna and mustard yellow. It looked like the banquet room was raining leaves. The tables below were skirted in black tablecloths. Mason jars, which were painted a rich chocolate and tied with a fall-inspired plaid ribbon, were filled with an array of warm, harvest flowers. Burgundy mini carnations, peach spray roses and butterscotch chrysanthemums encompassed all that I loved about the season. *It looks even better than it did on Pinterest.* My best decorating ideas were stolen from someone much craftier and more talented than me and the day's event was no exception.

"Flanagan, I have housemen that can do that." TJ appeared beneath the ladder.

"I know. But I like to do it."

"Just don't fall. I don't need an accident recorded in our department."

"Your concern is overwhelming."

"Nice boots." TJ held the ladder.

"You like that, do you?" *Why am I flirting?*

"Leather and…." He tried to peek up my skirt. "Lace perhaps?"

I kicked my heel toward him and purposely missed hitting him. "Easy, Tex. We don't want to make *that* mistake again."

We both laughed. It was the first time we had ever mentioned that night.

"That was kind of a disaster," he said.

"You think?" I rolled my eyes.

"Well, least it wasn't caught on security video." TJ tugged on the hem of my skirt.

"How did *you* know about that?" I asked of my singing performance caught on tape at Hank's.

"I was there, remember?"

"Yeah, but how'd you know about the video?"

"I asked Hank for the tape, but Bogart had already beat me to the punch."

"Oh." *Bogart.* My chest grew heavy.

"Yeah, he's a real bulldog when it comes to you."

"What do you mean?"

"It's nothing," TJ said.

"No, tell me. What do you mean?"

"It was bad enough that Jimmy caught us in the act," TJ said. "But then Bogart cornered me in the bar that night and really gave me an earful."

"What did he say?" I carefully stepped down from the ladder.

"What *didn't* he say?"

"Seriously. What'd he say?"

"Everything you'd expect from a guy who's in love with someone."

"He's *not* in love with me." I exhaled. *Not in the least.*

"Flanagan, I may not have a college degree, but I'm not an idiot."

"That's not what I meant. I don't think Bogart…. Well, he may have *had* feelings for me then but now…." I shook my head. "He's with Carmen."

"The little girl from the front drive?" TJ asked.

"She's not so little. She's beautiful."

"So are you."

I tilted my head and snorted a laugh. "Yeah, sure."

"Flanagan, that's always been your problem."

"What?"

"Your lack of confidence. You think everyone else is better

than you are and they aren't. You just don't see what you have to offer."

Huh. I listened as the guy I had lusted over and gone after gave me a new perspective.

"You're the smartest girl in the hotel, but the dumbest when it comes to men. And just for the record, you're wasting your time filing when you should be running the department."

"Please."

"You think we don't know who created these monthly breakfast functions? It has your stamp all over it. You care about people, Flanagan, and it shows. Holly doesn't give a flying whoop about the employees. She's got her nose so far up Jerry's ass," he said, referring to the general manager, "she wouldn't know how to motivate the staff if she tried. But you do. You know what makes people tick. I see it in the F&B meetings and your work with the housemen and their insurance paperwork."

I was speechless.

"But when it comes to guys, you seem to lose that confidence that makes you so attractive. I deal with a lot of women in my profession," he said of his interaction with the guests. "And there could be a room full of women, all shapes and sizes, but you know what's attractive?"

I shrugged.

"The way a woman carries herself. She could be three hundred pounds, but if she walks into a room as if she owns it, with her stride and confidence, she's the one all the guys are looking at."

"I'm not three hundred pounds," I clarified.

He let out an audible sigh. "That's not what I'm saying. It's all about how you carry yourself. And when you get around a guy, you lose that kick in your step that you normally have when you're cruising the halls doing your HR or F&B thing."

"I don't cruise the halls."

"Flanagan! For Christ's sake, are you listening?"

I gritted a smile and nodded.

"Hold up your head. You don't have anything to be ashamed of. I was just as much at fault as you were. But you didn't see me hang my head."

"It's different. You're a guy."

"That's bullshit. It's not different. I still got caught with my pants down, literally, by the director of Food and Beverage. No matter what you want to believe, it still didn't look good for me or my career. But I looked Jimmy in the eye and apologized."

"But you never apologized to me."

"You're right," he said. "And that was wrong. You accepted the blame for both of us, but you didn't need to." There wasn't anything he'd said that wasn't true. Still, it cut to the shame I carried and hadn't reconciled. "You've gotta let it go. It happened months ago."

"I have," I lied.

"No you haven't," he said. "And if you like Bogart, then you need to let this go and move on, so you two can be together."

"It's too late. He's with Carmen."

TJ shook his head. "He's not into her like he is with you."

"That's not what I saw last night."

"I don't care what you saw. Look at us. No matter what people saw, it wasn't the real deal. I mean, I like you and all, but I was just being a prick. I liked Jackie," he said. "But I was afraid."

"So you hooked up with me?"

"Yeah, because I was afraid."

"Afraid of what?"

"Jackie, and my feelings for her."

"So it was easier to be with me. With someone you didn't like?"

"Don't go there. I was attracted to you. Hell, I still am. You're the whole package," he said, and I flashed to Carmen's description of Bogart. "But my feelings weren't there for you in the same way they were for Jackie."

"I get it."

"Listen," he said. "Bogart likes you."

I looked into TJ's hazel eyes. They didn't captivate, mesmerize, or hold me like they had just a few months ago. TJ was TJ.

"Those eyes of yours," he said. "Now there's something to be scared of."

"Thanks." I laughed in surprise.

"No, I mean it. You look right through someone with those dark eyes."

I stood before him and smiled.

"Carmen isn't your problem," he said. "It's your confidence you should focus on. Get that back and you'll get Bogart. He needs to see that you're okay without him. Then he'll come knocking down your door."

I chuckled. "Seriously doubt that will happen."

"See," he said, nudging me in the elbow. "Confidence. Work on it. Don't settle for less. If you want to be with Bogart, then go for it. *You're* the only one in the way of making that happen."

I nodded with a smile. "Thank you."

"I'll send you my bill," he said. "Now, let's get this breakfast thing off the ground, huh?"

"Sounds like a plan."

We worked together to create a breakfast buffet worthy of the Waterfront Point Resort.

At 8:00 a.m., weary-eyed bodies came in for their monthly offerings. I surveyed the line but didn't see Bogart. *It was only a dream.* Pessimism crept in and crowded out hope. *Who knows….* I inwardly smiled. *He could still show. It could happen.*

###

The breakfast hour neared its end. I worked with the housemen to gather the leftover food to deliver to the cafeteria.

"Got room for one more?"

My heart leapt. I turned to find Bogart standing at the end of the buffet. There was a moment of silence before I remembered TJ's advice. *Be confident and you'll get Bogart.*

"Come on in, there's plenty of food." I smiled.

Bogart grabbed a plate and worked his way down the serving line until he reached the end where I was loading cartons of milk onto a dolly.

"Got milk?" he asked.

"What's your flavor? Low-fat, 2 percent?"

"None of that Sissy-Mary stuff," he said. "Give me the whole cow."

"No wonder you and Patrick get along so well." I handed him a carton.

"John Wayne didn't drink 2 percent," he said.

"Good to know." I grinned.

Bogart took a seat at a linen-skirted table. "The room looks great," he said with his head tilted up.

"Thanks."

"This is a really nice thing you do for the overnighters."

"It's not just me," I began, and then corrected my slouched posture and confidence. "Thank you. It's important to me that the graveyard crew gets recognized."

Bogart looked over and smiled.

"So you're on nights now?" I asked.

"I got called in last night."

Last night... when you were with Carmen? My stomach twisted in a knot, but instead of turning away I offered a smile in reply.

"So Patrick tells me you've totally revamped my car. Thanks, I really appreciate that."

"It was no trouble. I had a lot of fun."

"So maybe we should make a date." I watched his face shift. I wasn't sure if he was surprised or scared. "To exchange cars."

"Of course," he said, his cheeks taking on a slightly rosy tint.

Ahh. You thought I was asking you out. The knot in my stomach loosened. *Wow.* It was just like TJ said. *Who knew?* I felt possessed of a new power.

"How does tonight sound?" I posed with a false sense of confidence. *But hey, fake it until you make it, right?*

He stuttered, "T-t-t—" He cleared his throat. "Tonight?"

"Yeah. I'd like to get my car back."

"Sure. Tonight."

"Excellent. I'll drop by after work then?"

He nodded and then shook his head. "Actually, how about seven?"

"Seven's perfect. Do you want to meet at your house or would you prefer somewhere else?"

If shock and awe shared a joint facial expression, Bogart was wearing it. *Yeah, you're getting on with your life; so am I.*

"I'm fine with my house, unless you're not."

I shrugged as if I couldn't care less, which at that point I didn't have a hard time selling. TJ's little insider secret about confidence with men was gold. But then I suddenly remembered my apartment and the refrigerator I still needed to purchase. Ed had said I could store the refrigerator in the garage. And having two hours after work with Bogart's truck could save me on delivery charges.

"Actually," I said as Bogart put his glass of orange juice to his mouth. "Would you mind if we met at my apartment?"

I almost got sprayed in the face. His eyes watered and he swallowed hard.

"Are you okay?"

He nodded and cleared his throat. "Apartment?"

"Yeah, it'd be easier if we could just meet there. You don't mind, do you?"

He assured me with a grim certainty that he didn't mind.

"Great. It's on Main and Tenth. Look for the cute blue cottages. I'll be on top," I said.

His eyes widened, and a mischievous smile played on his lips.

"It's the only unit on the top floor," I said, ignoring the obvious chance to flirt.

"Right." Bogart shrugged his broad shoulders.

"Great."

My food cart was loaded, and if I stayed around any longer I might blow it. *Now to make a noticeable exit.* And thanks to my mom's latest shopping treat to her personal shopper, Stella, I was ready to shine. My gingham pleated skirt was like two skirts in one. The top layer was a sheer silk organza in a black gingham print that felt like I was walking through clouds. It billowed over a tight, white miniskirt that hugged my ass and slimmed my thighs. It was pretty much a miracle skirt. The sheer overlay flaunted the best part of my legs, hiding my imperfections. A long-sleeved black T-shirt and black boots completed the look. Stella had told me it would be an outfit that rocked the feminine vibe. I just wasn't so sure how well that would track with the masculine half.

"Okay, see you at seven." I looked back at Bogart, whose raised eyebrows and grin assured me that Stella hadn't been wrong. There was something to rocking the feminine vibe that crossed the gender divide. Or perhaps it was what TJ had said. Either way, I pushed the cart away from Bogart with the confidence of a three-hundred-pound woman.

CHAPTER **SIXTEEN**

The garage door was raised and the refrigerator stood upright in the back of Bogart's truck, strapped to an appliance dolly with a series of ropes securing it in place. Thirty minutes remained until Bogart was due to arrive at my new apartment to swap cars. I had half an hour to get the fridge out of his truck and into the garage.

I've got this.

And thanks to Jimmy's find on a rental appliance store closing its doors in Garden Grove, I had a relatively new recycled refrigerator. The downside was the color. There's a lot to be said about an avocado-colored refrigerator. I just hadn't figured out what. For certain, it'd bring a splash of color to the faux woodgrain cabinets in the kitchen. Plus, maybe it'd make the meals I prepared look better—or perhaps worse. Again, I wasn't sure.

I rolled down the windows on both sides of the truck and used the side mirrors to carefully back up, navigating the ginormous upright avocado toward the open garage behind me.

I've totally got this.

I stopped the truck just shy of the overhanging garage door, allowing enough room to back the fridge out of Bogart's truck. The guys at the appliance center had assured me it was a one-person job, although it took two of them to get the refrigerator into my truck.

I put the truck in park, set the emergency brake, and hopped out. I pulled down the tailgate, draped a blanket over the lip, and hopped into the back. I tugged on the four ties that had secured the refrigerator in the back of the truck, and they released just like the guys had said they would. I was left with the refrigerator strapped to the appliance dolly. *Perfect.*

I dusted off my jeans and straightened my sweatshirt. My hair had finally grown out enough that it fit into a ponytail. It bounced behind me as I surveyed the work still ahead of me.

"Oh boy." When the men loaded the refrigerator into the truck, they'd used the back of the truck and dolly as leverage to hoist it up. *But how the hell do I get it out of the truck?*

If I backed the dolly up and reversed it…. *That might work.* I turned the dolly around, walked the refrigerator to the edge of the tailgate, and looked down. *Huh.* It wasn't more than a two-feet drop, but the refrigerator was heavy as hell. I peered over the edge and bit my bottom lip. *I don't think I got this.*

"Wait!"

My head snapped forward.

Bogart ran toward me in a pair of jeans and a white button-down. Definitely not moving material. "Don't move!" He waved at me with both hands frantically. He rushed to the tailgate and slapped it like he had hit his destination, then drew in a ragged breath.

"You can't move this by yourself. It's too much."

I exhaled. "You're probably right."

"By the way," he said with a brow arched toward the refrigerator. "Nice color."

I stood beside the dolly and glanced down at him. The light from the September sun shone in his brown eyes and made them shine. *Oh, Bogart.* I felt my entire body light up in a smile. A heavy heart followed, knowing he belonged to someone else.

"It is a pretty *badass* color. It's vintage, I'll have you know. Newest trend in the OC. I practically made two housewives cry when I drove away with it."

"Oh, I bet they *did* cry seeing this refrigerator in any part of the OC." His deep, throaty laugh made me giggle.

"So where we taking this beauty?"

"Don't be a hater." I shook my finger and then directed it to my fridge. "Bertha here will know." I gently patted her side. I figured if Barbara named her computers, and I christened my car with a vintage classic like Scarlett, I might as well nickname my appliances. And nothing screamed avocado dream like Big Bad Bertha.

"Fair enough. Where are we taking *Bertha*?"

"That's better." I gave a pointed glance toward the upstairs unit. "I don't get to move in until mid-October because of work they're doing—carpet and paint. So… looks like we're storing Bertha in the garage."

"That's silly. Whatever renovation work they're doing, your refrigerator won't be in the way."

"You're probably right."

"Is the apartment open?"

I shrugged. "I only got this far. Plus, there's stairs involved."

Bogart frowned. "Stairs are the easy part. Getting a refrigerator *off* the back of a truck is the hard part. You *really* could have hurt yourself." The concerned tone in his voice matched what was reflected in his eyes.

"Who knew? I was trying to get your truck back to you and save on delivery charges." I stepped to the edge of the truck.

"You could have held on to my truck longer."

"Nah. I didn't want to bother you." I went to hop off.

Bogart held out his hand. I slipped mine in his and jumped down.

"I'll always help you." His hand remained tightly wrapped around mine.

"It's okay. I know how you feel about fixing me." I cleared my throat and looked away from his eyes that wouldn't stop staring into mine. I glanced toward the stairs that led to my apartment. "That doesn't look so bad. We can get Bertha up there."

He pulled me toward him. "Kates."

I gave a slow, weary shake of my head. "Don't," I said with my back turned to him. The pull and tug, and the pang in my chest, would only spread and magnify into a greater, deeper pain if I immersed myself in my desire for Bogart the way I had with TJ when I knew his heart belonged to someone else. Only it would be worse, because I was in love with Bogart.

"What's wrong? Why won't you look at me?"

With my free hand, I hiked my thumb behind me, making fleeting eye contact with him. "Let's just get Bertha into the garage, and I'll ask my landlord if his men can get it into my apartment."

"Kates."

My head dropped, my shoulders shook, and tears fell out of me like rain. He hadn't called me by that name in three months. He had barely even uttered my name.

"Hey, oh, what happened?" He still hadn't let go of my hand.

I turned to him and buried my face in his white cotton button-down.

"Kates."

"Don't." My voice was nothing more than a plea.

"Okay." He gently dropped my hand and wrapped both of his arms around me and tenderly pulled me to him. "I don't know what you don't want me to do, but I won't do it."

I smiled against him. His scent poured into me like a familiar friend returning after a long absence, and my body responded to him immediately. My shoulders relaxed, my breathing steadied and I found my center. My North Star. I looked up into his eyes. *Why can't I stay here?*

The pain was building and I had to release it. I couldn't contain it for another three months of hiding away from life and retreating from my feelings, hoping they could be filed away. I slowly stepped out of his arms. I had to stand on my own and do this.

"I know it's too late for us," I said, the tears pooling at the corners of my eyes and my face ready to dissolve into a really ugly cry any second, but I had to tell him how I felt. If not now, then when? I'd regret this for the rest of my life if I didn't.

"I am so sorry *for everything*. I know that I really blew it. And you're the type of guy most girls wouldn't blow it with." *Girls like Carmen.* "And I did. I blew it." I wiped my nose with the sleeve of my sweatshirt.

"We weren't even dating. You didn't blow anything."

It was a nice thought, but it didn't change the fact that my hallway hookup with TJ had altered our path. He knew it and so did I.

"If that were true," I said, "then we wouldn't have gone all summer barely speaking to each other."

Bogart gave a humorous smile. "*Touché.*"

"Listen, I'm having a hard enough time doing this in English. Let's keep the French to a minimum."

"I've missed you," he said.

"Don't."

The humor instantly faded and so did his smile. "There you go again with the 'don't.' But I *don't* understand."

Tears welled in my eyes and spilled unchecked down my cheeks. "What *don't* you understand? When I hear you call me Kates, or tell me you miss me, or just look at me… it about kills me."

"Gee, thanks."

I waved away his remark. "It's not funny. Each of those

moments is a reminder of what we could have had." I paused and looked at him. "We *could* have had something."

But he didn't respond. It hurt to breathe. My legs suddenly felt weak. If I just could get over to the stairs, I could collapse, lean against the railing, and fall apart. He could drive away, and I could get on with my big, sad life alone with Bertha. *Because he belongs to someone else.*

"Kates…?"

Dazed, I glanced up at him. "I'm okay. I'll be okay."

The sound of the waves crashed in the distance, ominous and low. The sky behind him was marbled in a dark blue and black. It looked bruised, ready to surrender. I understood. A storm was rolling in, and it felt like someone had dimmed the outside lights.

"We still can," he said.

"What?"

"We can still have something," he said huskily.

"You're with Carmen."

"We're just friends."

"Does she know that?" It was an honest question.

"Yes." He looked at me with intense brown eyes. "We've only gone out a handful of times."

"She may not know how you feel. She may think it's more serious."

Bogart rubbed the stubble on his chin. "I don't see how that's possible."

"Why?"

"Because all I've ever spoken about was you."

Tears once again blurred my vision. "Really?"

"Kates."

This time, when he said my name, I walked into his arms, leaned up, and with my lips inches from his, said, "Don't." I kissed his top lip. "Ever." I kissed his bottom lip, the one that always looked like an invitation to nibble. "Stop." I gently melded to him. He returned my kiss with a passion I'd only imagined. His lips were soft, tender, but heated. When he wrapped his arm around the small of my back and pulled me to him, he wielded the power of seduction and he wielded it well.

His body pressed against mine, and the energy between us grew as our mouths explored each other. His lips feathered kisses down my neck, biting my earlobe, heightening my desire for him—something I hadn't thought possible. My leg wrapped around his thigh and before long our kissing backed us against the edge of his truck.

"Not here," he said.

I nodded against his chest.

"Are the keys to my truck inside?"

"Yeah."

"Okay, I'm just going to move the truck forward so we can close the garage."

Bogart lifted the tailgate and I stepped aside. He carefully drove the truck forward into a parking spot without harming Bertha in the process. I closed the garage door.

Before he shut and locked his truck, I saw him reach into his glove box. When he returned, he held up his finger. "Wait here." He darted toward the stairs and took them two at a time. When he reached the top step, I held my breath. The moment of truth. Was the door unlocked? He shook his head. It wasn't.

I tilted my head back and stared into the sky that looked ready to erupt into a hearty storm. "It's okay. We've got to get Bertha out of the truck and inside before it rains." When I brought my head out of the clouds, Bogart was nowhere to be seen. *Where he'd go?*

Suddenly the front door to my apartment opened. "Looks like we'll be at your place," Bogart said between ragged breaths.

"What?"

"You have a balcony."

I grinned. "I have a balcony."

He cocked his head. "Are you going to join me? Or did I break into your apartment for nothing?"

I laughed aloud. "What about Bertha?"

He grimaced. "I don't think anyone's going to steal Bertha. And I don't think she'll melt if she gets rained on. In fact, a little rain might dust the old girl off."

I frowned.

"Now, your car's another story, but I added an alarm to it. And it's already set."

"My car? That's right! Where is my car?" I turned but didn't see it in the small parking lot.

"It's on a side street. I wasn't sure if you had your own parking space so I parked it where it wouldn't get dinged."

"Thank you." I walked toward him, and with each step, I ached to know what he felt like. But like my moment with TJ, I was ruefully unprepared.

Bogart flipped a switch, and a dome light positioned in

the middle of the studio flickered for a few minutes and then came to life.

"Hey! Look at that," I said, smiling.

"It's a cute apartment, Katie."

I playfully rolled my shoulder. "It is cute, right?"

Bogart picked me up and tossed me over his shoulder.

"Oh!" I laughed aloud. My arms dangled down his back. I spanked him while he walked. "My, my, my… what do we have here?" I slid my hand down the back of his jeans and cupped his ass. It was firm, but soft in all the right spots. Better yet, it wasn't hairy.

He turned into the bathroom, turned on the light. "Later," he said and flicked the light back off and headed back toward the front of the house where my bedroom and living room would coexist.

Bogart drew the shades, so the autumn moon could find its way into the main room and toward us. And it did. He gently laid me down on new, thick carpet. He knelt before me with wide eyes and a radiant smile.

"I don't have…." It was the start of the same conversation I'd tried to have with TJ, and shame overtook me and shut me down. But this wasn't TJ, this was Bogart. I leaned up on my elbows and squared him in my sights.

"I want to be with you. More than you will ever know. I ache to be with you. To know you. But I've only been with one other guy, my high school sweetheart. We even tried to make our relationship work in college, but when it ended…." My shoulders rose to my ears. "I got off the pill because I didn't just want to be with anyone." I half laughed. "I'm sure you're going to find that hard to believe, but...." My voice trailed off.

"Kates."

"I never screwed TJ." A tear fell from my eye.

He reached over and wiped it away with his thumb. "I'm sorry. I know you didn't, and it was an awful thing for me to say."

"Yeah, pretty much."

He laughed.

"So we can fool around and have some fun," I said, "but without a condom I can't let this go any further."

Bogart leaned over and gently kissed me. "But just to be clear, if we had a condom we could have *a lot* of fun?"

I chuckled. "We could have *the most* fun."

He reached into his back pocket and withdrew a strip of condoms.

"Dear God! What the hell?"

He shrugged. "It's an Eagle Scout thing. I keep them in my truck. Always be prepared."

"How many Cadets were you preparing for?"

A burst of color shot across his cheeks. Then he reached for my hand and pulled me into a sitting position. I sat cross-legged in front of him.

"Listen," he said as he held my hands. "There's no need to rush anything. I don't want to be the second lover you tell the next man about."

My chest rose and fell as he held my gaze in his. He cupped my jaw and brought my lips to his. "Kates. I don't want to be your second lover. I want to be your last lover."

It wasn't just a line or something he was saying to get me in bed, because there wasn't a bed and I had already offered myself to him. It was a man I was in love with declaring his love to me. A forever love.

Our lips met in a kiss that was unlike our first. And if it were possible, the kiss was more tender, more romantic and meaningful because any doubt had vanished. I was in love with Bogart and he was in love with me. The passion was more charged because now it wasn't just our bodies that were engaged, but our hearts.

I looked at him as I slowly pulled my sweatshirt off over my head. He reached behind me and gently released the ponytail that held my hair captive, letting waves of my golden-brown hair fall to my shoulders. My pink lace bra remained on.

I unhooked the top button of my jeans and kicked off my running shoes. I sat back and Bogart grabbed the frayed cuffs of my jeans and yanked. I giggled as they slid down my body.

Even though my stomach wasn't toned or flat like 99 percent of what was seen on the beaches in Huntington, and my thighs probably took up more space on the carpet than his, I didn't feel self-conscious in front of him. In nothing more than my pink bra and lace panties, I felt sexy and desired.

He slowly unbuttoned his shirt, and his muscular chest was finally before me. His body hair was dark and sprinkled along his chest, highlighting all the right spots, narrowing to a thin strip that led to the happy trail that dipped down below his jeans.

With a snap of his wrist, he unhooked his belt buckle and unsnapped his jeans. He knelt before me, and from the wanton desire in his eyes, my heart raced and my body tingled. But he waited. He didn't remove his jeans, and he didn't expose himself until I gave permission. I rose up before him, loosening the rest of his jeans to thankfully discover he didn't go commando. Instead a hint of color peeked through. I glanced up at him and smiled.

"Red's my favorite color."

A husky, sexy chuckle erupted from his throat.

I slowly pushed his shirt off his broad shoulders and let my fingers trail along his chest. I kissed the center and flicked my tongue along his nipples, inhaling what I had always been drawn to. And then there was something else. The more Bogart got aroused, the more primal he became, giving off a scent that attracted me to him with a drive and hunger like no other. I had to know if he tasted as good as he smelled.

My hands pushed his jeans down to his knees. He rose, standing before me fully aroused in red boxer briefs. The boxers hugged his hips and muscular thighs. My thumb slid along the red waistband, skimming the surface of hair. His breathing turned shallow and his thighs tightened. My tongue trailed his inner thigh along the edge of his boxer briefs.

"Katie…." His voice was unsure, but his body wasn't. His hips thrust toward me.

I reached beneath the cotton fabric and firmly cupped his ass. My index finger gently brushed between his cheeks—at times almost stroking and at times almost taunting him while my tongue continued to explore every part of him without ever delving beneath his boxers to the pulsing shaft that seemed to lengthen and harden with each lick. He had waited for my permission and now I awaited his.

I looked up and held his gaze. He knelt down before me. We kissed as I slowly lay down on the ground and he followed. His weight barely pressed against me; he rested most of it on his elbows.

"I won't break. I promise," I said, gazing into his eyes.

"I know."

His mouth again covered me with kisses as his hands caressed my body, gently massaging my shoulders and my arms. I melded into his touch. When he reached beneath me and unhooked my bra, it felt like it floated off me.

The warm heat of his breath against my breast made me arch to meet his mouth. His tongue slowly moved across my nipple, back and forth in the same rhythm as his other hand dipped below my panties and parted my thighs. My hands moved up instinctively to his dark thick hair as he swept his tongue across me and his finger suddenly, slowly found its way inside me.

I groaned or yelled. I wasn't sure which; I lost track of what was happening. I know I pushed his head further down my body to the throbbing that needed his lips more than my breast.

He knelt between my legs and slid my panties down, keeping them draped on one ankle.

"That's hot." His gaze flickered up to me.

My body trembled waiting for his lips, waiting for him to caress me, waiting for release.

His tongue discovered me in a way that was rhythmically and beautifully orchestrated in a series of soft circles that pressed against my clit without numbing it. The man was a genius. I had found Nirvana.

"Don't stop. Dear God. Please. Don't. Stop," I pleaded.

I was on the edge of release, and my hands dug into his hair. My hips rose to meet his tongue, but the throbbing wouldn't subside. Even with his finger moving inside me, it wasn't enough.

"I need you. I've got to have you."

He inched up my body until he knelt before me. He lowered his boxers and his full desire sprang out on display. I turned on my side, and my mouth trailed along the tip of him, teasing and exciting and sending little groans of pleasure out of his mouth.

His breathing turned shallow, and his body tensed as I ran my tongue slowly over his thick, pulsating shaft. His hands clenched. He tasted as good as he smelled—tangy, yet subtly sweet with a hint of saltiness that had an addictive edge that was all Bogart. My tongue lightly focused on the sensitive head until I parted my lips and took all of him in my mouth.

He groaned.

My tongue flickered across his head the same way he had carefully though brilliantly navigated my clit, knowing how to arouse without numbing. I brought him to the edge the way he had brought me to the same precipice.

"Kates, I think we better slow things down." There was an erotic rasp to his voice that spiked my temperature.

I gave him one last meaningful lick and caress with my tongue, drawing him deeper and deeper into my mouth all the while my hands wrapped around his ass, my finger playing between his cheeks.

When I released him, Bogart wiped the sweat from his brow and repositioned himself above me. I wrapped my legs around him.

He reached behind him for his jeans and the strip of condoms. He tore one open with his mouth and rolled it down the length of his shaft. My thighs ached to feel him between me. I was swollen with need, and the condom stretched so thin across him that I thought it was going to break. We were both on the razor edge of release.

But instead of slamming into me—which I would've been fine with—Bogart leaned over me and gave me a long, passionate kiss. He lingered on my lips. He kissed me again and again as he made his way into me. My legs trembled and then tightened around him as he drew deeper and deeper still. My hips lifted to meet each of his thrusts. We synchronized, our bodies working as one.

Our breathing grew more rapid and fevered as each of us reached that edge together. The pleasure was so intense, so fierce, that I thought I would pass out if I didn't reach that peak, which suddenly seemed so unattainable. My heels dug into his back and I screamed.

"Deeper!"

He pulled back and thrust into me so deeply that he hit my G-spot. I arched up and cried out as the sheer force of my orgasm shot through my entire body with a wave of heat that radiated shockwaves of pleasure that were beyond comprehension. From my scalp down to my toes, everything had gone from a heightened tension to an instant relaxation.

My body tingled. I hadn't even known an orgasm like that existed.

Bogart's breathing and groans grew more fevered as my release triggered his, and he climaxed inside me. He collapsed on top of me with his full weight and scent covering me. It was a feeling I had been longing for all summer.

CHAPTER **SEVENTEEN**

"You've got a degree in journalism, right?" Jimmy approached my desk as soon as I arrived for my shift. My Thursday was again his Friday, because he was leaving for a long weekend with his son and daughter.

"I sure do." Giddy was the only way to describe my tone. After my magical night with Bogart, nothing could rattle my cage, ruin my mood, or make me believe that love couldn't conquer the world.

My cell had chimed with texts from Bogart all morning. *When will I see you again? How about dinner? What are you wearing?* I had barely filed one folder in HR, spending my time replying to each of his texts, and never had my morning shift gone so well. Now my cell vibrated on my desk beside me.

"Come into my office." Jimmy's tone was low and

hushed—almost conspiratorial. He glanced down the row of administrative desks and back at me.

My cell thumped. I flipped it over and quickly read the screen. *Hey... whatcha doin'? Whatcha think Bertha's doin'?* We had left Bertha behind in Bogart's truck and I had driven him home in my new, souped-up car.

I grinned.

Jimmy wasn't someone to normally get in my personal space, but he leaned into my desk as if I hadn't heard him. "My office."

"Okie dokie." I gleefully picked up my pen, pad of paper, and cell phone.

He pointed toward my pulsating iPhone. "Leave that behind."

I shrugged. "Righty-oh." I plopped it in my backpack and practically skipped behind him into his office. *Ain't love grand?* I wanted to sweep my arms out and announce to the world that Bogart and I had spent the night together. I was about to when Jimmy stood behind his desk, pressed his hands into the thick leather desk blotter, and motioned his head toward the door behind me.

"Make sure it's closed."

My body suddenly drained of all its happy, in-love feelings, and dread inched up my spine and settled in the back of my throat. *Ah, sonofabitch. I'm getting fired.* And this was how they did it at the Waterfront Point Resort. They made the employee close the door before they quietly exited them off property. *Fan-freakin'-tastic.* Well, so much for love saving my ass. I was as screwed as that unassembled furniture I'd just bought from IKEA. *I wonder if I can still return it?*

"Go ahead and sit down." He pointed toward two chairs positioned in front of his desk while he sank into his oversized executive seat.

I sat farthest from the door and neatly crossed one leg over the other. Something like 70 percent of people did the same thing during an interview. A random fact I'd learned from one of Janet's many ramblings about the recruitment process. But the key was that body language spoke volumes. And the one-legged cross was considered the normal cross-leg position. My body language wasn't closed off, like if I'd crossed my arms along with my legs, which would definitely have indicated to Jimmy that I was blocked entirely to anything he had to tell me. Nor did I have my leg propped up on my knee with my hand clamped over it, locking it in place, which would be a clear sign to him that I was tough-minded, stubborn, and rejected any opinion other than my own. Nope, my body language was textbook perfect. If this was a firing, well, I was completely open to the execution—other than the sweat that began to collect beneath my knee, which was making it super difficult to maintain my one-legged cross. I looked at Jimmy, ready to face whatever he had to say.

"I want you to do something," he said.

Huh. My shoulders dropped, my one-legged cross slid into an ankle lock, which I think was considered a defensive position, but I couldn't help it. Relief washed over me. "Ohh-kay."

"There's going to be some changes happening around here," he said. "*Big* changes."

Their killing the overtime. I quickly tried to unlock my ankles, but they seemed twisted together.

"But it's not October yet. It's weeks away."

His gray-blue eyes widened.

Uh-oh. My knowledge of the Executive Board's plan was not a reveal I was supposed to make. I tucked my feet beneath my chair and clamped my hands over my knees. If my body language said anything, it was that I was incredibly interested in everything he had to say. Or I was just about to keel over and have a seizure.

"So you already know."

"What?" The ringing in my ears from my heart beating so loudly was compounded by the heat that lit my scalp on fire and poured sweat down my neck, forehead, and across my upper lip. My hands slipped off my knees. "Know, what?"

The gray in Jimmy's eyes seemed to match the silver threading along his temples. Even though I was sitting, I stared at it to try to keep my balance.

"Each fiscal year, the board drafts a critical course or outline for how the hotel should function to meet year-end goals. A preliminary copy of this confidential course was distributed to certain areas of the hotel, like Kitchen and Housekeeping. The administrative offices didn't appear to be targeted, and we figured that's because there's only one part-time person." Jimmy raised an eyebrow at me. "But apparently, that part-time person already happens to know about the upcoming changes."

I raised my sweaty hand in defense. "I didn't leak it."

"Well, someone did. Areas heavily populated with part-time employees were hit."

Jimmy stared at me.

"It was on the printer and I saw it." Was all I would confess.

"Well," he said, "it's out, at least to the majority of part-timers, but I'm sure it's circulating."

I vehemently shook my head, trying to cool off. "I didn't do it. I only read what the plans were." I tried to remember where the memo was. The last time I'd seen it was in my car with Bogart at the wetlands. That was months ago.

"Doesn't matter," Jimmy said. "Copies of it are out, and it's really put Jerry on the burner."

"Does he think I did it?" I asked, panic gripping me.

"God, no. They have no idea where it came from."

"How did you know it got out? I mean, did someone show you a copy?"

"The hotel has eyes," Jimmy said.

"But you said you didn't know who had circulated it."

"We don't. Jerry has his suspicions, but nothing's been confirmed."

"What'll happen?" I asked.

"Whoever did this will most likely get fired."

"Well that's unfortunate. It's not like someone was spreading rumors. Part-time staff will lose their overtime and be kept just under forty hours a week so that the hotel can avoid providing all the benefits that come with full-time status. But hey, sure, fire the messenger." I was tired of trying to conceal what I knew. If Jimmy wrote me up for insubordination or canned me, so be it. I crossed my arms defiantly across my chest. At that point, I didn't care what my body language said.

"It's that fire of yours I was hoping to tap into."

"What?" I blinked, but he continued to smile.

"Originally the idea was to hire seasonal staff to get us through the initial start-up and grand opening, but the hotel's bookings justified hiring permanent part-time staff—as long as they remained part-time."

"And I'm grateful that I was hired." I uncrossed my arms. "But to work 150 people, including me, like full-timers without the perks and benefits, well, it just isn't right."

"I agree," Jimmy said.

"So then why the closed door? Why the secrecy?"

"Kandy," he said, referring to Kandy Healy, the director of Public Relations and Marketing, "is apparently slated to write a press release on the hotel's winter bookings and holiday events just before we eliminate the overtime option. A PR move that, the majority of the Executive Board thinks, will counter any bad press generated if word gets out that half the staff is employed part-time but practically works full-time hours."

I slumped back in my seat. "They've thought of everything. They'll hit their numbers for year end, look good, and the executives will get a big bonus to boot."

"They haven't thought about everything. The release of the board's critical course was damaging, but not damaging enough," Jimmy said.

The expression on my face must have conveyed my dismay.

"Not everyone on the board is in favor of this solution to our year-end budgetary concerns. There're other ways to resolve this without eliminating overtime altogether or working our midlevel salaried managerial staff to the bone. But that boss of yours," Jimmy said heatedly, "spearheaded the whole damn thing."

"Holly? But she wrote a memo trying to increase my position to full-time."

Jimmy's eyebrows furrowed, pronouncing the worry lines that stretched deep and wide across his forehead. "And that surprises you? If she doesn't have overtime available for her part-time person, it leaves more work for her and that twit she calls a recruiter."

"Oh. I never thought of it like that." *Bogart was right. Holly was saving the position. She cares more about it than me.*

"Whoever released the critical course was on the right track." He wagged his finger in the air. "But the majority of part-time staff probably don't understand the critical course."

"That's why I created a Facebook page."

Jimmy's eyes widened.

My cheeks burned with heat. "I *did not* release the critical course, but I did create a Facebook page in an effort to explain the benefits and overtime issue so that everyone would understand it."

"So you're Pumpkin Spice?"

I gritted a smile and nodded. "Guilty as charged." I paused. "Does Mr. Adams know about the Facebook page?"

Jimmy nodded. "We have an IT team that is dedicated to media monitoring."

"Media monitoring?"

"They monitor the press, TV, radio, and Internet for any mention of the hotel. Any coverage—good, bad or indifferent is monitored. Our IT team spotted your Facebook page and alerted Terry. It's clever. I really liked your page on 'Top Shelf' benefits."

I genuinely smiled. "I may have gotten the idea for that page after I wrote the drink menu."

"It's smart to tap into social media, but it still won't have the desired effect for change."

"What would? A party?" I leaned forward in the chair. "Because I was going to have a housewarming party to unite everyone and explain what all this means and how it affects them. But that's like five weeks out. I won't get my apartment until mid-October." I suddenly remembered a reason to celebrate and snapped my fingers. "We could have a birthday party for you! Everyone would come to that."

Jimmy gently smiled. "I love your enthusiasm. The Facebook page and a party are all great ideas, but I was thinking more along the lines of striking for benefits and full-time employment."

If I weren't already sitting down, I would have collapsed. "Are you serious? A strike? We aren't a union hotel."

"It would be a staged walkout." Jimmy placed his aged hands on the desk before him.

"You're serious?"

"Do you have any other ideas?"

"What about a union?" I asked, repeating a conversation I'd overheard in the locker room. One of the housekeepers had said that if the Waterfront Point Resort unionized they couldn't pull half the crap they were pulling.

"No union. Union hotels are the worst."

"For you or for the staff?"

Jimmy grinned. "A little of both."

"But you think a staged walkout will work?"

"It's all about the publicity that can be generated from the event. Isn't your father a reporter?"

I exhaled. Suddenly, his interest in me became clear. "He's a *sports* reporter."

"But he writes for a newspaper," Jimmy stated rather than asked.

"Yes, my dad writes for a newspaper, but I—"

"Listen. You've got a degree in journalism. It's high time you start using it toward something more than just typing my memos."

"Why me?"

"Because you've got the skills and the talent. The staff respects you."

"I'm a secretary!"

"Shh," Jimmy said. "You're more than a secretary and you know it."

I gently swung my leg back and forth while I considered his plan. *This is what I've been trying to do.* Now the opportunity to really implement change had presented itself and I was frozen. I took a long, deep breath and looked up at Jimmy.

"So you want me to write a press release about the overtime being cut? Or that half the staff is part-time, but worked like full-time? Or both. I'm confused."

"No, about the staged walkout." Jimmy returned to his

desk and sat down.

"For it be *staged*, someone has to gather the staff together. I've been trying to do that for months, and let me tell you, it ain't easy, boss."

Jimmy chuckled. "I know." He raised his eyebrows like he was holding onto the best kept secret in the world. "But until today, you haven't had someone on the inside backing you. Someone who knows what you're capable of accomplishing if given the room to unify the troops."

"Oh, I don't know." My leg came to an abrupt stop. I planted both feet firmly on the ground and looked directly across the desk into Jimmy's gray-blue eyes. "I'm not happy about losing my overtime, but I don't want to lose my job. Not if I can help it. I'd love to write some *Spotlight* piece about the hotel. And I *want* to be your Norma Rae. Or Erin Brockovich. But I'm more like Annie Hall or Calamity Jane."

"Are there any other movie references you'd like to throw out there?"

I glanced at the overhead lights and purposefully paused, tapping my forefinger to my chin before I returned my focus to him. "No, I think I nailed them all."

"Okay," he said with a shine in his eye. "Just for the record, I don't agree with your self-assessment. However, if you're more comfortable behind the scenes, I'll get someone else to rally the troops. I still need you to write the release."

I thought about Bogart when he'd first read the critical course, and my chest swelled with emotion.

"I'm in it to win it. I'll do whatever it takes to right this wrong." I paused. If that were true, then why was I hiding behind the scenes? *You're the whole package.* TJ's pep talk about confidence. *So why couldn't I be the dramatic heroine instead of the comic relief?*

"I'll write the presser, and if you can't find someone to lead the troops, I will. I can do it. I won't hide behind a name, like Pumpkin Spice, or insecurity and fear. If I lose my job," I shrugged, "I'll land on my feet. I always do."

The smile on Jimmy's face was all the assurance I needed.

I swallowed the emotions at the base of my throat. *There's no crying in a staged walkout.* "So once I write this release, who do I distribute it to? The only contact I have in the media is my dad, and maybe my old editor at the radio station."

"Kandy is scheduled for knee surgery," Jimmy said. "The board was planning on hiring some college intern to handle the details of the holiday programs in her absence until we realized that Kandy had only sketched *out* the programs."

"Oh. It sounds like she's kind of behind the eight ball."

"In her defense, there's a lot of planning and paperwork involved," Jimmy said. "And she wasn't expecting to injure herself on a bike ride with her husband. It took her completely off guard. Luckily, she's completed the evaluation and aligned the print production."

"Evaluation? Print production?" Another department and another set of buzzwords and jargon to not only understand, but also to use correctly. Even though all the departments used nothing but the English language, it was all foreign to me.

"Kandy already finished the evaluation, which measured the impact this campaign would have financially on the hotel. The cost and revenue projections. We already approved the holiday programs because of the planning and the research she presented in her evaluation at our board meeting a few weeks ago."

"So if she already planned it, then what's the problem?" I said.

"No, I said Kandy sketched out her ideas and had the evaluation and data to back them. She also coordinated the print production, so all printed materials, like brochures and posters, will be ready once the copywriting is completed."

I nodded.

"Kandy handled and finessed the budget and worked with each department, so they know what rooms and staff to allocate in conjunction with her program ideas, but that's as far as it's gotten. They're just ideas with a budget and forecasted labor. But since the holiday programs are so integral to our fourth-quarter success, it's just not something we feel should be given to an intern. I suggested using someone in-house."

"So did you happen to mention anyone in-house the board could use?" I asked.

It was the first time in all the months I had worked for Jimmy that his cheeks tinged with color. The silver fox was blushing.

"Well, actually, your name was brought up."

"Uh-huh. By who?"

"Holly beat me to it. Though I was going to suggest you."

"And when did you two figure I'd do the PR and marketing work? I'm already working two jobs." I pointed my finger and thumb at him. "Oh, maybe it's that extra hour I have each week." I playfully smiled at Jimmy.

"Actually, Holly thought it was a good way to ensure you'd still make extra money. The reduction in overtime has been pushed up."

"Oh, no." My head reeled with information. I pressed my thumbs against my temples, but it didn't stop the throbbing. It did, however, serve brilliantly as blinders, allowing me to focus on the task in front of me. I needed the income. I hadn't expected the reduction in overtime to happen ahead of schedule. My emotions waged war against me. "Working for Kandy or working as Kandy." I shook my head. "How come I feel like a sellout? No one else is getting this reprieve from lost overtime wages."

"To begin with you won't be accruing overtime, so you're not a sellout to the cause. You're actually helping the cause. By filling a gap, you're not doing anything to hurt the hotel or its employees by filling in while Kandy's out on medical. Besides," Jimmy said as his sloped smile slide across his face, "just imagine how good it'll feel when your work gets published."

It had a Svengali effect. *Published.* Every writer's dream.

"We're going to start you on some simple press releases first. And then, once Kandy takes her leave, you'll be doing the marketing and public relations full-time until her return."

"Full-time? Who's going to handle the work I do for you? There's a lot that has to be done. You can't just go without a secretary. Who's going to type your menus, or take the minutes, or order those pens you like? You know, the black felt-tip ones...." My voice cracked and I felt my eyes sting with tears. "Why can't I just give up my HR job and work for you full-time? It's slated to happen in the New Year. Or it may. Why can't we just have it happen sooner?"

Jimmy's weathered face softened. "There's nothing I'd like more. But I'll be in good hands. I've already got Barbara slated to pitch in." He picked up a manila folder. "Here's your first assignment." He handed me the file.

"It's not going to explode after I read it, is it?" I eyed him playfully.

He rolled his eyes in return. "Take it home, study it, and come back on Monday with a draft of your first release."

"Monday? I haven't written a presser since college."

"Then take tomorrow off. I'm not going to be here anyway. Work on it at home."

"What about my hours? I know I shouldn't complain, especially since you're offering me temporary full-time hours, but I'm still part-time. I don't accrue sick or vacation time."

Jimmy tilted his head. His mane of hair didn't even move. "So no hours then."

"I'll cover your hours. But make it good, Katie," he said and stood.

I mirrored his movement.

"Kandy's top rate. She'll detect crap a mile away."

"Good to know." I glanced at the folder. Who knew a single file labeled "Christmas" could carry so much weight?

"Okay, see you Monday."

I waved the file. "See you Monday." I returned to my desk and opened it.

A budget, a labor sheet, and room rates were paper-clipped to the inside, and a handful of notes were scratched on loose-leaf paper. From what I could make out of her notes, it looked like Kandy had three ideas for holiday programs, all of which centered toward increasing room occupancy and filling seats in the restaurants. The most legible article was a memo from Mr. Adams addressed to Kandy.

With the holidays approaching, we need to finalize our Christmas program. I need copy no later than Monday, September 12.

My brain was a complete blank.

"Barbara?" I called.

"Yeah, hon."

"You've worked at a hotel before, right?"

"Twenty years at the Trinity," she said, referring to the popular Los Angeles hotel.

"What would you guys do for the holidays? I mean, for the guests," I said. My back was still to her. I was waiting for her reply when she suddenly appeared beside me.

"Meet me after work," she said softly and slid a business card on my desk. It had her home phone number and address on the back. I pulled out my cell phone and texted Bogart.

Gotta meet Barbara after work for this huge project. Wanna meet afterward?

I'd barely hit Send when his reply appeared on my screen. *You had me at huge.*

I snorted and burst into giggles.

"Are you still here?" Jimmy's gruff voice seeped out from beneath his office door.

"It's not five."

"Head out early," he said.

I picked up Barbara's card and my backpack and barely waited for my computer to shut down. When I passed Barbara's desk, I brushed her card along the edge and mouthed, "See you at five."

She nodded.

I had enough time to go home, shower, and freshen up for another magical night with Bogart.

CHAPTER **EIGHTEEN**

The rich hint of dark chocolate and roasted peanuts practically tickled my nose.

"Mom?" I headed into the kitchen where she was placing a cookie sheet filled with peanut butter dollops topped with a chocolate candy into the oven. A fresh batch of Texas kisses was cooling on the counter.

The melt-in-your-mouth cookies were sinfully delicious. "Yum." I was about to reach for one when I paused. Bruised knuckles had long ago taught me to ask before taking. My mom wielded a spatula like an old Catholic nun gripped a ruler. In either case, hands were going to bleed. "May I?"

"Just one," she said. "I don't want you to ruin your supper. Your brother's coming over."

"Patrick?" I asked.

"Katie, now really," my mom said. "No, Ian."

"Ah, I haven't seen him in a while, but…." I quickly grabbed a cookie before I told her the bad news. "I have to meet Barbara at five and then I was going to head over to Bogart's to work on this project for work."

"Who's Bogart?" My mom turned. "Is that the young man who drove you home the night you got drunk?"

"Yes," I said, realizing she'd probably always associate Bogart with my drunken debacle.

"Ian's bringing his girlfriend, Ashley, over for dinner."

"I'm sorry I'll miss them, but I *really* have to work on this writing project. And I need all the help I can get."

"Writing project?"

I tilted my head. "It's a long story. Suffice it to say, I'm going to *temporarily* fill in for the director of Public Relations and Marketing when she goes out on medical."

The spatula practically fell from my mom's hand.

I waved a cautionary finger. "No. It's temporary and it all depends on how well I do on this trial run they gave me. I have to set up an entire holiday program, market it with a timeline, and have all the press releases written by Monday."

"Katie, that's wonderful. But weren't you and Patrick picking up the rental agreement for your apartment? Didn't he want to check the lease agreement *before* you actually took occupancy?"

"My little brother could tell me the apartment was built on quicksand, and I'd still take it," I said.

"Still, wouldn't you feel more comfortable having him look over the lease agreement?"

I pursed my lips together and slowly shook my head.

"No, ma'am. I'm good. I know all I need to know about my apartment."

It's beautiful, I already christened it, and by mid-October, it'll be mine.

"Better yet." I danced around the kitchen. "I'll be settled and in my own apartment by Halloween!"

"Katie Maureen, you'll cause my cookies to drop. Now stop that nonsense."

"Ah, you're going to miss me." I wrapped my arms around her and kissed her neck. She giggled.

"That I will, but I will not allow you to ruin my cookies. They're your brother's favorite."

"Which one?"

"I'm home!" Patrick yelled, as if on cue, and we both laughed.

"This isn't your home," I reminded him when he came into the kitchen and grabbed a handful of cookies. My mother did nothing to stop him.

I shook my head.

"How was work?" He kissed my forehead.

"Gross, you're going to get chocolate on me." I rubbed my head against the shoulder of his blue button-down.

"I mean it. How was work?"

Don't you mean, how's Bogart? I couldn't very well tell my brother that everything with Bogart was beyond exceptional, that the man was a god in the bedroom and that I was about to head over to his house for round two, but I knew his concern was well-intentioned.

"Patrick, everything is perfect. Bogart and I worked things out. I got my car back! Did you see it? Isn't that a cherry red now?"

A full smile broke across his face.

The red licorice color had been upgraded to a shinier, glossier red. Thin silver pinstripes accented the side. Normally I'd hate the custom detailing, but it was barely noticeable and actually added a sleek look to my chunky little car.

"I'll soon be in my new apartment. Little brother, life couldn't be better."

"That's great. I'm really happy for you," Patrick said.

"Now tell him about your writing project," my mother said.

I sighed and leaned against the kitchen counter.

"What? What did you get yourself into?"

"I'm not sure." I recapped the conversation in Jimmy's office and the pending trip to Barbara's house.

"Stay out of it," Patrick said. "Go back tomorrow and tell them you don't want any part of it."

"Why?" I asked. "I was already doing this behind the scenes with my Facebook page. What's the difference now?"

"The difference now is that your name will be attached to the work. Katie, you're going to lose your job."

"I know you're worried," I said. "And I appreciate your concern. I do. But if I could actually help save people, including myself, from being treated unfairly, then I want to do what I can."

Patrick bit into another cookie. "*If* you play it right, but Katie, you've never been good at things like this." He shook half a cookie in my direction. Crumbs sprinkled toward me.

"Things like what?" I swept remnants of peanut butter and chocolate from the counter.

"Being deceitful. Cunning. Crafty."

"That's a good quality," my mom said.

Patrick leaned his head back. "Not in business. In business you can't show your hand." He dropped his head back to eye level with us. "And Katie doesn't have a poker face."

"Sure I do," I said and gave a visibly agitated glance in his direction.

"Gimme a break. You look constipated. Sister, you're in over your head."

"No, I'm not. I can do this. I'm just planning a holiday event and writing some press releases."

"Is Dad helping you?"

"I can write my own pressers," I said, trying to remember where I stored my public relations and marketing textbooks from college.

"When are they due?" he asked.

"Monday," I said.

"So you'll be up till what, midnight Sunday night?" he said.

"No," I said, though he was probably right. "Because I'm going to hop in the shower and get to Barbara's, then to Bogart's. Between the two of them, I'll get this thing hammered out."

"So you're going to tell Bogart?" Patrick asked.

I paused. "Yeah, maybe I shouldn't?"

"Why involve him further if you don't have to," my brother stated pointedly.

"No," I slowly shook my head. "No more avoiding the truth." *We already played that game.* "Besides, it's going to become common knowledge in the hotel that Kandy is going on medical leave and I'm filling in for her. He'll be happy for me. But I don't have to drag him into writing the presser. I can do that on my own."

"Yeah, sure," my brother scoffed. "By Sunday night you'll be up at the kitchen table with Dad."

"No, because I'm hoping she'll join me in the press box for the game." My father walked into the kitchen, surprising us all.

"I didn't even hear the front door close," my mom said and kissed him on the cheek.

"That's because it was wide open," he said. "So I closed it without slamming it shut."

A red flush rushed to Patrick's cheeks. "I may have forgotten to shut the door when I came home."

"What the hell?" I said.

"My hands were full." He shrugged coyly. "At least I didn't slam it shut. I had my laundry basket."

I slowly shook my head, laughing. "Seriously? You have mom do your laundry?"

"She likes to."

"Unbelievable." I turned away from my brother and walked toward my dad. "Hey, I'm about to jump in the shower. I'd love to sit in the press box with you on Sunday. Thanks for the invite."

Patrick held up his hand. "Hold up. Dad, I'll take Katie's ticket. She rarely goes and she doesn't understand the game. She'll talk nonstop. And when she's not talking she'll eat all the comp'd food. She'll probably get you kicked out of the press box. Let me make it easy on you and just take her ticket."

"Patrick makes some valid points, Paddy," my mom said. "Katie really doesn't understand the game."

"Hey," I said. "No one gets my tickets. I'm going."

It was as if the Devil himself had entered our kitchen. The dazed, stunned faces of my brother and mother stared at me. They were avid sports fans. I was not.

"What? I'm going to the game. Dad invited me and I'd like to go."

"Oh, Katie, that's just wonderful. You're going to love it." My father clapped his hands together and his brown eyes lit up. "It's the UCLA-USC game!"

"Ahh-yah!" I pumped my fists in the air.

"What?" Patrick's arms flew above his head like a gospel preacher's on Sunday. "Dad, you need to think this through. Katie thinks UCLA is what happens on a clear day in California. *You see LA.* And Trojans? She thinks the Trojans are prophylactics. You can't take someone like Katie to the biggest game in Southern California. Not with someone who thinks students at Southern Cal have Southern accents. Please, Dad." Patrick lowered his arms and put his hands into a prayer position and shook them at our father. "I beg of you, don't waste good tickets on Katie."

My dad chuckled and patted Patrick's shoulder reassuringly. "I've got extra tickets so you can all come, and each bring a guest." My father reached into his jacket pocket and fanned out the tickets. "This will give you access to your stadium seats, and after halftime, you can join me in the press box."

"I get Katie's extra ticket!" Patrick said, reaching for my

plus-one ticket.

I widened my eyes in disbelief and elbowed him out of the way. "Listen, hamster brain, I actually have a date and I'd like to bring him."

"Bogart?" Patrick's brows knitted together in thought. "That's cool. You'll like Bogart," he said to our parents.

"Gee, thanks," I said.

My father handed me my tickets. "Bogart. Is that his name?" he asked.

"Well, it's Chris Bogart. But everyone calls him Bogart."

"Everyone else may call him Bogart but you're not everyone else. You should call him Chris."

I questioned him with my eyes.

He patted my hand. "Trust me on this, Katie Maureen. An old man knows these things. Call him Chris."

"Chris? I don't know."

"Okay," my dad said, easing off the pressure. "When the two of you are together—alone. Call him Chris. Just try it."

His voice was sincere, his eyes gentle. My father, who looked like Charlie Brown, rarely asked for anything. And all he was asking was for me to consider something he thought would benefit me.

"I will."

His face again lit up in a smile. "Wonderful!"

I kissed his cheek. "Thank you for the tickets, Dad. These are great. I can't wait for the game."

I grabbed a cookie off the counter without asking. "Sorry I'm missing dinner, Mom. Thanks for the cookies." I hugged her and whispered in her ear, "Don't wait up. I think it'll be a late night."

"Be safe," she whispered in a nod.

"Always."

\###

Barbara's house was a narrow old home in downtown Huntington. The whitewash was worn and weathered from the ocean air, but the inside showed like a page out of *Architectural Digest*. Hardwood floors and a custom fireplace left the exterior impression long forgotten.

"It's beautiful," I said when I stepped inside.

"Thanks. My dad's a carpenter and my ex was a builder. Between the two of them, my house was always under construction."

"I bet."

"Get comfortable." She extended her hand toward the front living room.

I sank into an overstuffed velvet chair. Bowls of hard candy were placed throughout the room.

"Patrick would love it in here," I said under my breath as I eyed a dish of jawbreakers.

Barbara returned with a pot of hot water and packets of tea.

"Hey, these look familiar." I recognized the tea we served our guests.

Barbara waved her hand in my direction. "They don't pay me enough to afford the good stuff."

"But how do you get it out of the hotel?" I asked, thinking of the bare cupboards that would greet me when I got the keys to my apartment.

"Probably the same way you got the critical course off property," she said.

I practically dropped my teacup. "How'd you know?"

"Katie, the blue bomb," she said, referencing her computer, "keeps a log of all my printing."

"Oh my God."

"It's okay. I'm just happy you made it out of the hotel without getting caught."

"You knew?"

"Not until you had left."

"Why didn't you say something?"

"I didn't feel the need. The issue concerned you, so I didn't see any harm in you knowing that your position in HR was never going to turn into full-time, and that by October you'd be losing your overtime. Now, if you had taken something that didn't concern you, I probably would have asked for it back," she said.

"I'm so sorry." I felt like I had betrayed her trust. "I just wanted to print the memo Holly had written to Jerry, I mean, Mr. Adams, and his response. I didn't know the critical course was attached."

"Neither did I. Made me damn mad too when I realized it. I spent more than an hour trying to locate that stupid thing."

"I remember."

"So I noticed Jimmy took you into his office."

"Yeah, it was about this PR thing," I said, not wanting to reveal too much.

"So you're going to do it?" she asked and I realized she

probably knew more than I did on the matter. She did, after all, take the minutes for the Executive Board meetings.

"What do you think?"

"I think that you're wasting your talent being a secretary," she said. "Not that there is anything wrong with being an administrator. But you've caught on so quickly and perform your job so efficiently. You really should be doing more than just filing and typing memos."

"I don't know. I've never been much of a writer," I said, and instantly heard my confidence slip. "Correction. I've never really taken the chance to become a writer."

"See, then," Barbara said, offering me a cookie, which I accepted. "This is the perfect opportunity for you."

"Perhaps. I'm just not sure how I'll handle the other part of it," I said, hinting at Jimmy's plan for me to write a press release announcing a staged walkout to strike for benefits and overtime. I thought of what Patrick had said and of my ability to carry it off.

"You just write the releases, and I'll get them into the right hands," she said.

"Doesn't this seem a little clandestine to you?" I asked of this internal group that was forming.

"No more than the Board's decision to hire 350 positions in June knowing half that number would be employed part-time without any benefits."

"At some point, they had to realize what they were doing was wrong. Don't you think?" I asked. I had to know if I was working for an evil corporate hotel who just didn't care or if maybe it had been a gross oversight in the initial hiring phase.

"You're so sweet," she said, warming her focus toward me. "But Katie, darling, this is the Waterfront Point Resort. Employee morale isn't as high a priority as earning the coveted five-diamond rating."

"Even if that comes at the expense of their staff?"

"Especially when it's as simple as expending the staff," she said. "If a part-time employee isn't happy, there's another part-time person in the wings who's willing to work the extra hours." Barbara leaned in. "And they know that. What I know from sitting in the executive board meetings is that they never had any intention of bumping part-time employees to full-time. They have the money budgeted for more full-time employees, but if they can keep labor to an even split, with 175 full-time and 175 part-time employees, they'll be well below the year-end numbers."

"And then they'll meet their bonus," I said.

Barbara nodded.

The truth settled in my skin. A five-diamond rating was their first consideration and then maybe employee morale. Even though I had created a Facebook page and tried to educate other employees, there was always a part of me that felt like I was being disloyal to the hotel, when all the while the hotel's first loyalty was to earning the top rating and their bonus. *Well that sucks.*

But it was the catalyst I needed, and also why I had to make Kandy believe that I could write well enough in her absence. So when she was on medical, I could pen the press release that would place the Waterfront Point Resort at the center of a national media firestorm. And for that to happen, the critical course had to first be leaked to the media. Move over Norma Rae, Erin Brockovich, and the entire *Spotlight* team—I had work to do.

"Okay," I said, pushing up the sleeves of my blazer and pulling out a notepad and pen from my backpack. "What can you tell me about holiday functions at a hotel?"

CHAPTER NINETEEN

"Hello." His voice was deep, throaty, and pressed against my ear. I'd never spoken to Bogart over the phone. *Does his voice always sound this manly? Woof.*

"Hey." My entire body lit up in a smile.

"So whacha doin'?" he teased huskily.

"Driving toward you."

"Nice."

I bit my bottom lip. *Damn.* I swallowed—hard. "Okay, see you soon."

"Katie?"

I nodded. "Yeah?"

"I can't wait."

I was pretty sure the low-rise, all-lace panties that barely covered me were wet. The super sexy little panties were something my mom's personal shopper, Stella, suggested.

Stella said the lace disappeared under clothes. No doubt. The soft lace showed off more cheek than my baby pictures. And the front bow added an extra dash of wow. Or so I was hoping.

I jokingly called them my five-minute panties because I'd only have them on for five minutes before they'd be off. Or with Bogart, tangled around my ankle. I hadn't worn any of the dozen pairs I'd bought in a rainbow of colors. But tonight seemed like the night to test-drive "Key lime" and my five-minute theory.

I rapped my fingers against the steering wheel while I waited for the red light to change. Bogart's house was just around the bend. *Crappity crap. What am I doing? I can't pull off these panties. Five minutes or fifty.*

But I had two football tickets in my jacket pocket that were a good distraction. And my meathead of a brother guaranteed those were a "lock."

Confidence, I reminded myself as I pulled into his driveway.

I had dressed casually in a pair of ankle jeans and a formfitting tank that required no bra. Or so Stella told me. The shade of pumpkin hid the fact that I was braless, and so did my one-button navy blazer. White Converse completed the outfit. *Where would I be without Stella?*

The lucky Irish emerald my mom bought on one of her many trips with my dad to Ireland hung on a thin, silver chain and rested on my breastbone. I rubbed the princess-cut gem before heading to the front of Bogart's house. Before I could knock, the door opened.

"Hello." Bogart stood before me in jeans and an open flannel with a Trader Joe's T-shirt on underneath. His dark hair was a heap of messy spikes. He had this disheveled, just-rolled-out-of-bed-with-perfect-wearable-bedhead thing going on that made it hard for me to keep my hands to myself. *Holy hell. My boyfriend's hot. He is my boyfriend, right?*

"Hi." My stomach flip-flopped.

"Come in." He moved aside for me to cross the threshold.

"Thank you." *Relax. Stay calm—confident.*

"Hungry?" he asked as I followed him toward the kitchen. The scaffold was gone, and the entry hall was lit by a wrought-iron-and-crystal chandelier.

I stopped beneath it. "Nice choice." I stood with my head tilted up.

"You don't think it's too much?" He stood behind me.

"Not at all, it's beautiful. I like the way you went old-school."

His breath was on my neck. His lips grazed my skin. I closed my eyes and wanted to lean into him, but I wasn't sure. Suddenly, the last time I was there came flooding back to me. The hurtful words, the accusations, the outbursts of emotion. And all the doubt. I tightened my eyes, blocking out the memory, trying to shut out the uncertainty that heartache created.

Bogart wrapped his hand around my waist, pulling me to him. His warmth radiated against me, thawing the chill that had crept in like an unwanted guest. He placed his chin on my shoulder.

"Every time I walked into this hallway, I thought about that night," he said.

I leaned against him and he absorbed my weight.

"I had to make peace with this a long time ago," he said.

The only sound I heard was his voice. All I felt was his heart beating against me. With each breath I took I inhaled him, until our breathing became one. And when I looked up, the ceiling glittered in a play of light. Wrapped in his arms, there was nowhere I'd rather be. I was home.

"So it was either reconcile or move, and I *really* like this house."

My stomach shook against him when I giggled.

"It wasn't our best moment," he said.

I nodded. "It wasn't our best moment."

The crystal teardrops captured the natural light from the front windows as the autumn sun set, illuminating the hallway in a kaleidoscope of colors that surrounded us. He pressed his lips against my neck. I closed my eyes and savored his touch.

He tightened his hold around me. "We weren't together then, but we are now."

It was a declaration, not a question. It put to rest any insecurity, doubt, or confusion I had about our future. When he turned me around, I saw it as clearly as his eyes that locked on mine.

"If you think this is something, you've got to see the kitchen."

The countertops, which had been covered by plastic, now displayed his completed work. A mosaic of tiles trimmed the kitchen. Slivers of silver and veins of gray streaked the small squares, tinting the surface brilliantly. Bogart's remodel had flipped a normal kitchen on its head and made it shine.

The pop of light that shone from the bay window opened

up the room and made me feel like I had stepped outside.

"Oh." Surprise caught in my voice. "I don't remember this." I stood in front of the sink.

"I thought of it later." Bogart stepped up behind me, leaned in, and gripped the kitchen counter on each side of me. His forearms flexed. I flashed to the night at the club when I saw him standing at the bar. His back was strong, sexy—ripped. But for whatever reason, I'd lusted after another when Mr. Right was in front of me all along.

I gazed out the bay window that faced the backyard. The season presented itself in a vibrant tapestry. Feathery silver-green leaves topped with brilliant golden blossoms covered the garden. The California poppy was as beautiful as it was prolific. It blanketed the back berm that Bogart had created against his fence and added depth and dimension to his yard. It worked. And my focus was drawn to the white poppies with bright yellow centers spliced in between the golden poppies.

"The white poppies are beautiful," I said, pinned beneath Bogart, "but they're like crepe paper. Much too delicate for a vase."

His chin again rested on my shoulder. "And you'd know this how?"

"My father has the same flowers planted in his yard. Along with our state flower."

"Represent."

I shook my head and grinned. There were a few flowers I didn't recognize. Tall, fuzzy stalks with silvery leaves that had cup-like flowers in shades of apricot to watermelon red burst across the backyard. The stems shot high and the flowers hung low.

"What is that?" I pointed.

"Which one?" Bogart's laughter tickled my ear.

"The one that looks like it belongs in *Alice in Wonderland* or maybe *Willie Wonka and the Chocolate Factory*."

"Oh, that's the Desert Mallow, or some people call it the Sore-eye Poppy."

"What?" I turned toward him and our lips were inches apart.

His eyes twinkled and my heart skipped a beat.

"Some people call it Sore-eye Poppy because the leaf hairs are an eye irritant to some."

"Really? That's a bummer, because they're amazing."

"I've never had a problem but"—he shrugged—"I wouldn't want to have you find out…."

"And suddenly have a sore eye? Or eyes?" I looked at his lips.

"Exactly." His lips met mine. His mouth was soft and inviting. I reached around his neck and gently pulled him to me. He complied by pressing into me, the heat of his body against mine. When our lips parted, I looked into his eyes and softly smiled. I turned my focus once more to the bay window.

In the distance, snow dusted the top of Saddleback Mountain, and trees split in color as the vibrant foliage of autumn offset the barren branches of the coming winter. I stood in the heart of this beauty with Bogart against me, feeling the cadence of his breathing.

I gently kissed his hand and trailed his forearm with the tip of my tongue. I playfully dug my teeth into the bend at his elbow where his shirt was rolled up. The way we stood together felt safe, protected, and oddly sexy. With his arms still locking me securely, tightly, snugly against him, he nuzzled the soft hollow of my neck, sweeping hair away. He slowly pressed his lips into my skin with a single warm, sensual, melt-in-the-moment kiss—and I did.

I tilted my head to the side and he peppered my skin with teasing kisses that made me catch my breath. His mouth pressed against my ear.

"Take off your jeans."

His directive made me gasp and heightened my arousal. Turned away from him, I stepped on the back of my sneaker and shrugged it off my foot. I did the same with the other. Then I shimmied out of my jeans and as I did, my palm slid along his button fly, stroking him through the denim. He murmured.

With my jeans off, the only thing that separated Bogart from me was a little slice of key lime lace and my tank.

"Green's my favorite color," he said huskily. His hands roamed the lace, feeling the contours of my body. "Oh, yeah, those are nice."

I grinned, realizing he had just shot a hole through my five-minute theory.

His fingers inched my tank top up and over my head. My breasts bounced free, and his hand drew around and caressed each nipple, cascading wave upon wave of pleasure throughout my body.

He slid down me to the curve in the small of my back. His tongue flicked across my sensitive skin to the edge of lace where he worked my flesh with his mouth. I arched forward.

The sensation of his tongue was an erotic massage, relaxing and stimulating, causing me again to lose all sense of time, place, and control. Being with Bogart was like being in a bubble where nothing else but us mattered, and the world shut down. All I felt were his hands on me, his taste on my tongue, and his breathing heavy in my ear. I looked behind me as his lips turned up in a satisfied smile.

His fingers brushed beneath my barely-there panties. They glided over my wet core, tickling, taunting, teasing. I practically purred above him. His fingers delicately danced across my core in a ballet of movements that circled my clit, bringing it to a fevered pitch, and then he exited the stage like he had the last time, keeping me teetering on the edge.

I groaned in disbelief, noting a pattern I wasn't sure I wanted repeated. But like his scent—which was all over me—it had an addictive edge that was hard to deny. Bogart sensed my resistance because his kissing intensified, hungrily nibbling my skin while his hands braced my thighs. His tongue covered my backside, flicking in and out between my cheeks. I inhaled sharply. The sensation was new and drove me to lean into him. He responded to my desire by dipping his tongue into me. I closed my eyes as his tongue took me to greater, higher, unimagined pleasure. His tongue gyrated, and I felt myself about to come undone.

"Oh my God. Don't. Stop." I gripped the counter.

I could barely stand, almost collapsing on his face when his mouth wandered, making its way between my legs to my pulsating core. Instead, my knees buckled into the cabinets, trembling against the smooth pine. Each stroke of his tongue was like a magic wand against my clit.

"Mother of all things holy." My hold on the counter was slipping. Hell, my hold on reality was slipping. Bogart's tongue was a national treasure.

My legs shook, and I knew I wouldn't be able to keep an upright position much longer. His hand swooped around my waist, and I folded into him like a jackknife. He slowly brought me to the floor, cradling my head as he gently laid me down.

Bogart stood before me, slipped off his flannel, and whipped his T-shirt over his head. His muscles rippled across his chest when he tossed his clothes to the side like a basketball player taking a last-minute three-point shot. His torso was V-shaped, sensual, and something I would never tire of admiring. He wasn't wearing any shoes, and the sound of his belt buckle when it snapped back, releasing his jeans, had already created a Pavlovian response in me. Heat coursed through my body as he unhooked his belt and unbuttoned his fly. It looked like I'd be indulging in dessert before dinner.

He stepped out of his jeans, and his thighs were hugged by black, formfitting boxers that didn't hide his full, pulsating bulge. I wrapped my feet around his ankles, inching myself toward him, aching for him to be inside me. He slipped out of the last of his clothes, removing the boxers, and I found myself licking my lips while a smile curved his. He reached behind him into a drawer and turned around with a condom, which he rolled down the length of his shaft.

I unlocked my feet from his, and without looking away from him, I slowly lowered the lace from my body until it hung from one ankle. He knelt down in front of me and covered my body with his. I wrapped my legs around him, pulling the length of his shaft hard against me.

"Chris," I said.

Surprise lit his brown eyes.

Emotion caught in my throat, and tears pooled at the corners of my eyes. "I've never met a man like you."

He pressed his lips against mine and kissed me until I was almost breathless. His cheek grazed against my cheek. "And I've never met a woman like you, who I've wanted all to myself so badly it hurt."

My body rushed with heat as emotions flooded me. I tightened my hold around him. "You have me. I'm yours. And *only* yours."

His mouth claimed me as his shaft filled me. My legs dropped their hold around his waist while his thrusts started out slow, steady, and grew in heat and intensity. My hips rose to meet him, but his pace increased to the point that he almost dove into me.

"God, yes!"

He hit my center faster and harder than before. All I saw was white. All I felt was heat. And all I knew was that the dam was about to burst. My head fell back, my legs seized around him, and my mouth was not my own.

"Ohh!" I cried out. "That's right, give me the good wood."

Good wood? But then it became a sexy mantra.

"Good wood." The words barely passed my lips as I bucked beneath him, my breathing intensified, my body clamping down on him. "More." I dug my heels into his back. "Good. Wood."

"Sweet mercy," he groaned.

Ecstasy slid between us as the friction built to a climatic pitch. Bogart pulled back, and this time I rose toward him, my clit in a prime position against him, just as he plunged forward. Our bodies collided. Implosion. Back arched, he shot his release through me, his voice roaring in my ear. As he continued to pump his orgasm, it broke the dam wide open. My hips rose off the floor, my head fell back, and my fingers bored into his shoulders. I cried out as the orgasm shook my body, threatening to rip me apart, but Bogart rode it out. The dam released, heating me from the inside out with a wetter, wilder, more satisfying climax.

I collapsed against the floor with Bogart on top of me. Our breathing was ragged and he gently rolled off me. I laid my head on his chest and listened to his heart beat as it returned to a steady rhythm.

I gently traced the stubble on his chin. "*This* is our best moment."

He leaned over me, his eyes glowing down on me. "*This* is only the beginning."

CHAPTER **TWENTY**

By Sunday, Bogart and I had been together all weekend, moving boxes into the garage at my apartment. I hadn't opened a Word document, let alone typed a single word for the press release that was due on Jimmy's desk the next morning. And now I was headed, hand in hand with Bogart, toward our seats at the UCLA-USC game. My stomach should have been a bundle of knotted nerves, but it wasn't.

The Rose Bowl was standing room only. The stadium was divided by color and allegiance, with police patrolling the entrances and gate. Cardinal and gold filled one section while blue and gold burst from the other side of the stadium. The energy was palpable. Our seats were on the UCLA Bruin blue and gold side, center section, fifth row from the field.

"Thank you for bringing me as your date," Bogart said, squeezing my hand.

"They are good seats, but caveat emptor," I said. "Buyer be warned. My entire family will be here, so thank me *after* the game."

Bogart raised my hand to his mouth and kissed it. "Relax," he said. "I've already met Patrick."

I giggled. "Good point."

My little brother and his buddy from college, Mike Murphy, were already there, staking the middle two seats. Peanut shells scattered along their feet. Patrick popped a peanut in his mouth just as he stood to greet us.

"Hey, brother," Patrick said, slapping Bogart on the back. "Glad you could make it."

After he introduced us to Mike, he handed Bogart a cold water and a soft pretzel.

"Water?" I shook my head. "What the hell?"

"There's no beer or any alcohol sold during the UCLA-USC game," Patrick said.

"Damn. I was hoping for a cold one," I said.

"Here." Patrick grinned as he handed me his last bottled water.

I waved it away. "I'll go get a soda." I held out my hand and waited for him to place a roll of money in my palm. His eyebrows furrowed.

"I want my change."

"Sure, sure." I pocketed two twenties and had turned toward the center aisle when he called after me.

"Twiggy, get some of those ice-cream nugget things."

"I'd better go, too," Bogart said after Mike added to the order. "I just helped her move boxes. You've never seen her carry a box. I can't imagine a tray."

My little brother slapped his thigh and laughed.

"Har har. Those boxes weren't sealed shut *and* they were lopsided and I'm pretty sure uneven."

My brother rolled his eyes. "I don't think that's possible."

"And if I can't hold a tray, it's because I'm *not* a server," I said.

"No, you're just the flunky they've roped into writing your pink slip, I mean, press release," Patrick said.

I tilted my head. "Shut the hell up."

I grabbed Bogart's hand and rushed toward the aisle before Patrick said anything else.

"What's that all about?" Bogart asked as we descended the bleachers and headed in the direction of the concession stands.

While we stood in the concession line, I gave a CliffsNotes version of my new role in the PR department and the plan to stage a walkout.

"I was hoping the critical course would be enough," Bogart said matter-of-factly.

I turned to him in surprise. "What? It was *you*?"

Bogart said nothing. His eyes glittered darkly as he rubbed the stubble on his chin.

"You released and distributed the critical course through certain sections of the hotel?"

Again nothing, but his face spoke volumes. "And Patrick said *I* didn't have a poker face," I said. "You could lose your job if they find out."

He shrugged, but there was vulnerability there. Bogart

would never claim it, but he was the hero in my story and it pulled on my heartstrings.

"Why did you do it?"

"I didn't want to see good people lose their overtime, especially since it's the only benefit they have." He paused, his eyes drinking me in. "I didn't want to see *you* lose your overtime."

"But you sent it out when we weren't even talking. Why would you risk your job like that?"

He ran his fingers through his dark thick hair. Exasperation inched across his face. "Don't you get it?" His eyes searched mine for an answer.

I slowly shook my head.

"Kates, I'm in love with you."

My heart leapt in my chest. I raised a tentative hand to his cheek. "Oh, Chris, I love you, too."

He pulled me into his arms and kissed me. When we came up for air, the man behind us in line cleared his throat. "Uh, I think it's your turn."

Heat ignited Bogart's cheeks. He cocked his head toward the man. "Thanks."

I giggled and tucked behind him as we approached the beer counter.

"We'll take um… uh…." He suddenly stammered and looked over his shoulder at me. "How many waters do we need?"

"Six? And a soda."

Bogart's brows rose, his dark eyes holding mine. "Sure. Six, seven, what the hell. USC's going to lose, and we'll be up all night writing a press release."

I raised a hand in the air. "Ah-ya!"

###

"Bogart doesn't think what I'm doing is stupid," I said to my brother as I handed him his change.

"Bogart's been sniffing glue."

"I look at it like this," Bogart said as he took a seat next to Patrick. "She's already losing her overtime, and that's the only real benefit she had. So if she can help the crusade to strike for benefits and overtime, why not? She's definitely got the talent to write."

"I do? You think I have talent at writing?"

"I've read your memos."

"Memos." I rolled my eyes. "Well, there you have it. The girl can write memos. Great. Memos don't count."

"Don't do that. Don't underestimate yourself or your talent," Bogart said.

"You're just smitten with my sister." Patrick waved his hand like he swatting away a bug and my compliment at the same time.

"I am smitten, but she's the real deal. She can do it."

Ahh... and he's in love too. A broad smile filled my face and a warm glow radiated through me.

"Yeah, the only question is, when will she do it? You haven't even started on those press releases, have you?" Patrick directed his question to me.

I grimaced. "I've started them." *In my head.* "I just haven't finished them.”

"Aren't they due tomorrow?”

"I've got this. Once the game's over, I'll crank them out. I've got plenty of time.”

The game went into double overtime and LA traffic was a triple nightmare. But the Bruins crushed the Trojans, making it a victory worth staying late to see.

"You know I really want your help, but I think we both know that if we end up back at your place alone, we aren't going to get anything written," I said.

"Understood. But text or call if you get stuck," Bogart said.

"Will do." I kissed him quickly and practically shoved him out of the car when I pulled into his driveway. I drove to my parents' house and hoped my father was home from the game.

"I'm screwed." A document remained blank on my laptop screen with my notes from my meeting with Barbara propped beside me.

My father walked into the kitchen and sat beside me. "Need any help?"

"Oh! You're home." Then I thought of what my stupid little brother said about needing my father's help. *Dammit, I hate it when he's right.* "Yeah, I'd love it, but…."

"You want to do this on your own."

"Something like that. But I'm stuck. I mean, Dad, I am *really* stuck." My gaze fixed on his.

"That's because you're trying to write from here." He tapped my forehead. "When you should be writing from here." He gently poked himself in the chest. "The best stories are ones that are told from the heart, not your head."

"I love you." I leaned over and hugged him.

"I love you too, rabbit head. And I'd be glad to proof it for you when you're through. Even the best writers still have their work proofed. Saves time for the editor and prevents the hacks from slashing your work."

"It might be late," I said.

"I'll be up."

"Thank you."

"Katie, get out of your head and just write." He kissed my forehead before he left.

I plugged my headphones into my laptop and cranked up the volume. "Have Yourself a Merry Little Christmas" blared. And suddenly the rhythm of words fell onto the paper, and the splendor of the holidays came to life before me. When I was finished, I tilted the screen, sat back, and read my first press release.

The Waterfront Point Resort Offers Relief for Holiday Travelers

Huntington Beach, CA: What are the six most dreaded words travelers will hear from relatives this holiday season? "Of course, you'll stay with us." Fortunately for those out-of-town visitors who prefer a hotel suite with an ocean view to a lumpy couch with a pull-out bed, the Waterfront Point Resort is introducing its Winter Weekend rates. Guaranteed to make any traveler's holiday visit a true vacation.

From December 1 through January 15, the Waterfront Point Resort in Huntington Beach is offering 25 percent off its already reasonable seasonal rate.

I followed Kandy's evaluation or budget or whatever the hell it was called. All I know is that she had been authorized to offer 25 percent off rooms. The remainder of the release gave the room rates and the cancellation policy. The first press release in my series of "Holiday Happenings at the Waterfront Point Resort" concluded with my name and extension number as the contact for further information.

I was on a roll. I next drafted "The Waterfront Point Resort Offers 12 Reasons to Come to the Coast" as I created my own rendition of "The Twelve Days of Christmas." From Monday Night Football at the Coast to Sunday brunch in Cielo Grande, I covered every food and beverage outlet with any activity. I wrapped up my twelve days with the tagline, "Experience Christmas on the Coast at the Waterfront Point Resort."

I spell-checked my documents and saved them onto a Jumpdrive before printing out a copy.

"I'm done," I announced too loudly, waking up my dad, who had dozed off on the couch.

"Then I'll stick a fork in you," he said sleepily.

I sat beside him while he read through my copy.

"Now, Katie," he said. "This is just wonderful. You're

missing a comma or two, but this is outstanding."

"Really?"

"Darling, this is just wonderful."

It may have been the late hour but I leaned my head on his shoulder, and my eyes welled with tears.

"Thanks, Dad."

He patted my head. "You're my funny little valentine," he said.

I chuckled as tears streamed down my face.

"It's true. If you've ever listened to the words of that song, it mentions your heart and how you make me smile, and you've always been my sweet child."

Some of my best moments had been spent on the gold, plaid couch talking with my dad. It was where he always sat, waiting for me to return from a date, dance, or college class. We'd sit and talk for hours. Somehow he always made me feel like I was the only person in the room, when in reality with Patrick and Ian, it was easy to be overshadowed. My father always made sure I wasn't.

"I'm going to miss you," I said tearfully.

"Oh, now, Katie Maureen. You'll only be a few blocks away. Look at Patrick. He lives further away, and we see him every day."

I giggled.

"I guess that was lame, huh?" he said.

"Not at all."

"Somehow," he said, pulling on the sleeve of my sweater. "I don't think you'll be lonely at your new apartment."

I leaned away and looked at him.

"Bogart?" he said.

"Don't you mean Chris?" I said, smiling.

My father grinned. "Good girl."

"Thanks for everything, Dad."

He handed me my copy with the corrections circled in red and hugged me before I disappeared into my old bedroom. I printed the final version and tucked it into my backpack. I'd met my deadline. Sleep came easy as I drifted into a heavy slumber, thinking of the day ahead.

CHAPTER **TWENTY-ONE**

"Our timeline's been pushed up." Jimmy briskly walked into HR, closing the door behind him. It was exactly a minute after eight in the morning. He knew that Janet wasn't due into the office until eight thirty and rarely made it by nine—on a good day. And Holly never came in before nine thirty. *Salary slacks.*

"I don't understand," I said.

"The Board met over the weekend. Grab your stuff." He stood by my desk.

"What?" I looked up at him with a frown. "I'm supposed to be in HR now. I just got here."

"I texted Holly that I need you all day because I was out all day Friday."

"Yeah and I'm sure *that* worked," I said with a wry chuckle.

"It did." Jimmy wasn't about to argue with me. "*Vámonos.*"

I knew when he started speaking Spanish it was time to get

moving. I rolled the chair away from my desk, grabbed my backpack, and followed him. He ushered me out of HR and into his office. He closed the door behind us.

"They're planning on executing the cutback on overtime before the start of the fourth quarter."

"When?" I asked.

"Friday."

"That soon? We're barely into September. It's only the twelfth. You said it was being pushed up but this is *way* up. What about this?" I reached into my backpack for my file. It contained three sets of press releases and the "Twelve days of Christmas" promotion.

"I'll present it to Jerry just like normal. Only this," he said, taking the file from me, "won't be your first press release. You need to write one about the walkout today."

"Today? No way." I started to back away from his desk like a deserter. "I can't do it today. We don't even have a walkout planned. You said you'd coordinate all that."

"I have. We're meeting at five."

"Who's meeting? Today? At five?"

"I've assembled a group of hourly and salaried employees who want to participate in the walkout."

I shook my head. *It's happening too fast.*

He came around his desk and gently placed his hand on my shoulder. "I've got the walkout covered, and I know you can handle the writing part. You've got this."

His hand was as strong and determined as his confidence in me. My breathing steadied.

"Listen, all I need from you is the press release announcing the walkout."

"That's all, huh?" I looked up at him. His gray-blue eyes softened, and a crooked smile slid across his weathered face.

"When have we ever done traditional or easy in Food and Beverage?"

"Never." I smiled. "Never."

He gave me a hearty pat on the back. "Atta girl. That's the spirit."

"All right, give me the basics. When and where are you planning this?" I grabbed a pen and pad of paper off his desk and began taking notes.

"It's going to be Friday at 9:00 a.m., 2:00 p.m., and 5:00 p.m."

"Nine, two, and five?" I gave a puzzled shake of my head. "I don't understand."

"It's the hotel's address."

I turned to him in surprise. "That's brilliant."

"I thought so." Jimmy arched a salt-colored brow. "We're going to have three scheduled walkouts."

"At nine, two, and five, okay I've got it. We should create a hashtag: walkout925, or something like that." I tapped my pen on the desk. "I'll chew on it. But if we get this thing to go viral, it'll really help."

"That's a great idea," he said. "I'll be covering the three shifts: a.m., p.m., and the night owls."

"Excellent." My hand feverishly scribbled down the schedule.

"That should do it. So I'll need you to get back to your desk and carry on as usual."

"But what about the meeting? Where do you plan on having it without getting caught?"

"Leave that to me," he said with a wink. And when Jimmy winked, he restored the art of a good wink. "All I need from you is your best writing."

"Sure, no pressure," I grumbled as I exited his office and resumed my post behind my desk.

I was about to pull up a blank document and start hammering out the press release when I was bombarded by a sales group touring the property. *Of all the Mondays.* They wanted to see our "Business Center" and have a copy of our price list. Barbara pulled up and printed the menu of secretarial services and the fee that accompanied each one while I gave the men and women a tour through our administrative offices, highlighting the on-site amenities we offered. The entire process ate up two hours. I was back at my desk, digging through my backpack for my notes on the walkout, when I heard my name.

"Katie?"

I didn't recognize his voice or the shiny brown loafers that pointed toward the side of my desk. I deeply inhaled through my nose and plastered a smile on my face when I glanced up. Jerry Adams, the general manager, was front and center before me.

My heart leapt to my throat. "Yes, sir?"

"Do you have a moment?" He tilted his bald head toward his office.

"Absolutely." I stood and readjusted my lemon-colored cardigan squarely on my shoulders. I followed Mr. Adams, my hands smoothing down the sides of my pencil skirt. The blue-and-gray check was tightly woven and looked like a shimmering sunset over the Pacific Ocean. With each step, a wave of emotion rose before me. *Does he know? Am I being fired? How'd he find out?*

I passed Barbara's desk and eyed her skeptically. She simply smiled, as if to remind me to act normally.

Mr. Adams closed his office door. He motioned to a plush upholstered chair. I sank into its overstuffed fullness and crossed my legs.

"I didn't know you were such a gifted writer," he said, taking his seat behind his desk.

"I just got—" I started to say lucky, but stopped. "Thank you."

Confidence. I corrected my posture, which was nearly impossible in the marshmallow-like chair.

"Kandy likes it as well, which is what I wanted to talk to you about."

"Yes, sir?"

"You may or may not have heard, but Kandy is undergoing knee surgery."

I nodded.

"And we had planned on hiring an intern," he said.

Isn't that a contradiction? How can you hire someone who would work for free?

"But after reading your work, the Board was curious how you'd feel about becoming the new assistant director of Public Relations and Marketing?"

What? Did he just offer me a job? My body felt numb. Or

it could be the chair. It was hard to tell.

"It'd be a full-time position, with full benefits," he said when I didn't respond. "You'd be salaried, so the occasional overtime would be incurred. But nothing you're not used to."

Oh, so you know about my six-day-a-week work schedule. Nice.

"We'd like to start you at $50,000, and after ninety days, you'd be eligible for a bump in salary."

"Fifty thousand?" My voice could have cracked glass. A pleased smile crossed his lips. *Did I hear that correctly? Does he know I only make fifteen bucks an hour?* My math sucked but I knew I'd be close to doubling my income. And then a moment of reality sank in. "Why now?"

Mr. Adams continued to smile like the cat that ate the canary. "We just never knew the talent you possessed. It's been a little hectic around here, if you haven't noticed." He chuckled and it didn't help that with his full belly and rosy cheeks all he was missing to look like Santa Claus were the white hair and beard. But it wasn't Christmas, and the gift he was handing me was tainted.

I smiled in his direction, knowing that while my writing was good, it wasn't fifty grand good. Not when a majority of the staff would be stuck working without benefits or overtime at the cost of my promotion.

"We were hoping you'd help us with a sensitive issue that's on the horizon at the Waterfront Point Resort."

I raised my eyebrows and widened my eyes just a bit to really sell my curiosity. "Oh, what's that?"

"Well, we can get into the details later, but suffice it to

say we need a *real* team player on this one. A *legs, arms, and heart* of the hotel kind of person," he said.

Seriously? Did he just reference my Huntington Hopeful intro? Are you kidding me? I knew the game of using someone's tagline to gain their favor. *Hell, I'm the master of that game.* I wasn't about to fall for my own PR. Or even my own BS.

But unlike what my little brother might think, my face remained neutral. *Yeah, I so have a poker face.* I looked at him with a wide smile broadening my face.

"So are you on board?" he asked.

"I'm flattered you like my work." I purposely bypassed answering his question.

"Good, good, good," he said and just as quickly as he had steered me into his office, he swiftly stood and led me back to the administrative area. "We'll talk soon."

Dazed, I nodded and walked back to my desk. *Unbelievable.* I grabbed my cell phone from my backpack and texted Bogart. My fingers flew across the screen.

Got offer from GM to be VP of PR & Marketing. 50K. But before I could redirect convo or even divert him off topic, he just assumed I'd say yes. I never did. He thinks PR thing is locked down b/c he thinks he locked me down. He's wrong.

I hit Send and felt my pulse pounding. *What the hell?*

My cell flashed with a reply text from Bogart. *I'm so sorry that happened.* Another message followed. *He's a fool.* My heart rate was returning to normal when my cell dinged with another message. *Besides no one locks you down but me.* I giggled and tossed my cell into my backpack.

A stack of faxing that had to be completed for the sales group I had given a tour to was waiting for me on my desk. As much as I wanted to, I couldn't put it aside or push it off on someone, because that would raise suspicion. Instead, I ran to the back mailbox area and faxed what seemed like an inordinate amount of documents. *Why do people fax when they could scan?* But I wasn't about to present that option because I didn't want the task of scanning and then e-mailing the documents. So, while I waited for each individual fax to transmit, I sorted the mail, made copies for Barbara, and wished I had brought my cell with me. I punched numbers into the fax and listened to the machine squawk in reply. It was a slow, time-consuming process. When the last fax spat out a transmittal sheet, I paper-clipped it to the stack and tallied the total.

"Will you bill them?" I asked as I ran past Barbara's desk on the way to mine.

"How many?" she said with her head down.

"Thirty-two. All international," I said. "The Spice Corporation."

"I've got it."

"Thanks."

I was about to finally tackle the press release when Jimmy called me into his office. *For the love of all things holy.*

"Where are you at with that project?" he asked.

My face must have answered his question.

"The meeting is in fifteen minutes."

I shook my head. "That can't be right. You said it was at 4:45 p.m." I glanced at the clock on the wall behind him.

"What the…. I haven't even started the press—"

He cut me a look that silenced me.

Oops. My bad. "I haven't even eaten lunch." I offered by way of apology.

He passed me a card key.

"Room 1425," he said before slipping out of his office.

There were three things that anyone who has ever worked for the Waterfront Point Resort learned immediately: the guest was always right, there were a dozen different ways to avoid saying "no" to a guest, and the most important rule was that when a guest hung a Do Not Disturb sign on the outside of their hotel door, *you did not disturb.*

There could be a flood, a fire, or even an earthquake, but no matter the peril, no one broke a DND. It was the one and only automatically terminable offense. It was the only rule that applied to everyone, from the hourly line employees to the coveted Executive Board. No one broke a DND. Ever.

So it was with a smile that I clocked off work on Monday and headed toward the service elevator. The door was about to shut.

"Hold the elevator!" I ran toward the metal doors, which were being held by an outstretched hand.

I stepped inside and saw Carmen.

"Hey," I said. I hadn't seen her since the night she was with Bogart at Hank's.

She smiled.

"Thanks for holding the door."

"*De nada.*"

I grinned. "I'm so glad I ran into you. I've really wanted to talk to you."

Carmen took a step back in the elevator cab we shared and questioned me with her exquisite eyes.

"I never wanted to come between you and Bogart," I said.

"There was nothing to come between. We were always just friends," she said.

"I know that now, and I'm sorry if I did anything to put distance between the two of you. I want you to stay friends. And I want us to stay friends too." I paused. "I mean, if you want that."

"Katie, you were always my friend."

I walked toward her. "You know, I'm kind of a hugger," I said shrugging my shoulders. "You okay with that?"

Carmen laughed and wrapped her arms around me. When we parted she looked at me. "So how are you and Bogart?"

"We're good." I gently smiled.

"And TJ? How did things end up there?" she asked.

"Things ended that night you drove me to Bogart's—both for TJ, Bogart and me. I made so many mistakes, and I'm grateful that you were there that night. TJ and I recently talked and we knew it was a mistake. And to be honest, I'm still a little shocked that Bogart gave me another chance."

"He realized he was partly to blame with the mixed signals he gave you," she said.

I nodded. "Yeah, but he didn't get drunk and make out with someone on hotel property."

"Not yet," she said and nudged me.

I shook my head. "Yeah, I can't see Bogart *ever* doing that. He's a by the book kind of guy."

She tilted her head.

"Oh." It suddenly made sense. "You helped him distribute the critical course to the part-time employees."

She smiled. "He didn't ask, but I offered."

"But if you got caught, you could have been fired."

"It affects me and a lot of people I care about." She nodded toward me. "Like you."

"Wow." My heart was full. "That was pretty badass of you."

"And Bogart," she said. "Don't forget who spearheaded this."

"I could never forget Bogart."

She smiled. "I know. You two were meant for each other."

"Thank you. I'm crazy about him—but in a good way."

We were both laughing when the door to the elevator opened to the fourteenth floor. A Do Not Disturb sign hung from the brass door handle of Suite 1425.

I glanced at Carmen and inserted the card key Jimmy had given me and the door automatically opened. We walked in and the door shut quietly behind us. Mr. Clark, the director of Security, stood off to the side in the foyer. He nodded with a slight smile toward the living room area where Jimmy had positioned himself. The suite was packed with employees.

His bushy eyebrows shot up when I walked into the room. "Okay, we'll give it five more minutes then begin," he said.

I stood off to the side with Carmen, where I dropped my

backpack to the floor and glanced around the room for familiar faces. I knew everyone's name from filing, but I didn't always know their faces. Tucked in a corner of the leather sectional, Chris Colombo sat cross-legged in black slacks, a single-breasted black wool Armani jacket that showed a hint of his trim-fitted white dress shirt, and a cranberry-colored tie. I had found out that Stella was also his personal shopper. His white shock of hair no longer reminded me of the Keebler Elf. Sandy was a pop of color in a coral, sleeveless romper that flattered her hourglass figure. They were holding hands, and a platinum band with a stunning diamond solitaire shone on her left ring finger. An engraved invitation to their December wedding had arrived in the weekend mail. I softly smiled in their direction. They had found their happily ever after.

Beside them, Jackie and TJ cuddled together. TJ cocked his head and held his fingers up in a peace sign. I shook my head and laughed.

Carmen nudged me and cocked her head toward the corner of the room. I followed the direction of her nod and saw Bogart, who was partially hidden behind the bar. A surge of adrenaline shot through my veins. We looked at each other. He stepped away from the bar and toward me. I grinned and glanced at Carmen, who smiled.

Bogart leaned against the wall beside us and pinned me with his gaze.

"Hello," he said.

A wave of heat flamed in my stomach. *His voice. Was it always this sexy?*

"Hey." I tingled with the need for him to touch me.

"I think you all know why we've assembled," Jimmy said, redirecting my attention.

A heavy rap on the hotel door interrupted him, startling me and from the collective gasp in the room, everyone else too.

"Okay, just relax." Jimmy nodded toward Mr. Clark. "Bill, will you please get that."

Mr. Clark peered through the peephole. A slow shake before opening the door.

All eyes stared at the hotel door when Trish walked through. Her long, toned legs made an impressive entrance in a pair of white go-go boots. In a tight-fitting blue mini dress with pink cap sleeves and a scarf tied around her neck, her retro look was eerily reminiscent of the "I can be a flight attendant" Malibu Barbie I'd gotten on my eighth birthday.

"What?" she said to the stares.

"Trish, you're supposed to use your card key," Jimmy said.

"Oh, is that what this is?" She held up the plastic card. "I get these all the time from hotel guests."

The entire room broke into laughter.

Her nose wrinkled in confusion.

"Take a seat," Jimmy instructed his part-time hostess, who had just graduated to part-time go-go dancer and was breaking in her boots.

"I have a manicure appointment at six," she announced to the group.

"I'll do my best," Jimmy said.

"Okay." She took the only vacant spot on the wall beside me, Bogart, and Carmen. "Have you lost weight?" she asked me in a less than hushed tone. "Because you look great."

I weakly smiled.

"Really, have you lost any weight?" she pressed.

"Maybe. Or it could be that I'm just not eating in the cafeteria anymore." I smiled and turned my attention back to Jimmy.

"As I was saying, we're all here today for a joint purpose. It hurts morale when people feel like they aren't being appreciated," he said. "It ends up pitting people against each other. We're fortunate that the full-timers and part-timers are working together to bring about the necessary changes that are needed. I hear people every day talking about looking for other jobs and wanting to leave the hotel for a job with benefits that will make them feel like they are valued and appreciated. So I want to say up front, I appreciate everyone who showed up. Thank you."

I freaking love Jimmy.

"The more united we are, the better the outcome," he said. "There's power in numbers, and so we have a week to gather as many employees as we can to participate in the walkout."

"You want the night owls, too, right, Jimmy?" Bogart asked.

"That's right. Every shift and any person who is willing to walk off. Now, what that means is you have to clock off. You can't do this on hotel time or you can get fired. But if you clock out first then the hotel has less recourse."

"But we could still get fired," Barbara said, clearing away any misconception regarding our voluntary involvement.

"That's correct," Jimmy said.

"What do you need us to do?" Chef asked.

Chef? I almost got whiplash turning toward him. I hadn't seen him in the room. *I can't believe he's part of this. He gets paid a boatload.* I guess he really did care for his staff.

"I need you to exercise discretion, but talk to your people. Explain to them what's happening. The critical course's focus is on eliminating the overtime for part-time personnel, which will have a trickle-down effect to the full-timers. Those who are salaried will see an increase in their workload, and those that are hourly may be rotated to other positions to cover a shift that was handled by a part-timer earning overtime. I can't stress enough that for salaried employees, their load will double and as salaried staff that means no overtime. So this effects everyone."

"You have to admit, it's a genius plan on the part of the Board," Carmen spoke up.

"If you consider creating two classes of employees, one with benefits and one without, then yes, it's genius. But there are other ways to run a business without being divisive," Jimmy said coolly. His position on the Board placed his job in the greatest jeopardy.

That's my boss. A sense of pride filled me.

"We just received word that we earned the five-diamond award," Donna from accounting said. "We achieved the highest award in the hotel industry in less than four months of opening our doors. The majority of employees logged thirty-nine hours to forty hours each week, and I know because I see all the time punches. So it shouldn't be a system that only rewards the forty-hour week employees with benefits. *All* employees working thirty-nine hours a week should be entitled to healthcare, retirement savings, and paid time off."

Her comment was sobering. We had earned the prestigious rating in record time.

"So explain how staging this walkout will improve our jobs?" a part-time cook from the kitchen asked. He also worked part-time in the banquet department as a morning cook preparing personalized omelets for guests at corporate functions.

"It's about the exposure it will generate," Jimmy said.

"Exposure?" Trish asked. "What exposure?"

"Actually, Trish, you could be a wonderful asset in this endeavor," Jimmy said. "As a Pacific Pro calendar girl, we could use you as a part of our publicity."

Trish brimmed with excitement. I would have, too, if I held that title. Or looked that good in go-go boots. The girl had it going on.

"Okay," she agreed blindly.

"Did you get that, Gidget?" he asked me.

I reached into my backpack for my notepad.

"Katie is going to write a press release announcing the staged walkout, so it's paramount that we hit the streets at exactly nine, two, and five."

I smiled again at the symbolism of using the hotel's address as part of the plan.

"Actually, could Katie read us the press release?" Chef asked.

I'm pretty sure I stopped breathing. For certain, I know my face drained of color, because Trish elbowed me. "Are you okay?"

I shook my head and my breaths became short and rapid.

"Chef, I don't have the press release written yet." I thought I'd pass out.

If Trish knocking on the door had caused concern, my announcement practically brought the room to a fever pitch of anxiety.

"What?" Chef's eyebrows furrowed and worry tightened his face.

"All right," Jimmy said. "Katie, why don't you come up and explain what you plan to write in your release."

I knew failure wasn't an option, but knowing that so much was riding on this was almost crippling. The pressure felt like a vise on my head. I couldn't move, let alone imagine what I'd say to everyone. That's when Bogart gently leaned toward me and whispered in my ear, "You've got this."

I flashed to our first day and to the interview, when he'd stepped up for me. My breathing evened out. *I've got this.*

I turned to him. "Thank you." I watched a flicker of emotion cross his face, and his eyes brightened along with his smile.

I stepped away from him and stood beside Jimmy in the center of the room, and suddenly my father's voice surfaced. *Write with your heart, not your head.*

"I haven't written the press release yet." My voice was shaky and barely audible. "But"—I spoke louder, more clearly—"I will focus on the *heart* of the Waterfront Point Resort. And the heart of this hotel…." I paused for a beat and a breath. "Is everyone gathered here. It's the employees. And I know the employees. I know you."

I looked around the room. "Because for the last several

months I have lived in your files. I know that most of you have children. And that if you are part-time and your child gets sick, you can't work and you lose income. I know this because I filed your lost-time wage forms. I know that many of you attend community college before and after work because I file your bus pass forms for our ride share program. But you're not benefiting from the perk of tuition reimbursement like half the other employees are, yet you're logging nearly identical hours."

"That's great, Katie. I agree that the employees are the heart of the hotel and that they are one-hour shy of full-time, but how exactly will you draft that in a press release?" Chef asked.

My legs shook and my heart raced, but I continued because everyone was looking at me. This was important to them, and it was important to me. Tears stung my eyes because I didn't want to let them down. So I swallowed hard and blinked away the tears. I wanted to give them the hope that I knew Jimmy would have promised them. It's what I wanted to believe was possible—that our actions would prompt the hotel to change their mind and do the right thing. I knew it was a long shot, a Hail Mary pass. But if life had taught me anything lately, it was that when all else failed, you needed to step out of the familiar and take the risk. And then go see Stella to dress for the outcome.

"That's a good question, Chef. All the employees are the heart of the hotel and give it a pulse. We make it not only run, but function with life. *But* to make this press release truly stand out and to give it the energy and the traction it requires,

I'll have to do two things. First, I need to leak the critical course to the press."

The room fell silent. I felt Jimmy staring at me.

"If the media reads the critical course, they'll realize that the hotel planned to rewrite the rules in their favor for a stronger year-end bonus. By working employees just under forty hours a week, they ensured that benefits never became an issue. By cutting overtime in the fourth quarter, they were all but ensuring their year-end bonuses would be big. So after I leak the critical course to the media, which will show the board's intention, and their focus on *their* bonus, the second phase will be the press release. *This* is where I'll get personal. The more I can connect our employees to the community, the more impact it will have."

I smiled in Carmen's direction. "Carmen comes from Costa Mesa, which isn't a far drive, but she's part of the OC that rarely gets written about. We all know the community college in Costa Mesa gets all the love from the media, but what about the working people? I mean who doesn't smile when Carmen pulls up to the front drive in a guest's car and hands them their keys?" Everyone, including Jimmy, laughed. "I mean, that girl looks good behind the wheel because her personality shines through. She'll bring pride to Costa Mesa, and it's that connection we want to forge in the community so that they back us on this."

She tipped her hat toward me.

"And when a guest checks in to the hotel, is there *anyone* on property better dressed than Chris Colombo?" I paused. "Seriously?" Again laughter ensued.

"But Chris isn't just a sharp suit. He's first-class service—all the way." Heads nodded and Chris grinned brightly beside his future bride.

"Or even TJ's charming wiles," I said, playfully rolling my eyes, "that have calmed nervous brides and gotten them down the aisle for their beachside wedding."

"Amen!" Chef said.

"I'll second that," Jimmy said. "Those brides. They're a handful."

"Absolutely. But without TJ, where would we be?" I turned to Bogart and shrugged. "I'd probably have been better off." I chuckled and more than a few people laughed, enjoying the joke at my expense.

"But many of the employees you mentioned are full-time," Chef said. "Like Chris, and TJ is salaried."

"You're right. I just used them as examples. But one of the keys to this is to break the class division that's been created by the hotel who only reward forty-hour-a-week employees. So my press release will focus on the heart of the hotel and highlight certain employees to make it relatable. So while it's not written yet, I know the message we want to get out there and it's very personal." I paused. "Thank you for entrusting me with such an important job. I won't let you down." A tear slipped down my cheek and I quickly brushed it away.

"Why are you doing this? I heard you were offered a salaried position in PR," a houseman in Banquets asked.

Damn. The hotel did have eyes and ears. Either that or Jimmy told his crew to show them my loyalty to the cause.

"You're right, I was offered a PR and marketing job."

Emotion caught in my throat. "But for the first time in my adult life, a line has been drawn in the sand and I know what side I stand on. If I lose both my part-time jobs because of that…." I nodded. "I'm okay. If I did nothing, I wouldn't be."

Jimmy slapped me on the back. "We're not going to let anyone lose their jobs." Then he turned toward Chef. "Do you have any other concerns about Katie or her ability?"

"I do not. We're in good hands with Katie."

I softly smiled in Chef's direction and then returned to Bogart.

"Okay, everyone, I'll keep in contact with you, but it's imperative," Jimmy stressed, "that discretion is used." He turned toward Trish. "So the next time, use your card key."

She grinned, giving Jimmy a thumbs-up, and then tucked the credit-card-sized key into her cleavage.

The meeting ended with ten minutes to spare for Trish to make her six o'clock nail appointment. Mr. Clark began letting employees leave in groups of three. I was talking with Donna from accounting when I heard my name.

"Katie." Jimmy waved me over. He was huddled beside Barbara and Bogart.

"Yes?"

"So you've got an entire press release to write," Jimmy said.

"That's correct," I said. "And a critical course to leak."

"Listen," Jimmy said, "I've got the critical course covered."

"Really?" I shook my head. "How? You said you needed my dad and contacts in the media."

"I've got a few of my own," was all he'd say. "So focus

on the press release. Barbara's going to get you a laptop, and Chris is going to wire the phone so you can dial out directly."

"Ohh-kay." *What are they up to?*

"We need you to stay here until you get it finished."

"At the hotel? What if I get caught?"

"Not going to happen," Mr. Clark said. "I'm on duty tonight, and besides," he said, smiling and waving the Do Not Disturb sign, "no one's about to bother you with this hanging on your door and a DND flashing on the operator switchboard."

"Are you okay with that?" Barbara asked me.

"Sure, as long as I can phone my parents and let them know I'll be late. My cell phone died and my charger's at home."

"Tell them you're staying the night," Jimmy said. "You don't know how long it'll take you, and that'll prevent them from calling the hotel."

"Good idea," Bogart said. "I'll have some food brought up. I'm working the overnight."

"Perfect," Barbara said.

Wow. They had it all figured out. All I had to do was prepare the most important press release of my life.

Barbara returned with a miniature version of her blue bomb. The laptop was equipped with Wi-Fi, so I could access the Internet without using the hotel's system.

"In case you need facts or figures… or an online dictionary," she said. "This way no one from the hotel's IT department can trace your activity."

"That's great." Though the feeling in my stomach was anything but. *The IT department checks our Internet usage? How did I not know that?*

When Barbara left, I phoned my house and my brother, Patrick, answered.

"What are you doing answering the phone?"

"Hey," he said with his mouth full.

Cookies.

"I had some laundry to drop off."

"You know it's not the Flanagan House of Cleaners, and Mom's not your personal maid," I said, taking my frustration out on him.

"What crawled up your ass and died?" Patrick always had the ability to make me laugh when I most wanted to cry.

"I'm in the hotel," I whispered.

"Good," he responded in a hushed, conspiratorial tone. "Because that's where you work, dumbass."

"Patrick!" I snapped. "I'm *in* the hotel in a hotel room."

"Oh," he said. "Very covert."

"You've got to help me."

There was silence on the phone.

"Patrick?"

"Wait a second," he said, and I heard the distinct rattle of the lid of my mom's ceramic cookie jar being removed. Growing up, I had learned to master sounds.

"Patrick, this is important."

"So is my stomach. It's rumbly and tumbly inside," he said, quoting Winnie the Pooh.

I groaned. "You drive me crazy."

"So why are you calling me?"

"*I wasn't*. I was calling Mom's house, not yours."

"Point taken," he said, once again with his mouth full of food.

"I've got to stay overnight at the hotel to finish this press release. Not the two for the Christmas programs," I quickly added, to avoid some smart remark on his behalf. "I already handed those in. In fact, they liked them so much they offered me the assistant PR job at fifty grand."

A noticeable silence followed.

"Patrick?"

"I'm trying not to choke. Fifty grand? You took it, didn't you?"

"Well, I didn't decline it," I said. "But I didn't say yes either."

"Katie! Have you been drinking again?"

"Patrick, be serious. Don't you think it's a little suspect that they offered me this job today on the eve of cutting our overtime?"

"*Reducing* overtime could be seen by many as a prudent financial move on their part," he said as his financial fortitude stepped into the conversation.

"You're absolutely right. It is a prudent financial move on their part because it ensures they get their year-end bonus. But I can't in good conscience accept fifty thousand a year for a job when good people will lose their overtime, which is the only real benefit they have, all while they are still left working two jobs. I don't quite feel right about it."

"Well, there're *fifty thousand* reasons why you should. For starters, you could buy a condo and not have to rent. You could pay off your car—"

"I don't care about those things."

I could practically hear him shaking his head.

"We're just different," I said.

"No, we're not." He paused. "I just hate seeing you give it all up for a group of people who probably won't even appreciate your sacrifice." His voice was softer, gentler.

Ah, Patrick.

"No, they'll get it." I thought of the group that had joined Jimmy today. No one was mad or angry. They were grateful. Everyone wanted the same thing: to stand together and strike for equality in the workplace for everyone. "They're just regular people like you and me," I said. The words resonated in my head. "They're just regular people," I repeated.

That's it. Yes!

"Oh, brother. Thank you. Tell Mom and Dad I'm okay. But don't have them call. Okay? Patrick? Don't have them call."

"Got it, don't call. What room are you in?"

"1425, but you can't come to the hotel and don't call asking for that room. I'm not supposed to be on the property."

"I'm not stupid, but you know Mom and Dad are going to ask what room you're in, just so they know."

"You're right. Listen, I have to go. Wish me luck."

"Kates," he said.

"Yeah?"

"Go kick their corporate asses."

My entire body lit up with a smile. "Brother, you know I will."

###

I opened the sliding door that led to the wraparound balcony and let the breeze from the Pacific fill my lungs. It was better than twelve cups of coffee. White sandy beaches beckoned, and the Huntington Beach Pier was in the distance. A September sun was setting over the pier, and surfers were riding the last waves of the night into the shoreline. Surf City, USA. This was my hometown, my turf, and it was time to show the hotel gurus how Huntington protected its own.

I went back inside and sat at the desk with the drapes drawn and ocean before me. I didn't care if Jerry Adams or the entire board stormed into the suite while I started penning the press release. I closed my eyes. *Write with your heart, not your head.*

When I opened my eyes, I began to write. My fingers felt light as they touched the keys.

Hotel Employees Stage Walkout

Huntington Beach, CA— On other days, they are chefs, bartenders, bellmen, and maids, but on Friday you will see them in their front yard helping to secure their future by staging a walkout over unjust scheduling practices.

They are the employees of the Waterfront Point Resort. They'll be easy to spot… just look for the group on the front drive.

"In less than four months we earned the five-diamond award," Donna Dickerson said. "And this is the way they repay our hard work."

The single mom of two and part-time accounting clerk is referring to the forced elimination of overtime, which was scheduled to begin October 1, but was moved up to Friday, September 16, 2016, to ensure the executives met their year-end bonus numbers.

Dickerson works thirty-nine hours a week at the five-diamond resort and attends Orange Coast College where she is enrolled as a student. Dickerson is finishing work on her Associate of Science degree in accounting.

"This is my last semester," said Dickerson, who has balanced work, school, and family with one career goal in mind.

"When I applied at the hotel, I was told during the hiring process that once I had my degree I would be eligible to work full-time," she said.

With an end in sight, the news of the elimination of overtime hit Dickerson hard. The single mom has worked overtime on the weekends to earn the money needed to cover the cost of health benefits for her two daughters and herself.

"If I were full-time, the loss of overtime wouldn't be an issue because my girls and I would be covered with benefits provided by the hotel. But since I work one hour short of forty, I have to work six days a week. And cover all my tuition costs, which full-time employees are partially reimbursed."

The approach of the holiday season creates more stress for Dickerson. "I have two little children to support and finals to prepare for. My girls still believe in Santa. What do I tell them when he isn't able to show up this year?"

The only thing missing from my press release was Tiny Tim. After our meeting, Donna handed me a gold mine. I wrapped up with additional information about the elimination of overtime and how it would impact other employees. Then I provided the factual data—that half of the staff employed by the Waterfront Point Resort worked without benefits. At the bottom of the release, I proudly typed:

For further information and/or to set Wild Art for Friday, contact: Katie Flanagan.

"What's Wild Art?"

I jumped and shrieked. I turned to find Bogart reading over my shoulder.

"Don't do that!" I snapped. Tension tightened across my already stiff shoulders, making them practically rigid.

"I thought you heard me come in."

"Well, I didn't."

"Sorry."

"It's okay."

"So what's 'Wild Art'?"

"It's a journalism term for a standalone photo or photo op. Same thing."

"This is really good."

"Yeah?" My gaze fixed on his. "You mean it? You're not just saying that...." *Because we're in a hotel room.*

"No, it's solid." A mischievous grin spread across his face. "And I'm not just saying that because I've seen you naked."

I burst out laughing, and it helped relieve some of the stress stored in my body. "Thanks." I rubbed my eyes. My contacts were dry and burned.

"I thought you could use this." He handed me an evergreen-colored zippered cloth bag. The Waterfront Point Resort emblem was embellished in gold thread.

"Fancy, fancy." I unzipped it and discovered a much-needed toothbrush, toothpaste, a razor, and other sundry items. Tucked in the corner of the bag was a small bottle of contact lens solution and a carrying case. "Perfect." I glanced up at him. "But do you think I should stay? I mean, I already got the work finished."

I checked the desk clock. The red digital display flashed 8:00. "Oh, hell. Where did the time go?"

"You've been busy."

"I know, but man it flew."

"Hungry?"

"Starving, actually."

Bogart went to the door, checked the peephole, and then opened it and brought a room service tray inside.

"Whatcha bring me?"

He lifted a silver lid off a covered plate to reveal a white paper bag with "Hank's" stamped across the top.

"Oh, Chris." I swooned. "You're the best!"

"Patrick told me you never ate your double bacon cheeseburger that one night."

"Or my shake," I added, holding up my index finger. "Don't forget that seeing you and Carmen together caused me to actually leave a shake behind. Or rather, in my parents' refrigerator, but still it was traumatic." I placed my hand to my forehead for good measure.

"I'm sorry about that. Hopefully this makes up for it." He handed me a chilled triple-chocolate shake.

"It's a good start," I placed my hand over his. "But only if you join me."

"I was hoping you'd ask." He lifted a bag from beneath the room service cart to reveal a second bag of food.

"Let me take out my contacts." I disappeared into the bathroom that was the same size as my new apartment.

I pulled my hair back into a messy ponytail and washed away my makeup. When I looked in the mirror, the absence of concealer and two days of going hard at the computer with little sleep in between definitely showed. I pinched my cheeks, but it didn't wake up my pale skin and there was nothing to remove the dark circles beneath my eyes. *Well, this'll be the litmus test.*

I stumbled over an ottoman before I found my way back to Bogart, who I thought had placed our food on the nightstand beside him in bed. Either that or he was making paper bag puppets. My backpack had my emergency glasses. I hated to reach into the inside pocket for them, but I was virtually blind without them. I slid them on and spun around really fast, hoping I would be a blur in front of Bogart.

"Ta-da!"

"What?"

Befuddlement was the only way to describe the expression on his face. It was a mixture of bewilderment and confusion.

"You like 'em?" I swiveled my head from side to side like I was modeling a pair of Ray Bans and not a relic that belonged in the Smithsonian. "I call them my birth control glasses."

Bogart leaned on his elbows. "Your what?"

"Yeah... you heard me. My birth control glasses. With these bad boys on, there's no chance of getting laid, let alone pregnant."

"Actually," he said, inching down the bed toward me. "I kinda like the naughty librarian look."

I slowly waved my index finger back and forth. "There's something seriously wrong with you."

"No, seriously, with that little yellow button-up sweater thing you got going on, the tight skirt, and your hair pulled back, you look very…." His eyes skimmed my body while his mind seemed to search for the right word. "Strict."

"Strict?" I moved my hand up and down my body like one of the gals on a game show presenting a prize to the contestants. "*This* looks strict? That's the best you got?"

"Oh and I suppose you could have done *so* much better?"

"Ah, actually yeah.... I would've come up with something *a lot* more clever and sexy than strict. Like repressed." I started to slowly unbutton my cardigan.

His eyes widened.

"Or even reserved." I slid the cardigan off my shoulders and let it fall to the floor, revealing a low-cut, curve-hugging sheer bra that was the color of champagne.

"You had that on underneath your sweater all day?"

I shrugged and raised my eyebrows. "Those repressed, reserved, often *bottled-up* perhaps, librarians… well, you never know what they're hiding. I'd even go as far as to say they're stifled." I reached behind me and lowered the zipper to my silk-lined skirt, which hugged my waist. As soon as the zipper released, it slipped off me. My panties matched my bra, leaving little to the imagination but creating a wonderful visual.

A small gasp escaped Bogart.

"There's also constrained." My hands reached into my hair, releasing the ponytail. Hair fell around my face.

"But strict?" With a slow shake of my head, hair danced on my shoulders. "When I see a woman who is 'buttoned up,' as you said, what I see is a woman who is ready to take charge. Dominate." I kicked off my heels and crawled on the bed toward him.

"She's ready to have her way with whatever boy thinks he knows what she's all about." I pulled back his belt buckle with one cinch of the wrist. "Because in reality, the guy's got no clue."

His jeans and navy-colored boxers were off before I had a chance to admire them. His shirt was becoming a memory too. My tongue gently trailed the sensitive head and pulsating ridges of his long shaft.

"You're so damn sexy." He drew a harsh, ragged breath beneath me, his thighs tightening with the flicker of my tongue.

Heat coursed throughout my body. My fingertips gently brushed his nipples while my tongue taunted, playing, teasing, before I parted my lips, taking all of him. I slowly moved my mouth in rhythm with his hips. I left one hand on his chest, volleying it lightly between his nipples, and my other hand cradled his base while my mouth stroked him long and hard.

"Dear hell." He groaned in ecstasy. His fist tightened by his side. "Okay, we've got to put the brakes on...."

I took one long, last, meaningful lick, suck, and taste of his tanginess and crawled on top of him.

He reached behind me, and in one fluid movement, he unclasped my bra, slipped it from my shoulders, and tossed it off the bed. His hands cupped my breasts, his tongue moving back and forth with a hunger like I had never seen. His hand reached for my panties, pulling them down. I slipped them off, kicking them away from us.

Then suddenly he stopped. "Don't move," he said. "And don't lose the glasses."

He jumped off the bed naked and ran into the bathroom. When he returned, a condom covered his throbbing dick. He flipped me onto my stomach, causing me to get even wetter. His fingers danced, finding their melody across my clit. Instinctively my hips rose to meet him as he drove himself inside me.

I arched back and felt him lengthen inside me, heightening my arousal. His fingers gently caressed me in rhythm with his movements. The tempo of our bodies was perfect.

"Oh my God, that's it," I said.

"You like the good wood?" His voice was husky in my ear.

"Shut up and keep doing what you're doing."

"Strict," he said, claiming one of my nipples with his other hand. "I like that."

I gasped. His mouth pressed into my neck, teeth gently biting me. Wave upon wave, the ocean broke against the shore, echoing in the distance and matching our beat until everything blacked out, and all I felt, heard, or saw was Chris. All that mattered was being with him.

Our climax took me by surprise. The intensity was so powerful, deep, and surreal that for a second my entire body shut down and then reawakened, tingling like it had been brought back to life.

I collapsed and Bogart gently rolled away from me. The bag of Hank's was on the nightstand beside my milkshake, which had sweated into chocolate milk.

"I'm either going to lose a lot of weight in this relationship, or we're going to start getting food afterward."

He leaned over and cupped my face with his hands.

I love it when he does that.

"Afterward," he said. "Definitely afterward. I don't want you losing any weight. Your body's perfect."

"Good answer."

He brushed back my hair. His dark eyes were penetrating, and yet flirtatious. They drank me in while his lips claimed mine. Our bodies intertwined on the bed. I fell asleep with my head on his chest and awoke with him beside me.

"Hey," he said.

I smiled. "You're dressed."

"Yeah, I should probably go clock off work."

We both laughed aloud.

"You're salaried." I elbowed him. "You don't have a time clock to punch."

"But if I did," he said, "I got a little distracted."

"Me too."

"Mr. Clark left a change of clothes for you in the closet."

"He came in here?" I pulled the sheet around my naked body.

"No. He left it outside on the door hanger."

"Do not disturb," we said in unison and resumed laughing.

"I've got to go though." He gently kissed me.

"Will I see you tonight?" he asked.

"Absolutely." It was the first time I used a pat Waterfront Point response and meant it. "Maybe I can write another press release and get us a room."

He pushed hair from my face. "I love you, Katie Flanagan."

I nodded, my eyes filling with tears. "Me too."

I knew he was the man for me. *He is the one.*

CHAPTER TWENTY-TWO

By the time Friday arrived, I was a wreck. My nerves were shattered, and I seriously doubted one press release could turn the tide at the Waterfront.

"It's not going to work." I applied another layer of makeup. *What the hell, I'll look like a clown.*

"It'll work," my father said from the hallway. I had given him a copy of my press release when I came home after my hotel tryst with Bogart. I leaned my head out the bathroom door. "I don't know, Dad."

"Listen, your press release was solid, and that critical course that was sent got people talking around the water cooler."

"Really?"

"Yes, so just let go of the results."

"It's not that simple," I snapped. I had been biting people's heads off all week. *It's too much pressure.* The wait was killing me. *I just want this thing over with. Either way—success or failure—I just want it over.*

"I'm sorry." I stepped out of the bathroom with a compact in the palm of my hand. "Dad, I'm so sorry. I'm a mess. But if we don't get any press coverage out of this, if no one shows up…." I closed my eyes, willing the tears not to fall, but they still did.

His arms were around me, pulling me into an embrace. "Katie, I'd be nervous, too. But you don't have anything to worry about."

I rolled my head against him. "You don't know that. Dad, so many people are counting on me. And if I let them down…."

He kissed the top of my head. "If they don't get benefits and equal treatment, it won't be because of you or your press release or anything you could have done differently. It's admirable you're doing this. I'm very proud of you."

Emotions lodged at the base of my throat. "That means the world to me."

He gently leaned away from me. I had his brown eyes, and when they warmed back at me, I began to understand the power simple brown eyes could hold.

"Katie, you're going to surprise yourself today," he said. "And I can't wait to hear all about it at dinner. Now remember, Patrick's coming for dinner, too."

This actually made me laugh. "And that would be different from any other day?"

"Katie Maureen, your brother gets lonely."

"Oh, please."

My dad shook his head, smiling. "Now, you be nice to him. Your little brother adores you. That's why he's here all the time."

I titled my head. "Ahh, I love Patrick, too."

"Then we'll have a family dinner tonight and celebrate your victory."

I smiled. "Dinner it is."

I punched in to work promptly at eight. Jimmy had texted to remind all of us of the necessity to maintain our regular routines, especially in regards to the time clock.

There can't be any infractions with payroll. His text was ironic. Jimmy was conducting the staged walkout by the books.

Since I had passed my probationary period of employment, I had my own key to the HR office. I let myself in and found yet another purple note waiting on my desk with my instructions for the day.

"Holly." My shoulders dropped in defeat. *It's too much.* "I can't do this," I muttered.

"You can do it," Bogart said from the doorway. "Hell, you're the reason *I'm* doing it."

"Chris." My voice softened, and the tension in my body lessened.

"It's in less than an hour," I said in a hushed tone. "I'm the only one walking from this office. To my knowledge, Janet isn't. I don't think she even knows about it. She's full-time so there's no benefit to her. And if something doesn't benefit Janet, she doesn't do it. So I'm sure Jimmy didn't apprise her of it. I know I haven't. And I know Jimmy didn't tell Holly. So it'll just be me clocking out in an hour." My stomach suddenly dropped like I had just jumped on a roller coaster, ridden to the top of the highest peak, and plummeted to the bottom. "I think I'm going to be sick."

"You've got this. Just be yourself."

"This is me being myself."

Bogart chuckled. His two-way radio crackled and buzzed. He cocked his head toward me. "I've got to take this. I'll see you later. Remember, I'm on nights still, so I'll be walking out later. I'm only here now to help Jimmy with some behind-the-scenes stuff. If you need me, text. I'll be right there."

I hesitated only a moment. "I love you."

He looked at me with large brown eyes. "I love you, too."

I glanced at the clock when Bogart left. Forty-five minutes remained until the first scheduled walkout at 9:00 a.m. commenced.

I mentally reviewed the schedule for the three staged walkouts. The a.m. shift would clock off promptly at nine. At noon when the mid-shift arrived, they would work for two hours and then clock off. The night owls, who arrived at 4:00 p.m., would log on for an hour and then clock off at five. Nine, two, and five. Jimmy's use of the hotel's address still amazed me.

"Imagine that," I said, reading Holly's note. "More filing." I halfheartedly picked up a file and resumed where I had left off in the P's.

Mr. Adams's offer to be the new assistant Public Relations and Marketing director had guaranteed that my filing days were numbered. When he discovered that I'd penned the press release announcing the walkout, it wouldn't just be my filing days that would be numbered.

"Yeah, I'm screwed." My stomach churned. *How will I pay for my new apartment? Hell, how will I pay for my new car? What am I doing?* "I'm *really* going to miss it here."

"You're not fired yet." TJ appeared at the door to HR.

I looked up. "Hey."

"I read your press release."

"Shh!" My finger rushed to my lips. "Are you trying to get me fired?"

"No, I think we're all trying to avoid that."

"Good point." I giggled. "I've been a bit on edge."

TJ shrugged. "It's understandable."

"I mean, what if no one shows up? That could happen. Not the staff," I said. "But the media. What if they don't show up? I'd be happy if one or maybe *two* reporters or news crews came, but what if that doesn't even happen? What then?"

A dazed shake of his head. "Have you learned nothing?"

Now I shrugged. "What?"

"Confidence," TJ replied dryly.

I laughed aloud and felt heat rise to my cheeks. "Got it. I'll see you on the lawn."

He raised an eyebrow. "Not unless I see you first." And then he disappeared as quietly as he had entered.

My cell phone alarm rang at exactly 9:00 a.m.

"Okay." I shut the file drawer and placed the remaining files in a neat stack. I closed the drawer to my desk. I glanced at my assortment of colored pens and paper clips and left them in their place. *I'm a crusader, not a crook.*

Janet wasn't in the office yet, so I would have to close and lock the door. But before I did, I took one last look.

"Thank you," I said to no one in particular. I turned off the lights, shut the door, and locked it. I glanced across the hall at Mr. Clark, who softly smiled.

My nerves had settled, my stomach was calm, and my mind was no longer wrapped around the outcome of my press release. *Que sera, sera.*

I stood in line with the small gathering of other employees at the time clock waiting to quietly punch out. I swiped my time card before exiting the hotel off the loading dock.

I walked down the slanted ramp and thought back to the Saturday in June when my biggest ambition was to get a job to pay for my car. The hotel's mass hire seemed to fit the bill— even if it was in two departments. Five months later, I was helping to orchestrate a walkout. *Unreal.*

The ocean air was damp, brisk, and awakened me. The sun shone brightly, taking the chill out of the morning. It also reminded me of that Saturday in June and the original Huntington Hopefuls who had become close friends. We were taking action with no way of predicting the outcome. I caught a glimpse of a baseball cap and stood on my tiptoes, hoping it was Carmen. But it wasn't. The front entrance to the hotel where she worked was a rolling tapestry of green. The lawn was neatly manicured and bordered by fall flowers.

Row upon row of uniformed employees sat on the curb. Jimmy had also told us that we couldn't conduct our walkout on the Waterfront Point property, but beyond its reach was permissible.

I scoured the crowd for Jimmy and spotted him standing behind a group of housekeepers. I walked over and joined him.

"I don't see anyone from the media." My voice revealed that I wasn't completely resolved to letting go of the results.

Jimmy patted his shirt pocket and withdrew a cigarette.

"I guess I thought they'd be here. I wrote that we'd be walking out at nine, two, and five. Do you think they're coming? They're not coming, huh?"

Jimmy stooped down and struck a match against the sidewalk, lighting his cigarette.

"It was in the press release. Maybe Barbara forgot to send it?" I rambled.

Jimmy took long deep drags off his cigarette and suddenly the intoxicating smoke seemed like a good idea.

"Got an extra one?" I pointed to his cigarette.

"Not a chance, Flanagan," he finally said. "You're already giving yourself a heart attack. I'm not going to light the fuse." He started to laugh. It was the first time I had ever really heard him chuckle, and it was more of a wheeze, which made me giggle.

"But what if they don't show up?" I asked. *Is it a boom or a bust?*

"Patience," he said. "You've got to learn patience. Everyone's going to be looking to you to see how you weather this, and if you're a basket case then it's going to have a downhill effect. Got it?" The tone and the piercing gray-blue eyes that made me stand tall were pure Jimmy.

"Got it. Patience."

"Relax. Have some fun. Don't be such a grim reaper."

I rolled my eyes. "I heard you the first time. I'm just nervous."

Jimmy patted me on the back. "Listen, it's normal to be anxious, but I chose you because you're a leader. And I need to count on that leadership and fire you've got. *Comprende?*"

"*Si.*"

"Okay, I'm going to go check on Chef. There's a major VIP in-house that he's a little nervous about."

"Who's here?" I asked, but I already knew, walkout or not, Jimmy wouldn't spill the beans. The one thing Jimmy could be counted on for was his discretion. It was the only Waterfront Point policy he respected. Hotel anonymity was one of the marquee qualities the Waterfront Point was known for, which pulled in an A-list clientele. From the Hollywood elite, who wanted a weekend escape along the coast, to the Washington policy makers, the Waterfront Point never revealed its guest list. When the hotel had earned the coveted five-diamond rating, it had tripled its bookings overnight.

Jimmy crushed his cigarette with the heel of his shoe. "I'm leaving you in charge. I've got my cell, and once I see how things are inside, I'll be back to check on the troops."

I took my orders with a nod. "I'll be here."

###

Two hours passed and the only attention the walkout generated was from the Executive Board members, who came out periodically checking on our progress. Still, none of the employees clocked back to work. We all held our ground, literally and figuratively.

At noon, I watched the afternoon shift arrive and disappear into the hotel. They'd be punching in, and then in a few hours punching out. It wouldn't be long until they joined us. Meanwhile, the hotel was operating on a skeleton crew with executives doing a lot of staff work. Jimmy had texted me that Mr. Adams had sent some executives to strip and make beds for the noon arrivals and departures. I did take a certain satisfaction in seeing Holly push a laundry cart up the loading dock. *Try filing, sister. I'd rather strip beds. At least then there's a sense of completion.*

Jimmy ordered pizzas that were delivered for lunch, and even though no media had arrived, not one employee left. I feared that the first person who broke the walkout would cause a chain reaction. I continually felt like I was holding my breath. I was handing out a slice of pepperoni pizza when I caught sight of the first news van that pulled up to 925 Waterford Street. I placed the pizza on the napkin for the bellman before me and breathed a sigh of relief.

Cheers erupted, breaking the quiet and bringing an abrupt halt to the peaceful demonstration.

"They came!" Barbara came up to me.

I couldn't believe it. "It's only one van, but…." Another car pulled in with KXYZ on the side door. "What?" An enormous weight felt like it dropped from my shoulders. *This is it. It happened.*

I turned to Barbara, who was jumping up and down. My eyes welled with tears.

"Hey, hey, hey," she said. "You've got to stop that right now. You're our media liaison. You're going to ruin your makeup."

I delicately dabbed my eyes, straightened my blazer, smoothed down my skirt, and flashed her a toothy grin.

"Do I have anything in my teeth?" I was not going to face the cameras with a poppy seed or anything else wedged between my teeth. I hadn't eaten but I had learned my lesson.

Barbara quickly surveyed my appearance. "Nope, nothing in your teeth or hanging out your nose."

I giggled.

"You look fabulous. You really do, Katie. This is your time. You're going to shine."

"Thank you." I took a long steady breath and squeezed her hands. "This it is." I pulled my notebook out of my backpack, which had my press release and my notes on the strike. I waded through the crowd toward the media vans with confidence. A two-man team was assembling their crew. I glanced at my watch. It was ten minutes to two. *Perfect.*

"Hi, I'm Katie Flanagan." I extended my hand.

"I'm Bob Roberts from Channel 6," the reporter said. "Are you in charge here?"

"Well…." I hesitated. *Confidence.* "Yes. I'm the one in

charge. And your timing couldn't be better. We have three walkouts staged and the next one is scheduled for two o'clock. If you'd like to set your cameras up over here," I said to the other team that had joined us. "You'll be able to get better footage of the loading dock, where the employees will be exiting the hotel."

"Seems like you've done this before," one of the men commented.

"I've had a little practice with the media," I said.

"She's being modest."

Dad? I glanced over my shoulder. A reporter's notebook was in one hand and a tape recorder was in the other. A photographer stood beside him.

"You came?" My heart jumped to my throat. "But you're a sports a reporter."

"Sports or not, I wasn't going to miss the best story of the year. Not a chance."

And despite what it did to my makeup, a tear slipped down my cheek. I quickly flicked it away. "Thank you."

My father fell in line beside me as I led everyone to the back entrance of the hotel.

"It's not a very good shot," one of the cameramen said. Another cameraman rolled tape. "It's not that flattering. There's trash cans and dirt...."

I stood in the camera's line of vision beside the reporter. The red light began blinking, and I knew from my field work in college that it was streaming live.

"I'm here with Katie Flanagan at the new five-diamond resort in Huntington Beach. But it sure doesn't look like business as usual. What's happening here today, Katie?"

The cameraman looked toward me. It was now or never.

"It's a side of the Waterfront Point Resort most people don't see," I said. "But there's nothing glamorous about unjust scheduling practices and that's what's happened since the hotel opened its doors in June. Half the staff work thirty-nine hours a week, which is one-hour shy of full-time. So while they work as hard and almost as long as a full-time employee, they don't get any of the perks, like health benefits, tuition reimbursement, retirement and paid leave. And now with the executive board's decision to cut overtime, so that they can meet their year-end bonuses, they've stripped us of our ability to subsidize our income to afford things like the health benefits we aren't entitled to. I respect that the board doesn't want to incur overtime, but if their only motivation is to hit their year-end numbers for their bonuses"—I shook my head—"well, that's not right. Imagine if those bonuses were put back into the operating budget?"

And then the answer to the financial dilemma and counter to any argument the board could make against our stance, crystalized. I looked directly into the lenses.

"If the executives forfeited their bonuses like they want us to forfeit our overtime, it could be a real win-win. The critical course detailed that the budget allocated for more full-time staff and a bonus for the executives. Yet instead of promoting part-timers to full-time, they opted to make their bonus bigger by making their year-end numbers stronger. But with additional funding, like the year-end bonuses, the number of part-time to full-time staff could increase. It would eliminate the unjust scheduling practices and strengthen morale. While the executives would be giving up their bonus, they'd still maintain their six-figure salaries." *Bam!* I turned behind me as the doors to the loading dock opened and employees started filing out. I looked dazedly through the crowd for a familiar face. I gave a pointed glance in her direction, and she quickly joined me.

"Bob, I'd like you to meet Carmen Gonzalez from Costa Mesa."

I stepped out of the camera's view and Carmen stepped in. She took off her cap, her silky black hair fell around her shoulders, her blue eyes locked on to the cameras, and her butterscotch-kissed skin glistened beneath the Southern California sun.

"They can call it prudent financial forecasting, which is what I just overheard one executive say to a guest," she said. "But no matter how much they sugarcoat their decision, it doesn't make not having benefits or overtime any sweeter."

The reporter and cameraman smiled.

Yes! I pumped my fist in the air.

My father smiled in my direction, and my chest swelled with a sense of pride greater than any I had ever experienced. I might not become the next assistant Public Relations and Marketing director for the Waterfront Point Resort, but I realized that it would be their loss, not mine.

CHAPTER **TWENTY-THREE**

I watched the taillights of the last news van pull away before I grabbed my backpack and headed toward my car. It was hard to imagine that one press release could make a difference. But coupled with critical course and more than two hundred staff members who had walked off their jobs at nine, two, and five, by the six o'clock news cycle, the Waterfront Point Resort had made a public announcement that there had been a "misunderstanding."

Nothing brings about a "misunderstanding" more than having bad publicity air on all the local radio and television news stations. Let alone being tweeted with a hashtag that had trended fast on Twitter. The hotel was also featured in print by the newspapers.

I almost grabbed my first national story, when the VIP Jimmy was so worried about, turned out to be a network cable president. When he was denied room service because Chef wasn't there to make his eggs Benedict, he threatened Mr. Adams with airing the story on the evening network news, which would look bad for all the Point properties.

Jimmy's plan had worked. Despite my skepticism, it had succeeded. Later that day I formally accepted the Waterfront Point Resort's offer to serve as their newly appointed assistant Public Relations and Marketing director, making $55,000 a year. Turned out that a single press release also made a 10 percent difference in my starting salary. It didn't hurt that my mug had appeared on every news station. As the new spokesperson for the Waterfront Point Resort, "saving face" took on a whole new meaning. They couldn't afford to lose me, and I was beginning to recognize my value, which made signing on the dotted line a lot easier to accept.

When I reached my car, I looked out to the evening sun that was starting to disappear behind the horizon. A beautiful Southern California night stretched out before me. Dinner with my family was in an hour. Bogart was going to join us, but the next hour was ours.

"You weren't thinking about leaving without me?" His voice came from behind me. His arm wrapped around my waist, pulling me to him.

A smile spread across my face. "Never."

His chin rested on my shoulder. "Good, because I've been looking forward to this moment all day."

I turned to him. "What moment is that?"

His lips pressed into mine, and I melded into him. Tucked in his arms, his clean scent surrounded me, his hot breath in my ear.

"This moment. When I get to be with you." His brown eyes sparkled. "I was so proud of you today."

Tears blurred my contacts, but my gaze never left his. Nor would it. His were the only eyes I ever wanted to look into.

"Kates, I love you. And I want to spend the rest of my life with you."

I felt my heart skip a beat.

"Chris, there's nothing I want more. I love you too." Teardrops spilled down my cheeks.

Our kiss was the promise of a lifetime of kisses.

I looked across the street at the lighted boardwalk and smiled. "Want to hit it?"

He wiggled his eyebrows. "Thought you'd never ask."

I giggled, removed my jacket, kicked off my heels, and tossed the bundle into the backseat of my car. We headed for the beach hand in hand. A whole new life had opened up for us, and it was time to start living it.

EPILOGUE

It was funny how four little words could alter the course of my life, but they had. Ever since Bogart uttered those four simple words, "Will you marry me?" my life hadn't been the same.

For starters, I had no idea that planning a wedding would be so time consuming and stressful. In a word, I had been clueless. Every day it seemed like I had a new decision to make. And the current pressing issue was over chocolate-cream filling or custard?

"Does it matter?" I hesitated to ask my wedding planner, Donna. I watched lines cross her brow and instantly regretted my question. Apparently the filling in a wedding cake was extremely important.

"Well, Ms. Flanagan, should you choose the cream filling, then you would want to serve a lighter entrée for the main course, such as fish."

"Fish and chocolate-cream-filled cake?" I said. "That sounds disgusting."

And so did my wedding planner's face when I blurted out my assessment of her food pairing.

"All right," she said in an even tone. "The custard filling is also heavy but since it's not as rich, you could serve meat or poultry."

I nodded as if that made sense, which it should considering all the menus I had typed when I was in the Food and Beverage department.

"Where's Jimmy when I need him?" I muttered. But I already knew the answer. My former boss was retiring as the director of Food and Beverage at the end of the first quarter.

Some people lost their identity when they retired because their job was all they had, and they found themselves with nothing but time.

But not Jimmy. He'd gone beyond losing his identity. He'd become an entirely different person. It was almost as if he'd testified against the mob and went through the Witness Protection Program. Though, instead of driving at top speed in his high performance car, which I had dubbed Sterling, he now puttered around in a golf cart. I was still working on a name for his new mode of transportation.

His top-shelf martinis transformed to margaritas. He even traded his custom-made suits for off-the-rack Hawaiian shirts.

Yet his new wardrobe still hinted at his old life. Every Hawaiian shirt he wore was adorned with pineapples, the symbol of luxury and hospitality.

The only time I saw him at the hotel was when he dropped by to pick up dinner to go or to attend his weekly meeting. His golf game, though, had seriously improved, and he had acquired a tan that he wore almost as well as his Hawaiian shirts.

So besides planning my July wedding, I was also in charge of coordinating his retirement party, which was slated for the end of March. After a thirty-five-year career with The Point Resort, everyone from the corporate office, including the founder and owner, Michael Harpington, was flying in to attend the event. *No pressure.*

I looked at the pieces of cake in front of me. Normally the prospect of biting into two decadent desserts would be a real treat, but neither looked inviting. My stomach was in knots. It was probably the easiest decision I had to make—custard or cream filling— yet I couldn't decide.

"Can I come back with my fiancé?" I asked, hoping to buy time with someone else's taste buds.

"Your wedding is scheduled for July twelve, isn't that correct?" Donna said.

"That's right." I quieted the impulse to remind her that it was only December.

"Well, that doesn't leave us much time."

Us? Where was the "us" in this process? It was me. Bogart's promotion to the director of Engineering kept him busy handling every emergency that presented itself at the hotel. I was so proud of him, but I missed him.

I stared at the two slices of triple-layer cake.

"Well, my dad loves chocolate," I said, thinking of the

three layers of chocolate he would devour. "But Bogart's father, Harold, he's a custard fan." I glanced at the vanilla custard sandwiched between angel food cake.

"What do you like?" His voice came from behind me.

I didn't have to turn around, but I did.

Chris.

"Hey," I said as he sat down beside me.

"Tough choice," my fiancé said, picking up the fork and cutting off a sliver of the chocolate cake. He lifted it toward my mouth. "Close your eyes," he instructed and I blindly obliged.

I felt the tong of the fork touch my lips.

"Before you taste this, imagine your wedding day. Your groom's all decked out in a white tux with a blue ruffled shirt and shiny white loafers. Yeah, he's bringing sexy back," he said, making me laugh. "Ah, come on now. I'm told he's a good-looking guy. He's looking smart. Handsome. You've just had this incredibly long Catholic wedding ceremony that your groom didn't understand at all," he said with a chuckle and I smiled. "And now you're at your reception. You're happy, but hungry. You've missed dinner because you were taking photos with Aunt Gertie and Uncle Charlie." My cheeks hurt from smiling.

"So now," Bogart said, "it's the moment of truth. You place your hand on your groom's hand as you cut into this obscenely large, but tastefully decorated cake that equals a monthly mortgage payment."

I popped opened my eyes. Bogart removed the fork that remained at the ready with cake. "It cost that much?"

"Shh," he quieted me. "Close your eyes. Now, where was I? Oh, that's right. The cake cutting. It's the final event of the day. Well, at least the last one the guests get to watch," he said in a purposefully husky voice that made me giggle.

"So the cake had better taste amazing," he said. "After all, you're going to keep the top section in the freezer for a year so you want to make sure it's the cake for you. Imagine your husband," he said, "feeding you for the first time." He gently pressed the fork toward my mouth. "So it's got to be perfect." He passed the piece of cake between my lips.

With my eyes closed, my other senses kicked in. A rich, decadent chocolate mixed with the tangy sweetness of raspberries and blended together to create a truly exotic taste explosion in my mouth.

"Sinful." It was the first word that came to mind, yet I wasn't sure if it was the cake or my future husband I was referring to. I opened my eyes. Donna had left the tasting table and I was alone with Bogart.

"It's good, isn't it?" he said in a voice as velvety as the cake.

I nodded.

"Let's try the other piece," he said, but I slowly shook my head.

"No, I've made my choice."

"And?" He raised an eyebrow.

"And," I smiled at his playfulness, "the chocolate cream. But Donna said something about fish?"

Bogart wagged his finger. "Katie, this is our wedding. You can serve anything you want."

"Anything?" I asked.

"You name it and it's on the menu."

"Hank's. I'd like Hamburger Hank's at our wedding."

Bogart's laughter was a sound I would never tire of hearing. It was deep, throaty, and his entire face lit up. I grinned.

I leaned toward him and melted into his kiss. His lips were soft, full, and fun to nibble. When I slowly pulled away, I looked into his soulful brown eyes.

"So? What do you think? About Hank's I mean," I said.

"Oh, that's easy. Consider it done. Hamburger Hank's and chocolate cake," he said. "It's the perfect pairing." He kissed me again. "Just like us."

The End

ACKNOWLEDGEMENTS

So imagine receiving an e-mail on a Sunday regrading a manuscript submission. I saw the subject line for my book and thought, "Great, I'm getting rejected on a Sunday."

Becky Johnson and Hot Tree Publishing, thank you for being the highlight of my Sunday. From the cover design to creating the "bloody blurb," anytime I click on one of your e-mails, I can't help but smile. Thank you for believing in me and my work.

Every writer needs a good editor and I was given the best. Liv Ventura, your input propelled me to produce top work. Thank you. I'm a stronger writer because of your dedication to the craft and to me.

To the Cheyenne Writers Group that lovingly adopted me into their fold: John Schutlz, Anna Lane, Dave Lerner, Rene Minder, and Merissa Racine—when I wanted to give up, your e-mails kept my pen on the page. Thank you for always welcoming me when I pop into the group.

Mike and Jen Solis: It takes a tribe or really good neighbors, who step up and feed my children so that I can make my deadlines. In the game of Life, I'm grateful for your friendship.

Dana Volney, you're the best pitch writer ever. Thank you for giving me my tagline and supporting me regardless of what appeared beside my byline. For sending flowers before I went into surgery and posting my first review afterward. Thank you.

Jami Wagner, you remind me that happily ever after isn't just for our genre. It happens every day. Your dedication and enthusiasm for our craft is contagious. Thank you.

To my sister, Suzanne Billiter Cragin, where would I be without your phone calls and texts? Lost. You're always my first call and the voice that guides me back to our childhood and what Mom and Dad would say if they were here. We are #BilliterStrong. Thank you for being there, for praying, and sending me fabulous shoes. Life is better in good shoes.

Stephen Billiter, you're a mad genius who is always at the ready with a great one-liner. Thank you for always being there.

The Raven Media Group: Thank you for your vision for my work and working so hard to get me there.

And finally to my family. My children Austin, Kyle, Ciara, and Cooper and the Gullberg boys—Max and Dylan. You're the reason I fight breast cancer. I can't imagine my life without you.

Ron Gullberg, you've seen me at my absolute worst and stayed at my hospital bedside, sleeping in a chair so that when I woke, I wouldn't be alone. You are the hero in my story and I will love you forever. The very best is yet to come.

ABOUT THE AUTHOR

Mary Billiter is a weekly newspaper columnist and fiction author. She also has novels published under the pen name, "Pumpkin Spice."

Mary resides in the Cowboy State with her unabashedly bald husband, their combined children, and runaway dog. She does her best writing (in her head) on her daily runs in wild, romantic, beautiful Wyoming.

Connect with Mary:

WWW.MARYBILLITER.COM

WWW.TWITTER.COM/MARYBILLITER

WWW.FACEBOOK.COM/MARYMBILLITER

ABOUT THE PUBLISHER

Hot Tree Publishing opened its doors in 2015 with an aspiration to bring quality fiction to the world of readers. With the initial focus on romance and a wide spread of romance sub-genres, we envision opening up to alternative genres in the near future.

Firmly seated in the industry as a leading editing provider to independent authors and small publishing houses, Hot Tree Publishing is the sister company toHot Tree Editing, founded in 2012. Having established in-house editing and promotions, plus having a well-respected market presence, Hot Tree Publishing endeavors to be a leader in bringing quality stories to the world of readers.

Interested in discovering more amazing reads brought to you by Hot Tree Publishing or perhaps you're interested in submitting a manuscript and joining the HTPubs family? Either way, head over to the website for information:

WWW.HOTTREEPUBLISHING.COM